Richard Laymon was born in Chicago in 1947. He grew up in California and has a BA in English Literature from Willamette University, Oregon, and an MA from Loyola University, Los Angeles. He has worked as a schoolteacher, a librarian and as a report writer for a law firm. He now works full-time as a writer. Apart from his novels, he has published more than fifty short stories in magazines such as *Ellery Queen*, *Alfred Hitchcock* and *Cavalier* and in anthologies, including *Modern Masters of Horror*, *The Second Black Lizard Anthology of Crime* and *Night Visions 7*. His novel *Flesh* was voted Best Horror Novel of 1988 by *Science Fiction Chronicle* and also shortlisted for the prestigious Bram Stoker Award, as was *Funland*. He lives in California with his wife and daughter.

Midnight's Lair

Richard Laymon

Previously published as
Midnight's Lair
by Richard Kelly

Previously published as MIDNIGHT'S LAIR
under the pseudonym Richard Kelly

First published
in 1988
by W. H. Allen & Co

Reprinted in hardback in 1992
by HEADLINE BOOK PUBLISHING PLC
Reprinted in this edition in 1992
by HEADLINE BOOK PUBLISHING PLC

A HEADLINE FEATURE paperback

10 9 8 7 6 5 4 3

ISBN 0 7472 3896 0

Phototypeset by Intype, London
Printed and bound in Great Britain by
Mackays of Chatham PLC, Chatham, Kent

HEADLINE BOOK PUBLISHING
A division of Hodder Headline PLC
338 Euston Road
London NW1 3BH

One day, feeling oh so brave,
I went walking in a cave.

Now, I fear, I can't get out.
I'll die in here, I have no doubt.

I'll mold and turn to slimy bone
Here where the sun has never shown,
Where I'll lie in darkness all alone,
Here in my tomb of ancient stone.

Remember me, before you dare
To journey into midnight's lair.
Remember me, and what I write:

'Here lies one who loved the light
But he was curious and brave –
He went walking in a cave.'

'The Explorer'
Allan Edward DePrey

Midnight's Lair

1

Darcy Raines, standing at the bow with her back to the group, grabbed a spike jutting from the cavern wall and stopped the boat. Keeping her grip on the spike, she turned sideways.

Kyle Mordock stared up at her. The first of the boat's bench seats was vacant. He sat on the second, next to a young couple holding hands. *His* seat.

Every day since Darcy began working as a guide through the cavern two weeks ago, the kid had shown up for at least one of her tours. There were other guides but he never went on their tours, just Darcy's. He always stayed close to her, usually managing to get the same seat for the boat ride, the one directly behind her, the one with the best view – not of the cavern, but of Darcy. He rarely spoke. He simply watched her with his tiny, feral eyes.

Now, he was staring at her rump. The way Darcy stood, sideways with one foot propped on the bow, her trousers were drawn taut against her buttocks. She could feel Kyle's eyes.

A fifteen-year-old lech.

Boss's son or not, she thought, I'll have to do something about this nonsense before he drives me nuts.

Tom stopped the second boat behind Darcy's, and nodded for her to start.

'End of the line, folks,' she said. 'Everybody out.'

There were murmurs and quiet laughter from many of the people on the boats. Several glanced from side to side as if prepared to follow her orders, then caught the joke and laughed more loudly than the others.

'You go first,' called a man in the second boat.

'Actually, the water is only about waist-deep in the Lake of Charon at this time of the year, though the level rises considerably higher in the spring with the seepage from melting snow and rain. But I wouldn't recommend taking a dip. The water is about fifty degrees.'

She glanced at Kyle. He was staring at her face. She turned her head away, and nodded towards the rock wall in front of the boat.

'This barrier,' she said, 'marks the end of the portion of the cavern that's accessible to the public. The wall was constructed in 1923 by Ely Mordock. Originally, it was possible to explore the entire length of the cavern – just over a mile. For a number of years, Ely led parties into the cave through its natural opening on the steep slope of the hillside near the eastern border of his property. The trip was an all-day, difficult hike, and not for the timid. In those days, they didn't have the walkway or lighting. Ely supplied waders, picnic lunches and torches.

'But his dream was to make the wonders of the cavern accessible to the general public, not just a hardy few, so in 1921 he began construction of the elevators. The shafts were sunk 150 feet to provide an entrance at what had previously been the far end of the cavern. When those were completed, work was begun to install the lighting and walkway.

'It was then that tragedy struck. On June 12, 1923, Ely and his wife, Elizabeth, were roaming an area somewhere between here and the natural opening when she slipped and fell into a deep chasm.'

An elderly woman muttered, 'Oh dear.'

'Ely lowered himself into the chasm on a rope, but the gap into which his wife had fallen seemed bottomless and he was forced to abandon any hopes of saving her . . . or of retrieving her body.

'He was grief-stricken, and determined that the chasm would never claim another life. So he sealed the cavern's natural opening, and built this rock wall as a permanent barrier to prevent anyone from entering the hazardous eastern half of the cave. In effect, that entire part of the cave became the tomb of Elizabeth Mordock.'

'That was over sixty years ago,' a man called from the second boat. 'Aren't there any plans to re-open that end?'

Darcy shook her head. 'Ely's will stipulated that the barriers should never be breached. His descendants have chosen to abide by his wishes.'

'Seems like a waste,' the man said.

A husky teenaged boy in Darcy's boat raised his hand as if he were in school. She called on him. 'What does that wall there do to the stream?'

'Good question. The wall restricts the natural flow of the River Styx. Before it was built, there was no Lake of Charon.'

'So, it's like a dam,' the boy said.

'Exactly. The river in this part of the cavern was only a few inches deep before the wall was built, and people could stroll through here instead of having to go by boat. In fact, portions of the original walkway are still intact below the surface.'

3

'How come the whole cave doesn't flood?'

'Ely was smart enough not to block the opening completely. He left a space near the bottom of the wall to allow water to run out. Any other questions before we head back?'

'I have one,' said a young woman two rows behind the boy. 'With the cave closed up like this, where does the air come from?'

'Originally, there were three elevators down from the surface. After Ely blocked off the natural opening, one of the elevators was converted to a ventilation shaft. Fresh air is circulated from the surface, and that has the additional benefit of raising the cavern temperature during the summer months. It still may feel a little chilly to some of you, but the natural temperature of the cavern would be about fifty degrees Fahrenheit, like the water, if it weren't for the warm air from the shaft. That brings it up to about sixty.

'If there aren't any more questions, we'll head back now. Before you know it, you'll be up top again and sweltering.'

Her comment was greeted by the usual chuckles and moans.

Someone said, 'No rush.' But there weren't any more questions.

'You may have noticed,' Darcy went on, 'that the first row of seats in each boat was left vacant. That was no oversight. We've got this whole thing *planned*. It's a lot easier to turn *you* around than the boats. So, I'd like those of you in the first occupied row to stand up carefully, do an about-face, and plant your bottoms on the seats we so conveniently left vacant for you.'

Following her instructions, the three people at the

front of each boat stood, turned around, and sat down.

That included Kyle Mordock. Darcy was glad to be freed from his constant stare. Soon, she would be at the opposite end of the boat from him.

One row at a time, as she gave the word, the rest of the tourists reversed their positions by moving to the seats in front of them. There were seven benches in all. It didn't take long.

'Okay, now comes the fun part for me and Tom. If those of you on the left will scoot towards the centre, we'll perform our daring feat.'

'Drum roll, please,' said Tom.

Near the middle of Darcy's boat, a girl of about seven had her elbow on the gunnel. Darcy smiled at her and waved her in. Her mother pulled her out of the way.

Darcy let go of the spike. 'If Tom and I are very lucky,' she said, 'we may reach the other end of the boat without getting wet.'

The only guide to fall recently during this manoeuvre was Dick Hayden. He'd done it last week, on purpose as a treat for the tourists, and vowed he would never try that stunt again. When Darcy saw him step out of the elevator forty-five minutes later, his clothes were sodden, he was shivering and his face was blue. He came down with a cold, and missed three days of work.

Darcy knew of nobody falling into the cold water by accident. The walk to the other end of the boat might look tricky, but she considered it a cinch.

Arms out for balance, she stepped onto the gunnel. Though it was wider than her foot, she walked it as if it were a tight-rope. She saw Tom performing a similar act along the side of the other boat.

He disappeared.

Darcy felt as if her vision had been switched off.
She saw black.

Great time to lose the lights.

People gasped.

She wobbled, trying to keep her balance.

'SHIT!' From Tom.

Then a thud, a heavy splash.

Worried voices. 'Did he fall? . . . He fell! . . . Oh, my God!'

'Quiet!' Darcy yelled. 'Everyone stay seated!' She clawed at her side, snatched the flashlight from her belt, switched it on and swept its beam to the second boat. Tom wasn't there. Fear squeezed her chest.

'Tom!' she called. No answer.

Her pale beam darted over the water along the port side of the boat.

It's only waist-deep! Where is he?

She saw the blunt top of the stalagmite known as Satan's Buoy jutting from the surface less than a yard from Tom's boat.

He'd been next to it when the cave went dark.

That thud.

Oh Jesus!

Darcy pointed her flashlight at the gunnel in front of her feet and rushed along it. The passengers in both boats were silent, an audience captivated by a strange show. At the stern, Darcy raised her flashlight overhead and kicked out. The leap carried her out past the squared corner of Tom's boat. Frigid water sprayed her face, wrapped her legs, seized her groin like a hand of ice. Her feet hit the bottom. They started to slide. She hooked her left arm over the edge of the boat and caught herself.

Her flashlight probed the water. She could see the

bottom under its bent beam.

Tom was not beside the boat.

Turning, she swept the light over the surface on both sides of Satan's Buoy.

'Maybe he's *under* the boat,' someone said. 'I think I heard a bumping . . .'

'Take this.' Darcy thrust the flashlight at the nearest passenger. It was pulled from her hand.

She took a deep breath. Her lungs felt shrunken. Ducking, she slipped an arm under the metal hull. She thrust herself down. The chill water seemed to squeeze her head. It soaked through her jacket and blouse and bra. It gripped her skin.

Her eyes were open, but she saw nothing.

She waddled through the shallow water under the boat, the back of her head and shoulders rubbing along its hull, her arms waving, searching.

Her right hand swept against something round. Tom's head? She curled her fingers in, the middle finger finding a small ridge, the two on either side touching marble-sized . . .

His eyes. They felt *open*.

Darcy flinched and jerked her hand away. Then she reached out, arms spread to avoid his face. She found his shoulders, clutched his jacket with both hands, and dragged Tom sideways.

Clear of the boat, she straightened up. There was a splash as someone jumped into the water behind her. She jerked Tom, and he burst to the surface. The flash-light found his face. His head was tilted sideways. Water spilled from his mouth.

His open eyes were rolled upward, only the whites showing.

'Let's get him into the boat.' It was the man who'd

jumped into the water. He waded past Darcy, wrapped his arms around Tom's chest, and walked backward, pulling the limp body to the stern of the boat. The beam of the flashlight stayed with them. 'Hang onto him.'

Darcy hugged Tom to her chest. She felt his face against her cheek, felt his whiskers. He didn't seem to be breathing.

What if he's dead?

The man grabbed the side of the boat, thrust himself up, and climbed in. Bending over, he grabbed Tom beneath the armpits. As he started to haul the body up, Darcy released her hold. She clutched Tom's rump and lifted. He surged out of the water. For a moment, her hands were pinned between his buttocks and the gunnel, his open legs caught under her elbows. She slipped her hands free and raised her arms. His legs flew up and he dropped backward into the boat.

Darcy threw herself against the side in time to see the man lowering Tom onto the vacant bench. As she boosted herself up, the flashlight beam skipped from the man to Tom. She glimpsed the bloody right side of Tom's head. Then, the man was straddling him and bending down. Someone reached for Darcy, grabbed her upper arm, and gave her a helpful pull as she squirmed over the gunnel. She sprawled across that person's lap, slid off, and squeezed between his knees and the leg of the man on top of Tom.

'I know first-aid,' she said.

The man ignored her. His hand was around Tom's throat. Then he dug fingers into the mouth.

'Got a pulse?'

He nodded. His fingers came out, stringed with saliva. He tipped Tom's head back and blew into the open mouth.

He knows what he's doing, Darcy thought. Thank God.

She struggled to her feet and turned around. The flashlight was now in the hand of a young woman in the first seat. The woman kept it on Tom and the man.

Darcy heard a confused noise of voices all asking questions at once. She raised her hands for silence.

'I'm sure all of you are wondering . . . Tom fell when the lights went off, and I guess he hit his head on that stalagmite near the boat. But we have him now, and a gentleman's giving him artificial respiration. I think he'll be all right.'

'You're to be commended for your prompt action,' said a voice in the darkness.

There were mutters of agreement, scattered applause.

'The important thing now,' she said, 'is for all of us to remain calm.' She was shivering badly. She wrapped her arms across her chest. 'We've apparently had a power failure. I'm sure it's temporary, though, and the lights will come back on shortly. In the meantime, there's no cause for alarm. We're perfectly safe here. Hell, a cave is just about the safest place in the world to be, no matter what's going on topside.'

I shouldn't have said that.

The swell of murmurs had an uneasy tone.

'I'm not saying that anything has happened up top,' she added.

'What's the power source?' someone asked.

'Generators inside the complex.'

'This happened before?'

'Not that I know of. But I'm new here. Kyle!' she called. 'Have the generators gone down before?'

'Nope. Never.'

Shit.

'Something happened!'

'War,' someone muttered. 'A nuclear . . .'

'Don't be an ass,' Darcy snapped. 'It's probably just some kind of simple breakdown. They'll have it repaired in no time. So let's not upset everyone by making outlandish guesses about the . . .'

From behind Darcy came choking sounds. She twisted around. The man was rising quickly, turning Tom onto his side as watery vomit gushed and splattered from his mouth. It sprayed the pants of the woman holding the flashlight. Tom kept on heaving. Then he was coughing and groaning.

He's okay, Darcy thought.

But she felt no relief.

That jerk and his nuclear war.

My fault, she told herself. I probably put the idea in his head. Earthquakes and nuclear war. How a cavern's the safest place you can be. Maybe I'll knock that out of my spiel from now on.

But what *did* happen up there? Something sure as hell killed the power.

She thought about her mother, who had come to visit and was staying at the hotel directly above the cavern. What if there *was* a disaster?

'What about the elevators?' asked a voice from behind her.

She looked over her shoulder. 'They'll be out, too. But as I said, I'm sure the power will be restored shortly.'

'Terrific.'

'We're trapped,' somebody whispered nearby.

'I'm sure,' Darcy said, 'that we'll all be out of here in time for lunch.'

There were quiet voices, people discussing the situation, comforting their spouses and children, probably sharing their concern with friends and strangers.

Darcy turned again to Tom. He was standing up, coughing, pressing a folded handkerchief to the side of his head. The man held him steady with a hand on his shoulder.

'How are you doing, pal?' she asked.

He answered with a groan.

'Bad?'

'Shit warmed over,' he muttered.

It was good to hear his voice. Darcy's throat tightened. She ran a hand over the wet hair on top of his head. 'We'll get you out of here quick as we can.'

He looked up at her. The woman with the flashlight was smart enough not to shine it in his eyes, but the halo of its beam illuminated his face. His features seemed slack, eyelids drooping and mouth hanging open. 'What's . . . ?'

'Power went out.'

He sighed, and that triggered a coughing fit.

The man on the bench beside him stood up next to Darcy. 'Why don't you stretch out?' he suggested to Tom. 'We'll find something to cover you up.'

'He can have my jacket,' said the man who had pulled Darcy into the boat.

She eased Tom down. He raised his feet and rested them on the gunnel. Soon, there were three jackets and a sweater on top of him.

'You look good and comfy,' she said.

'We should get him to a hospital as soon as possible,' said the man beside her. 'He's probably got shock and a mild concussion, but the head injury . . . you never know.'

Darcy looked at him. He was a big man, tall, with a

broad face and wide shoulders. He wore a sweatshirt. 'Thanks for all the help,' she said. 'Are you a doctor?' He looked more like a football player than a doctor.

'I worked as a hospital orderly while I was going to law school. And I was a policeman for a couple of years. Maybe there is a doctor down here.'

With nearly forty tourists on the boats, there should be at least one doctor. Darcy turned her head around and asked.

No such luck.

'Well, it was worth a try.' She held out her hand to the man. 'I'm Darcy Raines,' she said, even though she had introduced herself to the entire group at the start of the tour.

'Greg Beaumont.' He wiped his hand on a leg of his jeans, reminding Darcy that it had been slick with Tom's saliva. She didn't care. She squeezed the big hand when he raised it.

'Thanks again,' she said. 'I don't know what I would've done.'

'You were doing just fine. But I'm glad I could help. Now, we'd better see what we can do about getting out of here.'

'We *can't* get out of here,' she whispered. 'The elevators are the only way, and . . .'

'We'd better at least go though some motions,' Greg said. 'These folks have been pretty good so far, but they're gonna start losing it.'

In the darkness behind them, a child began to cry.

2

They *will* start losing it, Darcy thought. But nobody was likely to get hurt as long as they stayed in the boats. The lights were sure to come on, sooner or later.

There was only one flashlight, unless Tom's still worked. In spite of the walkway and railings that led from the dock to the elevators, herding all these people through the darkness would be tricky. The walkway curved, sloped, had some stairs. A few falls were almost inevitable. And what about Tom? What if he couldn't walk under his own strength? He'd have to be helped along, or maybe even carried.

All to reach a pair of elevators that wouldn't function anyway, until the electricity was restored. At that point, the lights would be on. Why not just wait here, and make the return trip after the cavern was once again brightly lit?

What if that's hours from now?

What if that's tomorrow?

What if that's never?

The thought made Darcy feel tight and sick inside, and she realized that everyone on the boats must be wondering the same thing, feeling the same stirrings of terror.

She suddenly remembered Lynn's group. Had those people been trapped down here, too? Maybe not. They'd passed Darcy, heading back, quite a while before the blackout.

The tours were scheduled to overlap, each taking an hour and a half. So Lynn's group should have reached the top at about the same time as Darcy reached Ely's Wall.

It would have been close. Maybe they made it, maybe not.

A hand squeezed her forearm. She looked at Greg. 'Even if we've got nowhere to go,' he whispered, 'we ought to go through the motions. Better than just waiting here and letting everyone's worries build up.'

'I think you're right,' she said. 'But we can't pull the boats along on those wall spikes the way we got here. It's tricky enough when you can see what you're doing.'

'Tow them?' he suggested.

'It's either that, or everyone wades. I'll take this boat and lead the way. Are you up for a dip, or should we call for volunteers?'

'I'm already wet.'

'Thanks.'

'No problem.'

Darcy faced the passengers. Many were speaking to one another in hushed voices. The child who had been crying was now sobbing quietly. The talk faded when the flashlight lit Darcy's face.

'First, Tom seems to be doing a lot better. I want to thank those of you who gave up your wraps to help keep him warm. I'm very pleased with the way all of you have been acting in the face of this situation, which I'm sure will be over soon. While we're waiting for the lights to

14

come back on, Greg and I are going to hop back into the drink and take the boats to the dock. I'm sure everyone will feel a lot better once we're on dry land.'

'Then what?' someone asked.

Before she could answer, Greg said, 'Let's just take this one step at a time, people.' He patted Darcy's back, then leaped off the boat.

Darcy followed. The cold of the water was a shock, but it didn't seem quite as bad as before. She held onto the gunnel. 'You with the flashlight?'

The woman looked at her.

'What's your name?'

'Beth.'

'You've been doing great, Beth. Thanks. Now, just aim the light forward so I can see where we're going.'

'Fine.'

Darcy waded around the corner of the boat. She clutched its metal rim with both hands and leaned backward. It slid sluggishly toward her. She began walking, and it picked up speed. Once it was moving smoothly, she guided it away from the cave wall.

The chill water climbed her body. She gritted her teeth when it wrapped her breasts.

Think warm thoughts, she told herself.

You'll bake when you get out of here. They won't expect you to take down any more tours today. You'll have the afternoon off. Go to the hotel pool with Mom and stretch out on a lounge.

If you do get out of here. If there's still a hotel. If there's still a Mom.

Damn it, nothing's happened up there!

Then why aren't the lights on yet?

'How's it going, Greg?' she called to stop herself from

15

dwelling on the awful possibilities.

'No problem.'

She looked over her shoulder. The beam of the flashlight slanted through the darkness, making a shiny patch on the water several yards ahead. 'Aim it up, Beth.'

The light lifted. Near the dim end of its reach was the dock, a wooden platform stretching along the far side of the cavern. Maybe eighty or a hundred feet off.

'Just a few more minutes, everyone,' Darcy said.

'Let's lift our voices in song.' That was Greg. Darcy smiled. A few of the passengers laughed. A woman in her boat actually began to sing 'Darcy, tow the boat ashore.' More laughter. Nobody joined in the song, and her voice trailed off after the first 'hallelujah'.

Darcy stepped into emptiness. Her other foot slipped off its hold. Gasping with alarm, she sank to her chin before she could pull herself up. She hung on. The boat carried her backward. She felt her legs rise up beneath it, her knees lightly bumping the hull. The boat slowed. A voice from its other end said, 'Look out, there.'

'What the . . . ?' Greg.

Darcy's boat shook, lurched forward a bit.

'You okay?' she called.

'No problem.'

'He almost got squashed,' said a woman.

'It's okay,' Greg said. 'You run into trouble?'

'I ran out of bottom,' Darcy answered. She lowered her feet. They found rock. 'It's okay, now,' she said, and tugged at the boat. It inched forward again. 'Watch out for the hole, Greg.'

'Yeah. No sharks down here, I hope.'

'We're the only wildlife.'

'A fucking comedy team,' a voice said.

'Watch your language, mister,' Darcy snapped. 'There's kids down here.'

'Big deal.'

'Mister!' Darcy warned.

'Up yours.'

'Dad, stop it.' A boy. Darcy imagined he must be the kid, thirteen or fourteen years old, wearing glasses and a hooded red sweatshirt – the kid who'd walked the tour beside the man with the sour face. The kid who got his arm yanked roughly when all he wanted to do was pause for a second to look at Indian Face rock, and Darcy had wanted to smack his creep of a father.

This had to be the same pair.

' . . . speak to me that way,' the father muttered threateningly.

'Ow, don't.'

'Knock it off back there, Slick.' The voice of a different man.

'Mind your own business, you old fart.'

'Hey!' Darcy yelled.

'Okay, pal.' Greg. 'You're the fellow in the Peterbilt cap and cowboy boots. You're gonna shape up right now.'

Silence.

Must be a real shock, Darcy thought, the creep hearing himself described by someone who couldn't even see him in the dark.

She looked over her shoulder again. The flashlight still pointed at the dock. 'Pretty soon, now,' she said.

Only about forty feet to go. Though the boat didn't seem especially difficult to tow, Darcy was starting to hurt. Her arms seemed all right, just a little heavy, but her back muscles, especially behind the shoulder blades

17

and all the way down her spine, were hot and sore and felt as if they were bunching into knots. Her buttocks ached. So did the backs of her legs.

This is what happens, she thought. You hit twenty-one, the body goes. All downhill from here on.

She smiled.

Deke the Creep had grabbed her in the parking lot of Sam's after the party last month, tried to steal a kiss from the sloshed birthday girl, and she'd tossed all over him. The look on his face! Then *he'd* tossed, missing her as she whirled out of the way. The story went all over campus. They started calling her Barfin' Darcy with the Kiss of Death.

Thank God the semester ended soon afterwards.

By fall, she thought, it'll be ancient history.

By fall, *I* might be ancient history.

Her stomach knotted.

We'll be all right.

Forget lounging by the pool. I'll spend the afternoon soaking in a bathtub in water so hot it'll steam up the mirror. Then go with Mom to the cocktail lounge. Have a double something. Anything but beer. Maybe a Mai-tai. Maybe Greg will be there.

I wonder how he looks in the light.

He's older, but not very. Under thirty.

Darcy must have seen him before the blackout, but she couldn't remember. She wondered if he was alone.

He'll probably leave, anyway, once we're out of here. Everyone does. If people stay in the hotel, it's usually just for the night *before* they take the tour. After they've seen the cavern, they take off, either heading home or for the next place of interest marked on their vacation maps.

I won't let him get away, she thought. Not, at least, until I've bought him a drink.

Maybe he's with his wife.

I'll buy her a drink, too. We'll *have* to celebrate when we get out of this mess.

We *will* get out of this mess.

Darcy kept looking behind her. A few yards from the dock, she walked her hands across the boat's edge, moved herself around it's corner, and shoved. The boat eased away. 'Watch out behind,' she said. 'We're slowing.'

The boat slipped along in front of her. She was between its side and the dock. As it settled in the water, she clutched its gunnel with both hands and leaned away, her back muscles on fire with the effort. The boat moved slowly towards her.

A man at the front, the one beside Beth who'd helped Darcy aboard and was first to offer his jacket for Tom, sprang up and leaped to the dock. Beth followed him with the flashlight. Darcy watched him as she pulled the boat. He rushed over the planks, sat down quickly to her right and stuck his legs out straight.

Darcy let go of the gunnel. She turned away. The boat nudged her back, but she didn't need to worry, now, about being squeezed against the dock. The man held the boat off with his feet while she thrust herself up and scrambled clear.

They knelt side-by-side, pulled the outstretched arms of passengers, brought the boat in closer, then grabbed the gunnel and worked the boat forward alongside the dock.

'Everyone stay seated,' Darcy said in a breathless voice. 'Wait till both boats are secure.'

Beth and two other passengers disregarded the order and jumped out. Just as well, Darcy thought. Beth provided light for the man and woman, who were getting to their knees farther up the dock and reaching out for her boat. Once they had it, Beth hurried forward and held the light on Greg's boat.

Greg waded to the other side and pushed the boat close enough for Darcy and the man to take over. They brought it in against the dock and three passengers, including Kyle Mordock, hopped out and began tying its lines to the posts.

As Darcy got to her feet, she saw Greg in the gloom near the far end of the boat, climbing from the water. She went to him.

'So far, so good,' he said.

'I'll buy you a drink when we're out of here,' she told him.

'A nice hot steaming mug of coffee.' He pulled off his sweatshirt, held it at arms' length, and began to wring it out. He was a pale blur above the darkness of his jeans, but Darcy could see that his shoulders were hunched up with the cold. She heard water patter on the boards. 'You want to go back and get the passengers organized?' he suggested. 'I'll be along in a minute.'

'Sure,' she said, guessing that he wanted to wring out his pants.

He turned away and walked farther into the darkness.

Darcy's own clothes were sodden and cold. She thought of the grotto near the other end of the dock.

She faced the boats. The passengers were already stepping out. She made her way through them. 'Greg and I want to rest and dry off for a couple of minutes. Then we'll all take a hike for the elevators. In the meantime, everyone stay here and try not to fall in the lake.'

There were a few laughs.

The seat on the forward boat where Tom had been was empty. She found him standing on the dock, held steady by the man who'd helped her with the boats. His head was hanging. He still pressed the handkerchief to his wound. 'How're you feeling, Tom?'

'Guess I'll live,' he muttered.

'Thanks for the help,' she told the other man. 'Are you Beth's husband?'

He nodded. 'I'm Jim. Jim Donner.'

'You've been a lot of help, Jim. Beth, too. I appreciate it.'

'Hey, we're all in this together.'

'You want to look after Tom till I get back?' she asked.

'Sure thing.'

She reached for the flashlight clipped to Tom's belt, pulled it free, and thumbed the switch. A white beam darted out. Its brightness made her realize how weak and yellowish the other flash had become.

With a glance over her shoulder to make sure no one was following, Darcy hurried over the boards and reached the concrete walkway. A few yards farther, she found the stone stairs, rushed up them and entered the grotto.

It had been the size of a small, round closet when Darcy first saw it two weeks ago. Now, it was slightly larger. Near the entrance was a wheelbarrow loaded with chunks of limestone hacked from the walls. A pickaxe was propped against the side of the wheelbarrow.

Cubby Wales, Ethan Mordock's handyman, had been down here during the weekdays, enlarging the grotto.

Once it was big enough, Ethan planned to install a chemical toilet for the convenience of the tourists.

Too bad this is a Saturday, Darcy thought. Would've been nice to have another able-bodied employee on hand.

She set the flashlight on the wheelbarrow's piled rocks, pointing away from her. Its beam spread out against the side wall, filling the small enclosure with light.

As fast as she could, she took off her shoes and socks. The floor was gritty under her bare feet, so she spread her jacket and stood on it. She kept her back to the entrance as she removed the rest of her clothes. Though the garments were sodden and cold, she felt worse without them. The chilly air of the cave seemed to seep into her damp skin. She crawled with gooseflesh and her nipples felt hard and achy. Her jaw muscles were sore from clenching her teeth together.

For a while, she stood there shivering, hunched over slightly, legs clamped together for warmth, and briskly rubbed her hands over her nubby skin. That didn't seem to help much.

With a palsied hand, she lifted her panties off the wheelbarrow handle, balled them up and squeezed. Water spilled through her fingers. When she couldn't force out any more drops, she shook the flimsy garment open. Hopping from foot to foot, she stepped into the leg holes, and drew the panties up. They were damp, but much better than before. The snug cling of them felt good.

Not good enough. She was still shuddering with cold as she leaned forward and pulled her trousers off the wheelbarrow. She struggled to slide the belt out of the wet loops, and then emptied the pockets, dropping her change purse, keys, comb and handkerchief onto the jacket at her feet.

She twisted a long, blue leg of the trousers into a tight club and water splattered the tops of her feet. Gathering up the other leg she began to wring it out . . .

. . . and flinched at a quiet, scraping sound behind her. A footstep? She whirled around.

Kyle stood in the opening.

She jerked her trousers up to cover her breasts. 'Damn it,' she snapped. 'Get out of here!'

In the dim glow from the flashlight, she saw Kyle form a narrow smile. 'I thought you might like to have this,' he said, holding his jacket towards her. 'It's dry,' he added.

'Thanks.' Her voice shook. She clamped the pants against her breasts with a forearm, and took the jacket with her other hand.

'Let's see if it fits,' he said.

'I'm sure it will.'

'Oh, come on.'

'You've already seen me, Kyle.'

'Not on purpose. I just came over to do you a favour.'

'And I appreciate it. Now, please go on back. I'll be along in a minute.'

His grin stretched wider. 'Do you want my pants?'

Darcy shook her head. 'Your jacket's plenty. Thanks.' She was about to suggest again that he leave. Instead, she asked, 'Do you have any idea what happened to the lights?'

'Maybe someone switched them off.'

That possibility had never occurred to her. She'd assumed, from the start, that the lights had gone off because of a power failure. If they were only turned off, then the elevators could still be working.

'Glad I asked,' she muttered.

'But I don't think that's it,' Kyle said. 'I think it's the generators. I mean, who'd turn off the lights?'

Darcy shook her head. 'I don't know. Anyway, thanks again for the jacket. See you later.'

He turned around and vanished into the darkness. The sound of his footsteps faded.

Wouldn't surprise me, Darcy thought, if he sneaks back for a second look.

Weird little creep.

Take it easy on him, she thought. He brought me the jacket.

Just an excuse to take a peek. I should've figured he'd do something like that.

She turned her back to the opening, held the pants between her legs, and got into the jacket. It was a wind-breaker of synthetic fabric that felt weightless. It was slick and cool against her skin. Tucking her chin down, she bent over slightly to watch her trembling hands struggle with the zipper. And noticed how her damp panties clung like transparent skin.

She felt sick.

The bastard couldn't have seen more if I was naked, she thought.

Damn him!

At last, she fitted the zipper together. She slid the tab up.

And sighed, moments later, when she felt how the jacket seemed to trap her body heat.

At least I got the jacket out of the deal, she told herself.

Would've been better to freeze, though, than have that shit lay his eyes all over me.

Darcy continued to shake as she finished wringing the water from her pants. But the tremors weren't from the cold – she shook with fury and humiliation.

Bad enough he saw my breasts.

Maybe he didn't notice the other.

Fat chance. He's short and he was standing below me. He saw, all right.

She stepped into her pants and pulled them up. After filling the pockets, she worked the belt through the loops and buckled it. She squeezed the water from her socks, pulled them on, and stepped into her shoes.

It felt good to be dressed again. Though she was still wet and cold from the waist down, the jacket gave her enough warmth to make the discomfort seem minor.

She debated what to do with the remaining clothes. She certainly didn't want to put them on. She could bundle up the bra and blouse inside her jacket and take them with her, but that seemed like too much trouble. I'll just pick them up the next time I'm down here, she decided, and draped the jacket over the wheelbarrow handle.

When Kyle reached the bottom of the stairs, he took a few more steps to make Darcy think he was going away. The tourists were still gathered on the dock. Their bodies blocked most of the light from the other flash. He watched until he was sure no one was approaching him, then turned around and returned, walking slowly and rolling his feet quietly from heel to toe.

He stopped at the bottom of the six rock stairs, and gazed up at Darcy.

She had the jacket on. Her back was toward him. Her head was down, and she seemed to be trying to fasten the zipper. The jacket wasn't quite long enough to reach her hips. It left a band of bare skin above her low, brief panties.

Though her back was in shadow, he could see a hint of the darker, curving crease between her buttocks.

She zipped up the jacket, then started wringing out her pants.

Kyle stared at her long, slim legs, at the smooth mounds of her rump.

He wished she would take off the jacket and give him another look at her front. He wanted more than anything to see her breasts again. For just an instant, while she was turning around before, he'd seen them in the light. They were pale and the nipples were sticking out. Then, she'd covered them and her front had been in shadow.

She *might* take the jacket off, he told himself. She might go to get into her bra and shirt again. But she wouldn't have to turn around to do that.

Worth sticking around for, though. If she only turned sideways a bit, he'd at least get a glimpse.

Amy Lawson was nothing next to Darcy.

She's all yours, Dad had said.

What if he could do Darcy the way he'd done Amy?

Kyle had had that thought many times before, but now it was almost too much for him.

He rubbed the back of his hand across his dry lips. His heart was thundering. His erection, pushing hard against the front of his jeans, felt as if it might explode.

Do Darcy the way he did Amy.
Get her into Room 115.
She'd have to ride the chute, after. But that was okay.

3

It was a week ago, Friday, that Amy Lawson checked into the Mordock Cave Hotel. Kyle first saw her when she entered the restaurant for supper. It was his job to seat the guests as they arrived.

She came in alone. She appeared to be about Darcy's age, but wasn't nearly as beautiful. Her hair was long and brown, not short and golden. She was inches shorter than Darcy, with bigger breasts, but also a bigger waist and rump, and her calves below the hem of her dress were on the heavy side. She appeared to be stout rather than fat, but Kyle much preferred Darcy's slender shape. Her face was pleasant, though, and looked rather pretty when she smiled at him.

'May I see you to a table?' he asked.

'Please. Thank you.' Her eyes betrayed the usual amusement at realizing that a boy Kyle's age was acting as host. He didn't bother to explain himself. This woman would simply assume, as they all did, that he was a relation of the owner.

'Will you be dining alone?' he asked.

She nodded.

He led her through the dining room to a table for two which had a nice view of the gardens. He pulled out a chair for her. Her scent was sweet and cloying.

'I like your perfume,' he lied.

She smiled over her shoulder at him. 'Thank you. It's Rose Blossom.'

'Very nice.' He was glad Darcy didn't use a sickening perfume like that. He'd stood close to her in the elevators. She had a faint, fresh smell that made him think of a morning breeze.

'A waitress will be along in a minute to take your order,' he said. 'I hope you enjoy your meal.'

'Thank you very much.'

Kyle returned to his station by the entrance, hoping Darcy would show up. She had come in Monday night with that other guide, her room-mate, Lynn Maxwell. It made him ache, now, remembering how she had looked striding into the restaurant. Her sleeveless dress was white with blue flowers, the blue in the dress matching her eyes. The light tan of her skin seemed tawny next to the white, and the dress floated against her as she walked. Kyle made believe he was under it, watching the airy fabric caress her skin.

After Monday, Darcy hadn't come into the restaurant. Kyle supposed she only dined here that night because it was her first time at the hotel and she was celebrating. He found out later that she had started going into town with some of the other guides. It was the usual thing. A room at the hotel came with the job, but the employees had to pay for their own meals and the Cave Chalet was too expensive. They'd be eating up their wages if they didn't head into town for hamburgers or pizza or whatever.

Besides, the guides liked to get away. They didn't go to town just for the cheap food, but to have fun. From hearing their talk over the years, Kyle knew that they went to movies and bars. Some of them tried to pick up townies if they didn't have one of the other guides to mess with.

Not Darcy, though. Kyle could tell from the way she acted towards the male guides that she wasn't letting any of them get her. She was friendly to all of them, but there was no one special.

And she wouldn't do it with townies.

Lynn probably did. But Lynn was a slut.

Kyle doubted that Darcy would show up tonight. Especially since this was Friday. The guides *always* went into town on Friday nights. But each time the door swung open, his heart quickened until he saw who was entering.

By eight o'clock, he'd lost all hope.

Darcy had gone into town, all right, and would probably be out till midnight – or even later.

How about tonight? he thought. He began to tremble slightly. It was always exciting to enter a guest-room with the pass key and have a look around. He'd been tempted all week to try Darcy's, but he couldn't leave the restaurant until 8.30 and by then he was afraid the guides might come back from town and he'd be caught. This was Friday, though. He could do it tonight.

I will! I'll do it!

Waiting for 8.30 became an agony. His heart raced, his mouth was dry, his clammy hands trembled. Only twice did new guests arrive for dinner, and he was grateful each time for the interruption that briefly distracted him from dwelling on what lay ahead.

Darcy's room. Her clothes. Her personal things. The bed where she slept. The bathroom where she'd been naked in the tub.

He couldn't stand the waiting.

31

At twenty minutes after eight, he left the door and crossed the foyer to the cashier's booth. 'Minnie?' he asked in a pained voice. The scrawny little woman, leafing through a stack of bills, looked up at him. 'I'm not feeling real hot. Do you mind if I go now? It's only ten more minutes before . . .'

'You do look a mite puny, hon. You go on ahead. Your daddy won't never be the wiser on my account.'

'Thanks, Minnie,' he said, and made his way slowly to the door, hanging his head and holding his stomach just to make it look good.

Outside, he straightened up. After the air conditioning of the restaurant, the evening felt warm. He took a deep, trembling breath, and started along the walkway towards the hotel. His father would be manning the registration desk, so Kyle entered the side door at the end of the west wing and trotted up the stairs to the second floor. The corridor was deserted; his footfalls were quiet on the thick carpet. As he passed the main stairs at the halfway point, he saw a middle-aged couple on their way up. He slowed down. Glancing back, he saw them reach the top and turn the other way.

At the door marked 210, he looked back again. The people were near the far end of the corridor, the man unlocking a door. A moment later, they were gone.

Kyle listened. No sounds came from behind the door. Just to be safe, however, he knocked. If Darcy or Lynn should answer, he'd say that Dad had sent him to look for Tom, who sometimes watched the desk for him. Did they know where Tom might be?

Nobody answered the knock.

He dug a trembling hand into the pocket of his slacks and pulled out his key case. The keys clinked together, loud in the silence, as he fumbled for the right one. At last, he had it. He pushed it into the lock, turned it, gently twisted the knob, and eased the door open.

He saw no one, but he left the door open while he crept forward far enough to see through the alcove on the left. Nobody in the bathroom.

The girls were gone, all right.

He stepped back to the door and shut it.

I'm in!

He leaned against the door and took deep breaths, trying to calm himself. The curtains at the other end of the room were open. The wooded hills in the distance were gloomy with dusk. If Kyle didn't waste time, he'd be able to get by without turning on any lights – except in the alcove and bathroom, which didn't have windows.

He rubbed his sweaty hands on his slacks, and pushed himself away from the door. The alcove had clothes hanging along one side. He would give them a look later. And the bathroom. He moved on.

The twin beds were both made, but a little rumpled. Clothing was scattered on top of the nearer bed: blue pants lying flat with the legs draping the edge, a white blouse lying in a heap, a white bra. The pants had a wide waist. The bra had broad straps and enormous cups. Lynn's. So that must be Lynn's bed.

Because of the difference in the girls' sizes, Kyle had no trouble figuring out which drawers of the built-in bureau contained Darcy's clothes. The bottom drawer held sweaters, a sweatshirt, a couple of heavy shirts. They were all neatly folded. He lifted them, glanced at each, but took none of them out.

The middle drawer was more interesting. There, he found slips, pantyhose, a couple of T-shirts, a pair of faded blue shorts and a bright yellow jersey. He picked up the jersey and let it fall open. It was a nightshirt. It had slits on each side. Kyle held it against his body. He was shorter than Darcy. On her, it would hang only part-way down her thighs, the open sides leaving her bare to the hips. He could see her wearing it, the light fabric showing all her curves. He imagined how it would tremble over her breasts as she walked. Bending down, her rump would show, and if she reached for something high, the nightshirt would rise up and he'd be able to see between her legs.

The thoughts made Kyle hard.

He folded the nightshirt and placed it carefully into the drawer. Satisfied that it looked the same as when he found it, he slid the drawer shut and opened the top one.

Here were panties, brassieres, socks and two swimsuits.

One of the suits was bright blue and backless, the other a white string bikini. Neither had stains, and they both smelled clean. Kyle supposed that Darcy had packed them fresh and hadn't used the hotel pool yet. He'd checked it a few times on Wednesday and Thursday, her days off, hoping to see her there. Now, he knew that he hadn't missed her. He would keep a watch on the pool. Sooner or later, she'd show up.

Most of the bras were white with a lacy fabric for the upper half of the cups, narrow straps, and two fasteners in the back. But one was black and strapless. It was stiff along the bottom. It would hold her breasts underneath, and leave them bare on top. The other two bras were flimsy, shapeless things. One was pink, one blue. They fastened in front with a hook and eyelet between the cups. Holding them up, Kyle could see right through them and the wispy fabric felt slick against his face. The pink one smelled faintly of Darcy, that fresh early morning scent of a breeze blowing through the woods.

Kyle bent over to ease the pressure of his erection pushing against his pants.

He put the bras away.

He looked at the stacks of brightly coloured panties.

He was breathing hard, gasping. He was almost past control. If he didn't stop now, he'd mess himself for sure.

He slid the drawer shut.

I'll come back, he thought. Some other time. See the rest of it then.

On his way back to the door he glanced at the bathroom. He'd badly wanted to see the tub. Darcy was naked when she was in there.

Next time, he told himself. Next time, I'll see everything.

Right now, he had to get out before he burst.

He was in the corridor, pulling the door shut, when the sound of voices made him turn his head.

Out of the elevator near the main stairway stepped an elderly couple. And his father.

Dad had suitcases in each hand.

He glanced at Kyle, then turned away and led the couple towards the west wing.

Kyle felt sick. He went through the fire door, sat down on a stair and hunched over, clutching his knees.

Now what'll I do? He saw me. Shit, oh shit.

What were you doing in that room?

Maybe he didn't see me.

He looked right *at* me. Maybe he'll forget about it.

Fat chance. I've gotta have an excuse. Darcy phoned from town, said she couldn't find her purse, and wanted me to see if it was in her room? That won't work. How could I get the call? Dad would've been at the switchboard.

Dad doesn't *know* why I was there. He might think I wanted to steal something. That'd be better than the truth, anyway. But maybe he'll guess the truth.

I've gotta have a story!

How about if I say I was out back and thought I saw someone in the window? I knew Darcy and Lynn were gone, and thought somebody'd broken in, so I came up to check.

Okay? That's not bad. Okay, that's what it'll be. He might believe it.

The best thing to do is go see Dad right away. Tell him the story. That's what I'd do if I really had seen someone in the window.

Kyle sat on the stair, unable to move.

Dad'll never believe it. It never worked, trying to lie to him. He always knew the truth. Like he was a mind-reader, or something. He'll know what I was doing in there. He'll think I'm perverted.

Better not to say anything, Kyle decided. That way, at least, I won't get it for lying. Just wait and see what happens. See what he asks.

Kyle finally got to his feet and went downstairs. He pushed through the metal door. Feeling numb and shaky, he headed for the lobby.

Please, he thought, let Dad not be there.

Kyle's father was behind the registration desk and looked up at him as he approached. Nobody else was around.

'You have some business in 210, young man?'

'Darcy wanted to borrow a couple of my speleology books,' he said, and wondered where *that* idea had come from. 'I just took them up and left them for her.'

He nodded.

He believed it!

'Business pretty brisk at the Chalet tonight?'

'About the same as usual,' Kyle said. 'It was pretty full.'

'Glad to hear it.'

'Guess I'll go watch some TV, okay?'

'Go on ahead. I'll let you know if I need you.'

Kyle stepped around the end of the registration desk and opened the door to their rooms. He went straight to his bedroom and shut himself in. Immediately, he slid two of his speleology books off the shelves and hid them in the space behind some other volumes. Not that Dad was likely to check. But when you make up a story, you have to follow through with the details.

Once the books were concealed, Kyle felt a lot better.

He turned the television on, and sat in the middle of his bed.

He was too uneasy to follow the shows. Part of the time, he worried about Dad finding out the truth. (He's gonna. No, he won't. What if he asks Darcy about the books? What if he just *knows*?) Part of the time, he got past the worries and took himself back into Darcy's room. There, he lifted her things from the drawers, looked at them and touched and smelled them and dreamed of how they would look on Darcy.

Later that night, with the lights off, he sat propped up in bed and stared at the television and thought about the next time.

Next time, maybe he would take off his clothes. Maybe try on some of her things. (If he stole a pair of her panties, would she notice they were gone?) Maybe he would lie down on her bed, stretch out naked on the same sheet she slept on. In the bathroom, maybe he'd find a towel Darcy had used after a bath or shower. It might still be damp. A towel that had rubbed her body all over.

Someone shook Kyle's shoulder. He woke up, startled, and rolled onto his back. His father was leaning over the bed, face grey in the fluttery light from the television. The screen was fuzzy, the way it looks after a station has signed off for the night. Kyle glanced at the digital clock on his bed table. Two thirty-six.

'What's wrong?' he murmured.

His heart sped up. He knew what was wrong. Dad knew he hadn't been in Darcy's room to leave books for her.

'Get dressed and come with me,' Dad whispered.

This was strange; if Dad meant to give him a lashing, or even just a lecture, he'd do it here, wouldn't he? Maybe he had some other kind of punishment in mind.

Maybe he plans to make me face Darcy! *At this hour?*

'Where are we going?'

'Do like I say.'

Dad didn't sound angry, but Kyle heard a tremor in his voice. Was he scared about something? Excited?

Kyle climbed out of bed. His clothes were draped on a chair. With his back to his father, he dropped his pyjama pants and put on his jockey shorts. He started to step into the good slacks he'd worn for hosting at the Chalet.

'Not those,' Dad said. 'Put on some grubbies.'

Why!

He didn't ask. He went to his closet, and got into jeans and an old shirt. Then he put on socks and jogging shoes.

Dad led the way. The lights had been dimmed in the deserted lobby. The hotel was silent. Kyle felt as if the building itself were asleep.

Dad said nothing.

They walked down the corridor of the east wing, even walked past the door of 115, the final guestroom.

We're going to the stairs, Kyle thought. He *is* taking me up to Darcy's room.

But Dad stopped at the very last door before the corridor's end. It was unmarked. In the past, Kyle had tried to unlock it. This was the one door he'd found in the entire hotel that didn't open to the pass key.

Dad had told him, long ago and more than once, that it was a storeroom.

He's gonna lock me in!

You like sneaking into rooms so much, spend some time in this.

Dad took a leather key case out of his pocket. It was the one Kyle had given him for his last birthday. He unsnapped it. On one of the metal clips were two matching keys, one that looked shiny and new. He tugged the new key loose, and held it up in front of Kyle's eyes. It shone like gold in the dim lights.

'I had this made for you on your fifteenth birthday,' he whispered, still in that same tense voice. 'But I saved it till I was sure you were ready.'

'Ready for what?' Kyle rubbed his sweaty hands on his jeans.

'I saw you coming out of that room tonight, I figured it was time.'

'I didn't do anything.'

'Oh, I got a pretty good idea what you were doing. Used to do it myself. Then one day, my Daddy gave me one of these.' He handed the bright new key to Kyle. 'Go on, open her up.'

Kyle's hand shook so badly that the point of the key scraped the lock face. His father took his hand, held it steady, and guided the key in. Kyle turned it. He opened the door.

He glimpsed red curtains, an easy chair. Then Dad nudged him forward, followed him inside and closed the door.

The small room was dark except for a faint glow coming in around the edges of the curtains. A hand on Kyle's shoulder guided him, turned him.

'Now, don't yell or anything,' Dad whispered.

Silently, the curtains parted.

Kyle's mind reeled. His heart hammered. His breath rushed out.

He was standing no more than two feet from a window – not a window, exactly. It had to be a two-way mirror. A full length mirror like those on the bathroom doors of all the other units. This one, however, was obviously not on the bathroom door. It was set into the wall.

On the other side of the glass was a guest-room.

Room 115.

Its lights were on.

On the bed was the woman he'd seated at the Chalet, the one with the rose blossom perfume.

The bed covers lay heaped on the floor and she was squirming on the sheet.

'Name's Amy,' Dad said. 'Amy Lawson.'

She was naked.

A wide band of white tape covered her mouth. Her

hands were tied together with clothes-line, arms stretched overhead and secured to the wrought-iron bedframe. Her legs were spread far apart, tied at the ankles to the corners of the frame.

Kyle stared. He had never seen a real woman naked. Pictures in magazines, but never the real thing.

This was better than anything he had ever imagined.

Her struggles to free herself made it even better. She was rocking, twisting, arching her back, pulling at the ropes. Her big breasts bobbed and swayed. Her skin was shiny with sweat. It looked dark and polished from the sun, pure white where a bikini had kept the sun away. There were faint, reddish patches on her breasts and shoulders and thighs. Dad, Kyle thought, must've made those.

Dad, for sure, had done the number on her face. The face had been pounded pretty good. A cheek was red and swollen, and one eye was swollen almost shut.

'I always put the best-looking babes in 115,' Dad whispered. 'Sometimes, they're just for looking. This one checked in by herself. When they do that, sometimes they get the treatment. What do you think?' he asked.

Kyle muttered, 'Neat.'

He gazed at the writhing woman, hardly able to breathe. He felt trapped inside his jeans, his rigid penis threatening to ejaculate. It was the way he'd felt in Darcy's room just before he rushed out.

But some of the urgency drained away as his father eased him aside. The man crouched for a moment, then stood up and twisted a pair of latches near the top of the mirror's frame. Just below the latches were two metal handles. Dad gripped them and pushed the mirror outward. Stepping over a foot-high section of wall he entered the room, carrying the mirror in front of him.

'Come on in,' Dad said.

Amy made quiet whiny noises.

Kyle stepped into the room.

She stopped squirming. She watched him with wide eyes.

Dad propped the mirror against the wall near the opening to the secret room. Then he put a hand on Kyle's shoulder. 'She's all yours, son. I'll be back in an hour.'

Dad went out through the regular door.

Kyle stared at the naked, sweaty body.

This can't be happening, he thought. He felt as if his father had taken him by the hand and led him into a dream – an amazing, erotic dream that was too wonderful to be true.

It's not a dream, he told himself.

I'm really here.

And I've got an hour.

As fast as he could, Kyle took off his clothes.

4

In spite of her humiliation and anger at being seen half naked by Kyle, Darcy was glad to have the jacket. From neck to waist, at least, she felt warm.

Greg met her just before she reached the dock.

Now, if *he'd* been the one to show up at the grotto . . .

I'm sure feeling lively, she thought, and smiled at him.

'How's it going?' she asked.

'Not bad. There's a fellow with Tom who said he'd stick with him on the way out.'

'Okay, good. How would you like to take up the rear and keep an eye out for stragglers?'

'Fine.'

'I'll get the other flashlight from Beth. Here, you take this one.' She gave it to him. 'It's the stronger of the two. It should be good enough to keep things fairly bright for everyone.'

'We ought to count noses before we start out.'

Darcy nodded. Then she faced the group and called for attention. 'In just a minute,' she said, 'we'll start for the elevators. But I want to give you some instructions first. Most of you came down here with friends or family. I want you to stay close to those you came with. Hold

43

hands or something so you don't lose each other. Any of you who came alone, step up to the front right now, and we'll make sure you get a partner.'

Several people started working their way forward. They gathered in front of Darcy. One was Kyle. Four of the others looked around, formed pairs, and introduced themselves to their new companions.

'Why don't I be your partner,' Kyle said to Darcy.

'That'd leave somebody out,' she told him. 'Who's still alone?' she asked.

A girl raised her hand.

A blonde with a pony tail. She looked fifteen or sixteen. Darcy wondered what a girl that age was doing on the tour without her parents. 'What's your name?' she asked.

'Paula Whitmore,' the girl answered.

'Okay, Paula. Do you want to pair up with this young man?'

She looked at Kyle, smiled and nodded. 'Sure. If it's all right with him.'

He shrugged and said, 'I'm Kyle.'

'Okay,' Darcy said. 'It's you two, then.' She felt guilty about sticking Paula with Kyle. It seemed like a dirty trick, just a way to keep the jerk off her own back. Hell, she told herself, it's only natural to pair them up. They're the same age and everything. And Paula could have objected. The girl might actually enjoy having a male escort.

Darcy turned her attention to the rest of the group. 'Okay, now. Does anyone *not* have at least one partner?' Nobody responded. 'Once we start out, I want each of you to be responsible for three things. First, stay beside your partner. Second, keep track of the people directly in front of you. If it's too dark to see them, keep a hand on one of them. Third, pay attention to the people right behind you. Don't leave them behind. There's no hurry.

'With a flashlight at each end of the group, there should be at least a little light. Some of you have matches, lighters, and cameras with flashes. If necessary, use them. But don't waste them. The trip will probably take about an hour, and we really don't know how long we'll be in the cavern before electricity is restored. I think we should try to get by with the flashlights, and save the matches and things in case we need them later on.

'If anyone has trouble along the way, call out and we'll stop immediately. Any questions?'

'Couldn't we make torches or something?' It was the voice of the boy who'd asked about the damming effects of Ely's wall.

'I guess we could,' Darcy answered, 'but I don't think it's really necessary. The flashlights should be enough to keep us in light until we reach the elevators.'

'Are there any bats down here?' asked a woman near the back.

'No. Bats used to inhabit the cavern, but they didn't last long after Ely Mordock sealed the natural opening. The same goes for cave rats and other wildlife. So you don't need to worry about running into any nasty critters down here.'

'Well, thank goodness for that,' the woman said.

'Any more questions?'

'We gonna stand around here all day?'

Greg swung the flashlight across the group and found the face of the man in the Peterbilt hat. Squinting against the glare, the man turned his head away.

'Any *other* questions?' Darcy asked. When no response came, she said, 'Let's have Tom at the front here.'

He came forward, walking slowly, Jim and Beth Donner on either side of him. Darcy was glad to see that they weren't holding him up. A belt was wrapped around his head to hold cloth pads against his wound.

'I'm going to lead the way,' Darcy announced. 'Greg will take up the rear. He has a flashlight, and he'll keep an eye on everyone.'

'You'll need this,' Beth said, and gave her flashlight to Darcy. It seemed only about half as bright as the one Greg held, but it was still strong enough to do the job.

Greg put a hand on her shoulder; it felt big and warm through the jacket. 'Whenever you're ready,' he said, speaking quietly. 'I'll stay put and count them as they go by.'

'Great,' she told him. She faced the others. 'Everybody ready?'

'*Head 'em up, move 'em out!*' The kid who'd asked about torches. Darcy was starting to like him.

She turned around, then raised the hand with the flashlight high overhead, swept it down, and started walking. The wooden planks of the dock creaked under her feet, and rumbled as those behind her began to move. A few strides took her to the concrete walkway.

She kept the beam aimed low, lighting the area just ahead of her feet. Soon, she spotted the steps to the grotto on her right. The encounter with Kyle forced its way into her mind. She felt herself blushing.

The little creep's probably thinking about it right now.

Kyle, watching the dim shape of Darcy beyond the three

46

people in front of him, saw her head turn. The grotto's over there, he thought, and felt a warm stir in his groin as he remembered the way she'd looked.

Nothing on but her panties, and he could see right through those.

He'd been in her room three times, so far, and now he'd seen her nearly naked. The next thing was to *get* her.

Put her in 115.

Dad won't let that happen, though. She's a guide. She's not like Amy Lawson, someone you can just get rid of.

There must be a way.

The girl beside Kyle suddenly stumbled and grabbed his arm. Steady again, she muttered, 'Sorry,' and released her grip.

'It's all right,' Kyle said.

'I'm such a klutz sometimes.'

'Maybe you should take my hand,' he said, so polite, as if he were hosting at the Chalet.

She put her hand in his. It felt warm. Kyle looked at her. He couldn't see much, just that she was wearing glasses. But he remembered what she looked like. Even though he'd kept his eyes mostly on Darcy during the tour, he'd checked out all the other females. This one had blonde hair in a pony tail, and was kind of pretty in spite of the glasses. She was wearing a white blouse, an open white sweater, a plaid skirt with pleats, and knee socks. Kyle recalled that she had big breasts for someone so slim.

He noticed, now, that she smelled good. Not fresh like Darcy or flowery like Amy. It was an aroma that made him think of cotton candy.

'Where are you from?' she asked.

'Oh, I live around here.' He decided not to tell her that his father owned the place. 'How about you?'

'I'm from Santa Monica, California.'

'You're a long way from home.'

'We're visiting my uncle in Albany. My dad's brother. We rented a car so we could explore around for a few days.'

'You and your parents?'

'Just my dad and me. My mom died three years ago.'

'Oh, I'm sorry.' He wasn't sorry. He didn't even know the girl's mother. But it seemed like the right thing to say.

She squeezed his hand. 'That's okay. What about you?'

'Mine ran off with somebody.'

'So you live with your father, just like me.'

'You live with my father?'

She laughed quietly. 'Silly.'

'What are you doing down here without him?'

'He's got claustrophobia.'

'You're kidding.'

'No, honest.' The way she sounded, Kyle guessed she was grinning.

'And he brought you to a cavern?'

'Well, I saw it in the guide book and I said it sounded neat. So here I am. He's probably shitting bricks, if you'll pardon my French.'

'Shit ain't French.'

She giggled, and the pale blur of her right hand darted up to cover her mouth. When it lowered again, she said, 'You're weird, Kyle.'

'I'm not weird. Shit's English. It's in Chaucer. Past

tense is shat. He shat a brick.'

Stifling more giggles, she bumped her shoulder against Kyle. 'That's *awful*.'

The woman just in front of them, who was walking beside Tom, looked over her shoulder. She said nothing. A moment later, she faced forward again.

Kyle gave her the finger.

Paula bumped him again.

This isn't bad, he thought. She likes me. Maybe I can cop a feel before we get out of here.

Carol Marsh flinched as Helen put an arm around her back.

'You're shaking like a leaf,' Helen said.

'I'm freezing, that's all.'

'You should've paid attention. I warned you it would be chilly down here.'

Yes, Helen had warned her. Helen was full of advice. She was thirty-six, only five years older than Carol, but she treated Carol like a child. Too many years in the classroom with kids short on common sense.

She'd been that way since Carol started at George Washington Elementary School. Carol's first day on the job, the more experienced teacher took her under her wing. And kept her there ever since.

The mother-hen treatment never bothered her much until this trip. Being in Helen's company day after day, night after night, Carol had started feeling smothered and annoyed by the treatment.

By now, the fifth day of their vacation, she had it up to her nose with the constant advice and the underlying assumption that she was incapable of running her own life.

49

This morning in the hotel room when Helen had said, 'You're not going on the tour in *that*, I hope,' she replied, 'I don't see anything wrong with it.'

It was a yellow sundress.

'Well, at least put on a sweater. You don't want to catch a cold.'

'It's ninety degrees outside.'

'We'll be a hundred and fifty feet below ground in a chilly, damp cave. And the guidebook . . . Let me get it.' *She's going to read me a lesson.* Helen found the booklet, opened it to a map she had used to mark her place, and read, ' "Mordock Cavern, while warmer than many similar caves in summer due to its unusual ventilation system which circulates air from the surface, none-theless remains chilly. Those wishing to take the tour in comfort are advised to wear sweaters or light jackets." '

'I think I'll live,' Carol said.

'Well, it's up to you, of course.'

'Yes, it is.'

Now, Carol wished she'd chosen a different issue for her small rebellion. The cool of the cave had felt good for a while, but soon it began bothering her. She'd been shivering ever since the lights went out. She suspected that the shivers had less to do with the temperature of the cave than with fear. Whatever the cause, however, warmer clothes would have improved the situation.

Her sundress didn't cover much. It was cut low in front and back, sleeveless and short. The fabric was so light it seemed to float around her, barely touching her skin. It let the air in. Wonderful in hot weather. Not so great down here.

Helen's arm felt warm and good on her back. She put her arm around Helen.

Felt the thickness of her friend's cable-knit sweater.
I wonder if she'd let me wear that for a few minutes.
No way am I going to ask, Carol told herself.
We'll be out of here before long.

She looked up. Light from behind brushed the shoulders and heads of those in front of her. Its glow lit the slick grey wall of the cave to the right. She saw a ruffled slab of flowstone that the guide, Darcy, had talked about on the way in.

We're more than halfway back to the elevators, she realized.

Helen suddenly seemed to stiffen. Her hand pressed more tightly against Carol's side.

'Are you all right?' Carol whispered.

'I'm sure . . . we're not actually trapped.'

'No, of course not. It's just temporary.'

'Perhaps they had to send to town for an electrician. That might take a while.'

'They won't leave us down here, Helen.'

'I understand that. I'm certain we'll be out of here in a matter of hours, at most.

'Probably,' Carol agreed. 'I really don't think anything *serious* happened up there.'

'A short circuit, something of that nature.'

'Can you believe that cretin suggesting there'd been a nuclear attack?'

'I suppose it is a possibility. It's *always* a possibility.'

'But remote,' Carol said. 'This is bad enough without dreaming up catastrophes.'

Helen patted her side.

They walked in silence.

Carol forgot about the cold. She struggled against an awful feeling of loss. What for? she thought. There certainly wasn't any goddamn nuclear war. Probably.

Even if there was, I don't have any family. If everyone got wiped out, I'd lose a few friends. Helen's probably my best friend, and she's safe down here with me.

Isn't that fine? No one to lose. No husband, not even a lover. No child. You're thirty-one, and you've got nothing. You blew it with Derek, you blew it with David. You wanted your space.

You'll have all the space in the world if it's been levelled.

'Carol?'

'Huh?' she asked, glad to have such thoughts interrupted.

'I left my insulin in the hotel room.'

'Are we almost there yet?'

Wayne Phillips looked down at his daughter. Katie was walking between him and Jean, holding a hand of each.

'Almost where?' Wayne asked.

'Don't be dumb, Daddy. The elevator.'

'We'll be there in fifteen minutes or so, I think. If the monsters don't get us.'

Katie jerked her hand away and punched his hip. 'Mommy, tell Daddy to stop. He's talking about monsters.'

'Really, Wayne, I don't think this is a good time for that sort of thing.'

'You're right. Besides, I haven't seen any. Yet.'

'Daddy!'

'He has monsters on the brain,' Jean said.

'And a good thing, too,' he told her, 'or we wouldn't be able to afford this fine vacation.' It made him feel good to think of the $7,500 they'd just received, the first half of the $15,000 advance for his new novel, *Lurker in the Dark*. The other half was due in nine months or on publication, whichever came first.

'I'll get a book out of this, for sure,' he said. 'What a terrific premise. Forty people trapped in a cave.'

'Didn't we see an Irwin Allen movie like that?' Jean asked.

'That was a disaster movie. This'll be horror. There's something *nasty* in the cave. Something that creeps out of the darkness and . . .'

'Stop it, Daddy. I don't think you're funny.'

'I'm not trying to scare you,' he protested. 'I'm just thinking out loud.'

'I wish you'd think to yourself.'

Seven years old, he thought, and she's already giving orders to men.

She's scared.

She loves spooky stories and horror movies, but this is getting to her. This is the real thing. No zombies or madmen or scuttling aliens (not yet), but we're in just the sort of place they might really go for, and she knows it.

And so do I.

There's no one down here but us, Wayne told himself.

And he suddenly remembered the clay people from one of those Flash Gordon serials he used to watch on television. It was the same story that had the forest people, those freaky folks with the wild hairdos who swung through the trees – and got either Flash or Happy with an arrow from one of their weird little crossbows.

Good God, Wayne thought. I *used* the forest people. They'd shown up as the Krotes in his second novel.

Until now, he'd never realized the connection.

So how about the clay people? he wondered. They were every bit as frightening as those creeps in the trees. They kind of looked like mummies. They were *in* the walls of the caves. You couldn't see them at all. They were just part of the rock (or clay) until they decided to move around, and then they sort of unblended and lurched along.

A *lot* like mummies. Maybe that's what made them so creepy. And the fact that they could be anywhere. You lean against a wall of the cave to rest, and maybe you're leaning against one of *them* and the next thing you know it grabs you.

They turned out to be good guys, Wayne remembered. Getting turned to clay was punishment for screwing up. It wasn't Ming doing it. Some babe. Some evil queen or princess.

Pretty far-fetched. Maybe you could get away with stuff like that in 1938 or whenever, but not today.

Still, it is a spooky concept.

All around us. Right in the walls. After we pass by, they materialize – grey, misshapen creatures of the cave. They're hunched over. They don't walk so much as shamble. And they start to stalk us.

Something snatched Wayne's hand. He jerked rigid and sucked a harsh gasp.

His hand had been snatched by Katie.

She started to laugh.

'You scared the bejabbers outa me,' he whispered.

Katie laughed even harder.

He knew that giving Dad a good scare, even if done by accident (like this time), was seen by Katie as one of life's genuine joys. It ranked right up there with talk of boogers, barf, butts and farts.

With tastes like that, he thought, she'll end up preferring to read Stephen King instead of her dear old dad.

Wayne noted that the couple ahead of him were carrying on a conversation – and not likely to hear his whispered words. 'You scared me so bad, I think I blew a hole in my unders.'

'Turn them into a Hershey factory?' Katie asked.

'Who *have* you been reading?'

'She's been listening to *you*, dear,' Jean informed him.

'And me a Nestlés man.'

Calvin Fargo had long ago lost track of the number of broken bones in his body, but he suspected he could count them up now without much trouble if he had a mind to. Each of the old fractures seemed to be clamouring for attention. The dank chill was doing it.

Calvin had been a stuntman for over thirty years, spent a good part of that time in the saddle, and bit the dust in more than a hundred movies. He'd been trampled by horses and cattle, been run over a few times by stage coaches and buckboards (and by a chariot in the remake of *Ben Hur*), taken falls off balconies, roofs and bluffs. It all added up to more fractures than a human has bones.

The hand-carved mesquite walking stick with its brass stallion-head handle had been a gag gift on his fiftieth birthday. Busted up as he was back then, he could still get around on his own two feet without the help of a cane. But it came from Yakima Canutt, who was not only his old pal but also the greatest stuntman of all time, so Calvin cherished the cane and took it with him everywhere – even if he didn't need it.

Today, he was mighty glad to have the help.

But the cane was enough. He sure didn't need Mavis trying to keep him up.

'Leave off my arm, there, sugar,' he said when he realized she wasn't just holding his arm, but lifting on it. 'I don't need a woman tugging at me.'

'Don't be such a chauvinist, honey.'

'I'm sure the lucky one,' he said. 'Married to the only gal in the country still talks like a sixties issue of *Cosmo*.'

'Oh, quit your complaining.'

'Then you quit dragging on my appendage.' She stopped helping him along, and merely held onto his elbow. 'Much obliged.'

'Pride goeth before a fall.'

'Shitfire! Now she's into scripture!'

He heard Mavis chuckle softly. 'You old coot. I don't know why I put up with you.'

'Cause I'm the hottest cocksman north of the Rio Grande, that's why.'

'Shhhh. Someone's gonna hear you.'

'Let 'em hear. Tell the truth and shame the devil, as you're so fond of saying in between calling folks chauvinists.'

'You're certainly cantankerous today.'

'Pissant called me an old fart.'

'Well, you shouldn't have interfered.'

'A man can only take so much, watching that son-of-a-whore bullying his boy. He's damn lucky I didn't lay into him.'

'You just forget about laying into anyone, Calvin Fargo.'

'Got no right to treat his boy that way. Your children, they're the best thing you get out of life . . .'

'Well, thank you very much.'

''Cept, of course, for a good horse, old boots, a warm place to shit, and a tight . . .'

'Don't you *dare* use that word in public.'

He laughed. 'Shitfire, honey, I just wanted to include you in, that's all.'

Mavis squeezed his arm. 'Your compliment is duly noted. Just don't go announcing it to the world.'

The walkway ended, and Darcy stepped onto the rock floor of the area known as the cathedral. She raised her flashlight. Its beam wasn't strong enough to reach the far end of the chamber, but she knew that the elevators were just ahead in the darkness.

The area seemed deserted.

'Hello?' she called.

No answer.

So Lynn and her group had made it to the top before the power failure. Lucky for them.

We've been pretty lucky, ourselves, she thought.

She could hardly believe that the trek had gone so smoothly. There'd been no shouts of alarm. Apparently, no one had tripped or strayed from the route or panicked.

She turned around and walked back. Greg's light was a beacon, held high and shining down on the tourists, sweeping from side to side, up and down.

'We've made it, everyone!' she called.

Her announcement was greeted by subdued applause, a few cheers and a whistle.

Facing forward, she spotted the elevator doors at the faint, far end of her light. She walked toward them.

5

Leaning between the elevator doors, rump against the rock wall, Darcy asked, 'Any trouble?'

There were murmurs. Nobody spoke up.

'I want you all to stand still for a minute. Greg's coming up, counting noses to make sure we didn't lose anyone.'

She switched off her flashlight to save whatever dwindling juice might still remain in its batteries, and watched Greg move through the people.

What if we did lose someone?

Unlikely. Possible, though.

I'd have to go back and search.

Greg walked up to her. 'They're all here,' he said. 'Thirty-eight, including you and me.'

'I'd say we pulled that off rather smoothly. Thanks for all the help.'

'Am I dismissed?' he asked.

'Do you have someone to go back to?'

'All by my lonesome.'

'Then stick around, why don't you, and help me hold up the wall.'

'I won't be needing this.' He handed the flashlight to Darcy, then took his place against the wall close by her side.

Darcy raised the flashlight. 'Okay, folks,' she said, 'the tricky part's over. All we have to do, now, is sit tight and wait. Obviously, none of us knows the reason for the power failure. I don't think that speculating on it will do anyone much good. Let's just look at it as an irritating fact of life – like a traffic jam.

'I don't want to raise any false hopes,' she continued. 'It may be a while. God knows, I never expected it to last this long. The important thing to keep in mind, though, is that we aren't in any danger. None at all.

'If you get cold, snuggle up with someone. We have plenty of water. As for food, I can't promise that we won't get hungry. But nobody is going to starve. I can't imagine that we'll be down here for more than a few hours. It may be just a minute before the power is restored. They know we're down here, and I'm sure that getting us safely to the top is the major priority right now.

'Why don't you all sit down and make yourselves as comfortable as possible? If you want to smoke, go on ahead. I'm going to turn off the flashlight in a minute to conserve the batteries, so it will be totally dark in here, and I'm sure a few glowing cigarettes would be welcomed by everyone.

'If anybody needs to go to the bathroom, call out and either Greg or I will come to you with a flashlight. The important thing is for nobody to go wandering around in the dark.'

Darcy played her flashlight over the people until everyone was seated. Then she turned it off. For a few moments, there was silence. Darcy heard her own heartbeat and the quiet whisper of the River Styx. Then came a few soft voices.

'Black.'

'Christ on a crutch.'

'Can't see my hand in front of my face.'

'Are you there?'

'Is that you?'

Darcy spoke up. 'Unless you've been in a cavern before, probably most of you have never experienced this kind of darkness. This is a total absence of light, darker than any night. As an experiment, a man once left a roll of film exposed in a cavern for two weeks. When the film was developed, it was found to be completely blank.

'Living creatures that have adapted to cave life are usually blind and without any pigmentation due to the lack of light.

'Which reminds me – though your are adjusting to the darkness, you won't be getting any night vision. There has to be a small amount of light for that, and there is none.'

Darcy stopped talking. There was silence. Then the voices started again. She thought it sounded like a classroom when the teacher was out, a dozen or more quiet conversations going on at once, creating a steady murmur.

Here and there, matches or lighters flared. They fluttered in front of faces with cigarettes or cigars clamped between lips, and formed pools of light throughout the group. Darcy saw that everyone was seated. Most were in small clusters of two or three. The brightness didn't last long. Then the chamber was dark except for half a dozen spots of glowing red.

'Guess I'll sit down and make myself comfortable,' she whispered.

She sat on the stone floor and crossed her legs. Something bumped her knee.

'Sorry,' Greg said.

'It's okay.' She reached out and touched his leg. He was beside her. Before she could bring her hand back, he took hold of it.

'Do you mind?' he asked.

Darcy answered by squeezing his hand. 'It's nice to have a friend in the dark.'

'Or any other time.'

'How'd you end up here?' she asked.

'One of my secretaries told me about it. She got married in the Bridal Chamber.'

'Recently?'

'Six years ago.'

'I wasn't here, then,' Darcy said.

'No kidding. You would've still been in diapers.'

She laughed softly. 'Thanks a bunch. I'm not *that* young.'

'Let me guess, then. You look about eighteen, but the way you've been handling yourself, you act about thirty. Add them up, divide by two, we get your true age of twenty-four.'

'Nifty gimmick, but you're three years high. What kind of law do you practise?'

'Some criminal, mostly personal injury defence. And I do the usual odds and ends – probate, divorces . . .'

'Like it?'

'It's exciting. Though not as exciting as being trapped in a cavern.'

'This is a thrill I could do without.'

'This wouldn't be so bad,' Kyle whispered, 'if it weren't so cold down here.'

'I don't think it's so bad,' Paula said.

Neither do I, Kyle thought. But he made his voice shake as he said, 'That's because you've got a sweater. I wasn't cold, either, when I had my jacket. I gave it to Darcy.'

'The guide?'

'Yeah. I figured she needed it more than me – after being in the water.'

'That was a sweet thing to do.'

'Sweet, but dumb.'

'Want to wear my sweater?'

'Maybe if I just put my arm under it. That'd help.'

'Sure, okay.'

He trembled as he slipped his hand beneath her sweater, but it had little to do with the chilly air. Paula's back felt warm through the thin fabric of her blouse. She wore a bra with a wide strap.

Kyle moved his hand across her back and curled his fingers into the warmth of her armpit.

'Just don't tickle,' she warned.

'I won't.' He uncrossed his legs and scooted closer until he felt his hip against her.

Paula put her arm on his back. 'Is that a little better?' she asked.

'A lot.' He could feel the soft warmth of her breast pushing his side.

'For me, too.'

This isn't too bad at all, Kyle thought. She's no Darcy, but she's okay.

And cooperative. So far.

With the hand that was under her arm, he could reach her breast.

Don't try it, he warned himself.

You spook her and you'll blow it.

It's so dark in here, I could do anything. Anything at all, as long as Paula stays quiet.

He would need to keep her quiet.

Kyle patted the pocket of his jeans and felt the knife inside. Moving his hand over a bit more, he gave his erection a gentle squeeze through the heavy denim, felt a surge of pleasure, and imagined sliding it into her.

Then imagined the lights coming on suddenly.

Forget it, he warned himself.

Even if he had all the time in the world and could somehow find his way around the entire cavern, there was no place to get rid of the body. There'd be a search as soon as they got out of here, and she'd be found.

Only one way to have Paula – she has to go along with it.

'Just for the fun of it,' Darcy said. 'The pay's not good, but this is pretty interesting for a summer job.'

'What's your major?' Greg asked.

'You tell me. You probably have a theory.'

Greg laughed softly. 'Majoring in tour guidance?'

'Yeah, sure.'

'The obvious, of course, is geology.'

'Wrong again.'

'That was an observation, not a guess.'

'So, what's your guess?'

'Psychology.'

'Oh, come on. Only fruitcakes go into psychology. You think I'm a fruitcake?'

'No, your head seems pretty well screwed on. How about phys-ed?'

'Now I'm a jock. Thanks.'

'Jocks are air-heads, right?'

'You got it.'

'But they're also physically fit and graceful, so you shouldn't consider my guess to be an out-and-out insult.'

'Okay, I won't.'

'How about a clue?'

' "It is an ancient Mariner, and he stoppeth one of three." '

'Seamanship.'

Darcy elbowed him.

'Archery?'

She looked at him with surprise. There was nothing to see. 'You do know your literature.'

'I wonder if someone down here recently murdered an albatross.'

'Not me,' Darcy said.

'We could ask around. All this might be punishment for some kind of transgression.'

'Right.'

'As a matter of fact, I'm serious.'

'You don't sound serious.'

'I find it intriguing. You take life, a lot of nasty business goes on.'

'I'll buy that.'

'It all comes down to one of three things,' Greg said. About fifty per cent is crap that just happens, nobody's fault, just God or Mother Nature or Fate or Chance dropping on you like a ton of bricks. The other half of the bad stuff is caused either by human evil or ignorance. Evil and stupidity are about equal.'

'Nifty theory.'

'I think so. Now, you take our present situation, I figure the odds are fifty-fifty that we're victims right now of somebody doing what he shouldn't.'

'Twenty-five per cent that somebody shot an albatross.'

'Right.'

'So where does that leave us?' she asked.

'Right where we were before I started my lecture.'

'Except I'm wiser, now.'

Greg laughed softly.

'And we're a few minutes closer to getting out of here.'

'I sure hope so.'

Darcy didn't like the sound of that.

'Have you thought about . . ?' He stopped.

'What?'

'You said, yourself, we don't know what happened up there. We've been assuming that, whatever the problem is, it'll be fixed before long. But what if it's not? I think we have to . . . consider the possibility.'

'Great. Thanks. I've been trying like hell *not* to consider that.'

She felt Greg let go of her hand. He stirred beside her. Then his arm went across her shoulders, and she leaned against him.

'I figured to give it a couple of hours,' she whispered.

'Then what?'

'Then, we get our asses out of here.'

'That's what I like, a woman of action.' She thought she could hear a smile in his voice. 'But how do you plan to accomplish this feat?'

'With great difficulty.'

When Paula began to sniff, Kyle thought she had a runny nose. Then he wondered if she might be crying.

'Are you okay?' he asked.

Her voice trembled as she answered, 'Not very.'

She *is* crying.

'What's wrong?'

'I'm just . . . so scared.'

'Hey, there's nothing to be scared about.'

'It's so dark. Why aren't the lights on yet? What's taking so long?'

'They'll be on pretty soon,' Kyle said. He hoped not. It'd be just fine, he thought, if the lights stayed off for hours. Maybe we could even spend the whole night down here.

He liked the blackness. He liked the feel of Paula, and wanted more. The moment the power came back on, that would end it with her.

'Maybe you should try to take a nap,' he whispered. 'It'd pass the time.'

'I don't think I could sleep.'

'My butt's already fallen asleep.'

Paula made a loud, wet sniff. 'Mine, too.'

'Let's try lying down. Even if we can't sleep, it'd be a lot more comfortable.'

'All right.'

Kyle took his hand out from under her sweater. He felt her hand on his shoulder as he lay down. The chill of the cavern floor seeped through the back of his shirt. He rolled onto his side.

'This isn't all that comfortable,' Paula whispered.

'Here.' He touched her hair, then slid his arm under her head. He put his other arm around her back. 'Is that better?'

'Yeah.'

Paula's hand found his side just below the ribcage. But she didn't move any closer to him. Their bodies were apart.

A couple more inches, Kyle thought, and we'd be touching.

She's probably worried about that.

He could feel her shaking.

'Cold?' he asked.

'A little.'

He scooted himself closer. Her breasts pressed against him. He felt their warmth, and the warmth of her belly and thighs. Instead of moving away, Paula tightened her arm around his back and she squeezed him to her body. She sighed. 'This is nice,' she whispered.

'Yeah.'

'You feel so warm.'

'You, too.'

He wondered if she could feel his hard-on. She must. It was pushing right against her. But she didn't try to get away from it.

Maybe she likes it, he thought.

He'd never messed around with a girl his own age, never even taken one out, but he knew guys who had and sometimes they bragged about scoring. Unless those guys were lying, there *were* girls who put out.

Maybe Paula's one of them.

Even if she's not, Kyle was pretty sure that a lot of girls her age would let you do other stuff – everything *but* that.

He slid his hand down her back and rested it on her hip. Her dress was a soft fabric. He moved his hand over it, feeling the curve of her rump.

Her head moved. Kyle felt her face against his. Her lips brushed over his cheek, then found his mouth. She kissed him. It wasn't a noisy smack like he got on the cheek from his aunt and grandmother. It was a soft, quiet suck on his lips, and afterwards her mouth didn't go away.

Nobody had ever kissed Kyle this way.

She was a girl his own age, kissing him because she wanted to.

She must like me, he thought.

He pressed his lips against hers. He was hard and aching and wanting Paula more than ever. But there were new feelings: amazement, gratitude and tenderness.

This must be what it's like, he thought, to have a girlfriend.

But she'll go away when the elevators start up.

It isn't fair.

I'll still have room 115, he told himself. And I'll still have Darcy.

But I won't have Paula anymore.

He felt a tightness in his throat.

Even if she does like me, she'll go away.

The hell with her.

Keeping his mouth on Paula's, he twisted enough to make room between their bodies, and closed a hand gently over her breast. She made a small gasp and stiffened.

'Kyle, don't,' she whispered.

'It's all right.' He moved the sweater out of his way. He squeezed her breast through the blouse and bra. 'Nobody can see anything.'

'What if the lights come on?'

So it was okay with her; she just didn't want to get caught. 'If they do, I'll stop.'

'I don't know.'

He covered her mouth with his lips. She was breathing

hard and trembling. He fumbled with buttons, opened a way in her blouse, and slipped his hand inside. Some of her breast wasn't covered by the bra. He caressed its smooth warmth. She moaned into his mouth, a moan that seemed partly desire and partly protest. Then Kyle pushed his fingers under the bra. She flinched and squirmed.

'No, don't.'

'It won't hurt anything,' he said, digging deeper into the yielding flesh until his fingertips found the rigid post of her nipple.

She yanked his hand away. She held it motionless by the wrist. 'I told you no, Kyle.'

'I thought you liked me,' he said.

'I do. But . . . you're going too fast. I've never let anyone . . . There are people all around us.'

'I don't see any.'

'Silly.' She squeezed his wrist. Then she guided his hand through the blackness and placed it on her breast. He felt the blouse. 'Outside my clothes, okay?'

'But your skin is so smooth and nice.'

'Kyle.'

'Please?'

'Do you promise to leave my bra alone? And not go below the waist?'

'I promise.'

'Okay.'

She released his wrist.

Kyle unfastened the other buttons, then slid his hand inside her blouse.

Pretty soon she'll let me undo her bra, he thought. Pretty soon, she'll let me do everything.

'She took your car?' Darcy asked.

'And my stereo and VCR and all the cash in the house.'

'That's awful. After everything you did for her.'

'Well, she was such a mess,' Greg said. 'I was pretty upset for a while, but I was relieved, too. It was no kind of relationship. Once the shock wore off, I realized how lucky I was to be rid of her.'

'Did you love her?'

'I don't know. I thought so. At first, anyway. She was very attractive and vulnerable, and she needed me. There was certainly a strong element of sexual attraction. But putting up with her . . .'

'It must've been terrible.'

'On top of everything else – her fits of rage and jealousy and all the rest – she tried to commit suicide twice, and one night I woke up and found her holding a butcher knife to my throat.'

'Good Christ.'

'She said I'd put a radium bulb in the bedside lamp to poison her chromosomes.'

'I don't know how you could live with that kind of thing.'

'It wasn't easy. I kept hoping she'd get better. But she'd come back from the clinics and be fine for a while and then it would all start up again. I felt totally trapped. I really wanted her out of my life, but she was so dependent on me – I knew she'd go off the deep end if I tried to throw her out.'

'Why did she finally take off like that?'

'I don't have any idea. As crazy as she was, maybe she decided I was plotting against her. Maybe she met someone at one of the bars. I just don't know. I'm just thankful that she left.'

'Do you think she'll come back?'

'She's been gone more than a year, now, so I doubt it.'

'And you haven't been . . . involved with a woman since she left?'

'No. And it's been wonderfully peaceful.'

'So, you've let your experiences with Martha turn you off completely to . . .'

'Not turn me off, just make me careful. The last thing I need is to get messed up with another emotional crip – what's that . . .?' His voice stopped.

Darcy tensed.

Greg's hand tightened on her shoulder.

She listened. The sound came from behind her – from the elevator shafts? A far-off, skidding rumble that reminded her of a subway train approaching a station. It grew louder, louder.

Greg's hand darted under her armpit. Her other arm was grabbed and she felt herself being lifted, hurled forward through the blackness with Greg at her side until they stumbled over people who yelped with alarm.

Greg, on Darcy's back, pressed her down onto a squirming body.

She heard the roar, shouts and screams, a tremendous crash.

Greg rolled off her. Raising her head, Darcy saw that she was sprawled on top of Beth Donner. The woman's face glowed with fluttering yellow-orange light. She had a look of terror in her eyes.

'Sorry,' Darcy muttered. 'You all right?'

Beth nodded.

Darcy pushed herself up. She looked over her shoulder.

Into the flames.

The elevator on the left, its wooden doors blasted apart, was a closet of fire.

Darcy squinted into the burning, twisted wreckage of its car. She saw no bodies.

That's something, she thought. At least . . .

There came another roar.

Another crash.

The doors to the second elevator burst apart in a spray of slabs and splinters.

6

That morning, after coffee and a sweetroll from the snackbar, Chris Raines walked with her daughter to the area beyond the giftshop where people were standing in line to buy tickets for the tour.

'You sure you don't want to come down for another look at the wonders of the cavern?' Darcy asked.

'I don't think so. But maybe tomorrow. I suppose I should see it once more before I take off.'

'What'll you do with yourself all day?'

'I'm sure I'll think of something. Sit around and relax, I suppose. This *is* my vacation.'

'If you get really bored or something, you can always drive into town.'

'Maybe later on. I'll stick around long enough to have lunch with you, though.'

'Fine. Whatever. See you.'

'Have fun.'

As Darcy walked towards a doorway beyond the ticket booth, several of the men waiting in line turned their heads to watch her.

My kid, Chris thought, and felt the familiar stir of pride and concern. Darcy had always been beautiful. When she was a child, it had been women who seemed to make most of the comments: store clerks, people waiting in supermarket lines, strangers passing on the sidewalk. Later, the women stopped remarking on her beauty at about the same time that boys and men began to notice her. And stare. And often get awkward. Chris's male friends, after meeting Darcy, rarely failed to say, 'She's going to break a lot of hearts.'

She probably did, too. But never on purpose, as far as Chris knew. The girl accepted her beauty, realized it was nothing more than a lucky accident, and never let it go to her head, never dumped on people because she considered them inferior.

It was Darcy's own heart that ended up broken, so often, when she let herself fall for guys who turned out to be creeps.

Comes with the territory, Chris thought. All the men want you, but so often it's the wrong kind who comes along with the right moves. God knows, she'd had to struggle with that, herself, all her life.

Darcy's father was a prime example.

Don't ruin a lovely day by thinking about him, she told herself, and started walking quickly through the tourist centre. She opened a door at the front, and entered the hotel lobby. On her way to the stairs, she glanced at the registration desk. Ethan Mordock was there.

Speaking of creeps, Chris thought.

Fortunately, he was on the telephone with his back turned.

The man had been perfectly polite and friendly the few times she'd spoken with him, but he had that look in his eyes. Like a vulture inspecting its next meal. He might be looking at your face and chatting about the weather, but you always had the feeling he cared more about the colour of your panties.

A real sleaze.

And Darcy's boss.

Chris hurried up the stairs, and felt a little relieved once she turned at the landing and knew she could no longer be seen by him.

She had warned Darcy about the guy. 'I'd keep my guard up around him, if I were you.'

'Oh, he's all right.'

'If you don't mind a man undressing you with his eyes.'

'Depends on the man.'

'Very cute. I'm serious.'

'Don't worry, Mom. He's not my type.'

'Is he married?'

'Interested?' Darcy asked, that glint in her eyes.

'Right. I'll run right down and throw myself into his arms.'

'He'd probably go into cardiac arrest.'

'I take it he's not married.'

'I've heard his wife ran off with someone a few years ago.'

'Well, just watch out for him.'

'Don't worry. He starts any trouble, I'll give him the ol' one-two and knock his lights out.'

The kidding around, Chris knew, was simply her daughter's way of dealing with the problem. The warning had been heard and accepted.

And probably wasn't necessary in the first place. Darcy was a sharp kid. But a little motherly advice never hurt.

Chris searched her shoulder bag as she made her way

along the corridor. She found her room key, stopped at the third door from the end, and let herself in.

With the door shut, she turned the latch.

Don't want Ethan the lech coming in with a pass key while I'm undressing, she thought.

The pits to think he can let himself into any room that suits his fancy.

Good thing Darcy has a roommate.

Chris wondered if they used the inside latch. They certainly should.

Remember to mention it at lunch.

Oh, Mom, you worry too much.

The man is probably harmless.

I latched my door, she thought, and I'm sure I'm not nearly as tempting to a man like that as Darcy is.

She suddenly remembered Arthur, one of her boyfriends. Oh, that bastard, that bastard. She hunched over, hot and sick, no longer in the hotel room but home and waking up in her dark bed and wondering where Arthur had gone and looking for him and finding him in Darcy's room, crouched over her bed, touching her while she slept.

Darcy, only sixteen.

Thank God she didn't wake up. She never found out about that disgusting episode.

Days later, she asked, 'What happened to Arthur? You dump him?'

'He was a shithead.'

That grin. That glint in her eyes. 'Hey, I could've told you that.'

And no man, not one, ever slept over again.

Chris looked at herself in the mirror. She was bent over, her face red, as if she'd taken a punch in the belly. She straightened up.

She took her clothes off.

And felt stupid gazing at her reflection.

But it helped.

'Not bad for an old bag of thirty-nine,' she said. Then she got into her swimsuit.

Hank Whitmore looked up from his paperback when the woman entered the pool area. He watched her stride past the end of the pool and choose a lounge chair on the far side.

The scenery, he thought, has taken a definite turn for the better.

She was a tall, slender blonde, probably in her early thirties. As Hank watched, she removed her long white shirt. Her swimming suit had thin straps that formed an X on her back. Except for those, her back was bare to the top of her rump. Shiny white fabric hugged her buttocks.

Hank pursed his lips.

And Paula felt sorry for me, he thought. Poor Dad has to wait around for an hour and a half with nothing to do.

The woman turned slightly and bent over to drape her cover-up on the back of the lounge. Her side was bare all the way down to the hip. Though the suit clung to her breast, it didn't quite reach far enough. The very base of her breast, where it just began to rise from her chest, was left exposed.

Hank forced himself to look down at his book.

No better than a peeping Tom, he thought.

But my God, what a gal.

He looked up again.

She was facing the pool, maybe considering whether to go in for a dip. A couple of kids were splashing around in the shallow end.

Hank wished she would take off her sunglasses.

Her face – what he could see of it – looked just as fine as her body.

She took them off.

Even at this distance, Hank could see the blue of her eyes.

Christ almighty, he thought, I'm in love.

He looked at her left hand. No wedding ring. No ring at all, on either hand.

Her only jewellery was a thin gold chain around her left wrist.

She's not wearing a wedding ring and she's alone.

That doesn't mean she's available, Hank told himself. Maybe she's got a boyfriend who'll be along in a minute.

A gal who looks like this simply cannot be unattached. It's against the laws of nature.

Maybe she's gay.

There's a cheerful thought.

Maybe she's a hooker.

Now there *is* a cheerful thought.

Hank had never been with a prostitute. Not even in Viet Nam, which amused his buddies no end. Over the years since then, he'd frequently toyed with the idea – some were absolutely gorgeous and he knew that they'd do just about anything – but they were so *experienced*. Somehow, he'd always been sure he would commit a blunder and end up totally humiliated.

The woman on the other side of the pool was now sitting on her lounge, spreading suntan lotion on her sleek legs.

Hank looked at his wristwatch. He still had more than an hour before the tour ended.

He thought about his money. He had close to two

hundred dollars in his wallet, plus five hundred in traveller's cheques. And he'd heard that the classier hookers often took credit cards.

I could do it.

Jesus H. Christ.

He was trembling badly.

To spend an hour in bed with someone like that . . .

He'd always dreamed of having a really beautiful woman. Just once in his life.

What if she's got AIDs or something?

He'd noticed condoms in the hotel shop.

Go for it, man. You may never get another chance like this.

Hank folded his book shut, forgetting to mark the place. He got to his feet. His legs felt shaky and weak. He began to walk.

What'll I say?

What if she's not *a hooker? As great as she looked, she was awfully old to be in that line. Weren't most of them supposed to be teenagers?*

Who knows.

Nothing ventured, nothing gained.

Oh God, I must be out of my mind.

He walked around the end of the pool.

The woman was leaning back, spreading lotion on her arms.

Whatever you say, Hank told himself, *don't sound like a jerk.*

He stopped beside her lounge.

'Excuse me,' he said.

She looked up at him.

Say something.

'I'm Hank,' he said.

81

Hello, Hank. Fuck off.

She smiled. It was a fine smile, nothing superior about it. 'Hi,' she said.

He rubbed his hands on his shorts. 'I've got an hour or so to kill.'

'That's a terrible thing to do to an hour.'

'Kill it? Yeah. Well, I guess I'd rather make the most out of it.'

'Reading's a good way to do that.'

She'd noticed him with the paperback. Had she also noticed him staring at her?

'The book won't go away,' Hank said.

'And I will?'

'Good chance of it. Are you with someone?'

'My daughter's down in the cavern.'

Hank realized, with mixed disappointment and relief, that she undoubtedly was not a hooker after all. So much for fantasies. But they both had daughters in the cavern. That gave them something in common. Though he wouldn't be getting her into bed, at least he could pass the time with her and enjoy the view. 'Really? My daughter's down there, too.'

'I'm Chris,' she said. She lifted her hand toward him, then hesitated. 'Oh, it's all yooked . . .'

Hank took her hand. It was moist and slick with suntan lotion. 'Nice to meet you, Chris. I'm Hank.'

'I know. Feel free to pull up a seat, if you like.'

'Thanks.' He grabbed a nearby lounge and set it next to Chris's – at an angle so he could look at her without twisting his head halfway around. 'How come you're not taking the tour?' he asked.

'I went yesterday.'

'Didn't your daughter go with you, or . . ?'

'She's a guide. I'm staying here at the hotel for a couple of days, just visiting.'

'Your daughter's a *guide*? They use kids?'

'Everybody's someone's kid.' She laughed softly. 'Don't worry, your daughter is in good hands. Darcy's twenty-one.'

'Gee, you must've been ten when you had her.'

'And then some,' Chris said, her face taking on a red hue. 'What about your daughter? How old is she?'

'Paula's sixteen.'

'She went down alone?'

'I'm not big on caves. She wanted to see it. I didn't think I should deprive her of the experience just because I wasn't interested.'

'That's pretty neat of you,' Chris said. 'Most parents wouldn't do that.'

'Most parents would see the cave with their kid.'

She frowned slightly. 'If you feel that way about it, how come you stayed behind?'

'I figured maybe I'd latch onto some fabulous babe by the pool.'

Oh shit, why did I say that!

Chris laughed.

'As a matter of fact,' he said, 'I've got a touch of claustrophobia. I don't do real well in tight places.'

She looked interested. 'Were you always that way?'

'Something I acquired in the service.' He felt his heart speeding up. 'Do you have any phobias?'

'Getting a splinter in the eye.'

'Ow!'

'Fortunately, it's never happened. But I'm careful about walking close to shelves. Libraries make me very nervous, which is something of a handicap.'

'Why is that?'

'I'm a researcher. I freelance at it. Basically, that means I do the dirty work for lazy writers. How about you?'

'I teach.'

She raised her eyebrows. 'You don't look much like a teacher.'

'You don't look much like a researcher.'

'Because I don't wear glasses and wear my hair in a bun?'

'Among other things.'

She blushed again. 'If you're a teacher, it must be PE.'

'Me, a jock?'

'You obviously work out a lot.'

'I do body-building to work off the tension of the job.'

'So what *do* you teach?'

'Driver's education.'

'Oh shit, you're kidding.' She slapped a hand across her mouth as she started to laugh.

My turn to blush, he thought as he felt his skin heat up.

'I'm sorry. It's just that . . . driver's ed. In high school?'

He nodded.

'It's just . . . I can't picture you. My driver's ed teacher was such an incredible old fart. His name was Deederding and he looked like one. He had this high, squeaky voice. And a nervous tic.' She demonstrated the tic, twitching her left cheek.

God, she was cute doing that!

'Deederding. He was so awful. But there's nothing intrinsically funny about being a driver's ed teacher. I shouldn't have laughed.'

'As a matter of fact, there's plenty intrinsically funny about it. Most people do laugh. They picture a nervous nilly cringing and covering his eyes.'

'I'm sure you're not like that.'

'I do cringe a lot. I rarely cover my eyes.'

'Where are you from?' she asked.

'Santa Monica.'

'You're a long way from home.'

'Where are you from?'

'Da Big Apple.'

Hank felt a tug of disappointment. *We're from opposite sides of the country. I'll never see her again. Today is it. Probably.*

'My daughter's a student at Princeton. She's here on a summer job. I hadn't seen her since spring break . . .' Chris lowered the back of her lounge. She lay down and folded her hands behind her head. 'If you're planning to stick around, she said, 'why don't you bring your stuff over? No point in taking up two places.'

'Right,' Hank said. 'Save my seat.'

She smiled.

He got up and started making his way around the pool.

She likes me, he thought. *Man, why couldn't this happen back home? Why couldn't she be from Santa Monica or Brentwood or some place? Just my luck. I have to be three thousand miles from home when I meet a gal like this.*

Not only gorgeous, but nice. And she likes me.

And we'll be leaving in an hour.

Shit.

Who says we have to leave? The thought struck him hard, knocking him breathless. His heart thudded.

We could stay here tonight. All I have to do is check us in, if they've got any vacancies. Paula wouldn't mind. Cancel out on Cooperstown. She wasn't all that eager to see the Hall of Fame, anyway. Stay here tonight. Maybe take Chris and her daughter to dinner. Who knows what . . .?

Maybe Chris wouldn't want to do that.

Ask. Nothing ventured, nothing gained.

Hank pulled his shirt off the back of his chair and picked up his book. He walked back around the pool. When he reached the lounges, he saw that Chris's eyes were shut. He sat down and looked at her.

She's shut me out, he thought.

Probably thinks I'm a nuisance, after all. Was just being nice, did her bit for the sake of politeness, and now she wants to be left alone.

So much for my grand schemes.

At least with her eyes shut, she can't see me looking at her.

So Hank looked. She was smooth and tanned and her swimsuit hugged every curve and hollow and mound. But he took little pleasure from the view. His hopes had been smashed, and he felt only loss.

You never stood a chance, he thought.

She's gorgeous, and you're a nonentity.

The tip of her tongue slid out and wetted her lips.

He could *feel* those lips.

You never will.

'If you aren't in any big hurry,' Chris said, 'maybe you and your daughter could join us for lunch.'

Chris woke up. She hadn't meant to doze off. Turning her head, she saw that Hank's lounge was empty. Except for his book.

He'll be back, she thought.

She wondered how long she'd been out.

Maybe the tour's over and he went to get his daughter.

She didn't want to move. The sun felt like a hot, heavy blanket. But she needed to use a toilet, and this was as good a time as any.

Sitting up, she mopped her damp face with a towel. Then she put on the oversized white shirt, buttoned it, and stepped into her sandals. She left her suntan lotion and sunglasses on the lounge to show that she would be back. She picked up her shoulder bag.

No need to return to the room, she thought. She could use the ladies' room in the hotel lobby.

Just ignore Mordock.

The lech.

Walking toward the doors, she smiled. How come Mordock's a lech and Hank isn't? He couldn't take his eyes off me. So what's the difference?

Hank's sweet.

Mordock's a sleazebag.

You can't get much more different than that.

Chris pushed open one of the glass doors. Entering the lobby, she saw Hank at the registration desk. He reached into a rear pocket of his shorts and took out his wallet.

What's he doing?

Checking in?

Because of me?

Good Lord, she thought. She entered the ladies' room and went to one of the stalls. She set her bag on the shelf. She draped her shirt over the door. The toilet looked clean, but she pulled a paper seat cover from its dispenser, tore out the inner sheet, and set it in place. While she was peeling her swimsuit down, an end of the

87

paper slipped and dropped into the water.

'Damn,' she muttered, and brushed the rest of it into the bowl.

She got a new cover, put it down, and sat quickly.

So Hank is checking into the hotel, she thought. In a way, it was almost alarming. But nice, too.

Maybe it has nothing to do with me.

Of course it does. We hit it off, and he decided to stick around for a while to see what develops.

What can develop? He lives in California.

Maybe he's hoping for one night.

Sorry, buster, but if you think I'm going to hop in the sack with you . . .

Santa Monica wouldn't be such a shabby place to live.

You don't even know the guy. Hardly.

He's checking in.

God almighty.

Finished, Chris stood and pulled her swimsuit up. She slipped the straps over her shoulders, turned around and balanced on her right leg while she stepped on the flush lever with her left foot.

The toilet water started to go down, then didn't.

Great, Chris thought. Plumbing problems. She wondered if she should mention it to Mordock.

Let someone else. I'm not talking to that guy if I can help it.

She put her shirt on, slung the bag strap over her shoulder, unlatched the stall door and stepped out.

Hank. He checked in.

Smiling, she shook her head.

The guy really has nerve. Of course he does – he's a driving instructor.

And Darcy was afraid I might get bored.

She stepped to a sink and twisted a faucet handle. Water trickled out. She tried the other handle, but still no more than a thin stream ran from the nozzle.

Forget it, she thought.

She went to the door and reached for its handle.

And the roar of gunfire pounded her ears.

7

The man behind the registration desk handed the credit card back to Hank and gave him a room key with a big plastic tag. 'Checkout time is eleven a.m.,' he said.

'Thanks.' Hank, turning away, stopped abruptly to stare at the man striding through the lobby doors.

He was about twenty, fat and wearing glasses. His face was scarlet, dripping with sweat, and his cheeks jiggled as he walked. Clamped between his teeth was a lighted cigar.

He carried a bucket in each hand.

The buckets were full. Liquid sloshed over their rims as the man lugged them along.

Hank smelled the pungent stench of gasoline.

'Holy shit,' he muttered.

'Outa the way,' the man said in a high, girlish voice.

Hank backed away from the desk.

The man walked towards it.

The hotel man looked stunned. 'I told you, fella . . .'

'Fuck what you told me, Mordock.'

Hank kept backing away.

The guy with the cigar set one of the buckets on the floor. He lifted the other and swung it with both hands.

The amber liquid surged out, splashing the face and

91

chest of Mordock who shut his eyes and mouth tight as the flood hit him.

'What did you do with her?' the fat man asked. He took the cigar from his mouth and tapped ash onto the counter.

Mordock, dripping gasoline, squinted at him with one eye and shook his head wildly. 'I told you, nobody named Amy Lawson ever checked in. I showed you the cards. I never heard of her. Put that cigar away! Come on, mister!'

'She was here.'

'If something happened to her, it wasn't my fault. I had nothing to do with it.'

'Then why'd you get rid of her registration card?'

'I didn't. I tell you . . .' Suddenly, Mordock had a revolver.

Hank threw himself at the floor. The first shot crashed in his ears an instant after he hit. He saw the fat man flinch and toss the cigar like a dart. Mordock kept blasting as the cigar sailed toward him. The slugs pounded the fat man. Some came out his back, puffing out his white shirt and throwing sprays of blood. Another caught his face. The back of his head flew open.

Mordock got off his last shot, which seemed to miss, just as the cigar touched him off.

He was a torch. The fat man was shot apart.

They faced each other for a moment – two dead men.

The fat man fell forward. His chest hit the edge of the counter. His knees folded. As he dropped, the edge caught his chin and knocked his head back. He tumbled sideways. His shoulder struck the bucket of gasoline on the floor and overturned it.

Mordock started screaming.

Hank pushed himself to his hands and knees. An arm went around his back.

'Hank! Hank!'

Chris was crouched beside him.

Staring at Mordock, he got to his feet.

The man was shrieking and flapping his arms. He was all ablaze, his face bubbling.

He vaulted the counter.

'No!' Hank shouted.

Mordock's feet came down on the belly of the fat man. He stumbled off and fell to his knees, igniting the puddle of gasoline from the second bucket. He squealed, got to his feet, and ran for the doors.

He left flaming shoeprints on the carpet.

He crashed head first through the glass door on the left, fell flat on the concrete just outside the hotel, and lay there.

Chris was already running towards him. Hank chased her, caught her by the shoulder, and pulled her to a stop.

'We've gotta help him!'

'Forget it. He's finished.'

'What'll we do?'

A drop of water splashed the side of Chris's nose and slid off.

Hank looked up. The ceiling sprinklers had been set off, but they weren't showering water down – they were dripping. He couldn't believe it. 'Crazy son of a bitch must've turned off the water.'

He whirled around. The area surrounding the registration desk was an inferno, flames climbing the wall behind it, engulfing the counter, lapping at the ceiling, spreading over the carpet.

He spotted a pair of pay phones near the restroom doors. They were clear of the fire, for now. He grabbed Chris's hand and pulled her towards them. 'Got any change?'

'I think so.'

They reached the phones. She dug into her bag, came out with a change purse, opened it and took out a quarter. 'You call,' Hank said. 'I'll be right back.'

As she lifted the handset, Hank dashed for the tourist area. He pulled open a glass door. There must have been nearly a hundred people in the huge room: wandering the gift shop, standing at the snack bar, sitting at tables, waiting in line for the next tour to start.

'Give me your attention!' he yelled. A few people looked at him. Others continued about their business. 'There's a fire in the lobby! Everybody get out! Stay calm, you've got plenty of time.'

People started shouting, 'FIRE!'

Couples grabbed each other's hands. Parents clutched children, picked up the small ones. Everybody began to rush for the exits along the side and rear of the room.

There were plenty of exits.

They'll be all right, Hank thought.

At the rear of the room, two elevator doors slid open.

A tour group returning from the cavern.

'Thank God,' Hank muttered. He ran for the elevators as they began to empty.

It's too early for Paula's group, he thought. No, it's not. She's here. Please!

He scanned the people leaving the elevators. Must've been thirty of them. He couldn't spot Paula.

He was nearly there when a fire alarm began its deafening honk.

The guide, an attractive young woman, turned to her group and raised her arms. 'Everybody stay calm!' she shouted. 'Follow me. We'll be outside in a few seconds.'

Hank reached them. 'Paula!' he called. 'Paula!'

Not there.

Clamped with fear, he rushed to the guide. 'Are you Darcy?'

She shook her head. 'I'm Lynn. Darcy's down below. What's going on?'

'Fire in the lobby.'

'Oh, wow.'

'Take 'em out,' Hank said.

Lynn started leading her bunch away.

Hank rushed past them.

The alarm went silent. The lights went off. He threw himself into one of the elevators and pushed its 'down' button. Nothing happened, he pushed it again and again.

Not going anywhere, he realized. Power's out.

Something seemed to collapse inside him.

Paula.

My God.

He told himself she would be safe down in the cavern.

Safe, maybe, but trapped.

Chris. Her girl's down there, too.

Chris, holding the glass door open, gazed into the tourist area. The huge room was deserted except for a few people in a bunch near one of the side exits. And Hank.

Hank was running towards her.

Chris stepped through the doorway. Hank stopped in front of her. He looked grim. Chris took hold of his arms. 'What's wrong?'

'Paula and Darcy are still in the cavern. The other

group got out just in time, but they're . . . the elevators . . .' He shook his head.

Chris felt a numbness spread through her.

'I'm sure they're safe,' Hank told her. 'The fire can't get to them. It's just that . . . I don't know how they'll get out. Did you get through to the fire department?'

His voice seemed far away.

'Chris? The fire department?'

Darcy can't get out.

'Chris!' He grabbed her shoulders, shook her. The fog in her mind seemed to lift. 'Did you get the fire department?'

'The phones were dead.'

'How . . .? The crazy bastard must've cut the lines.'

'But I found the fire alarm. I broke the glass, and . . . that'll bring the fire department, won't it?'

'I don't know. I doubt it.'

Chris felt warmth on her back and looked over her shoulder. Flames danced beyond the glass door. They hadn't reached the door yet, but they were close.

'Come on,' Hank said. 'Let's get out of here.'

'Shouldn't we . . . there might be people in the rooms.'

'They would've heard the alarm.'

Chris nodded. The alarm hadn't lasted long, but it had made a terrible clamour. Nobody could have slept through it.

'What about a deaf person?' she asked.

'Do you know of a deaf person staying here?'

'No, but . . .'

'If we ran around knocking on doors, he wouldn't hear that, either.'

'No. Yes. You're right.'

Hank put an arm around her shoulders and guided

her diagonally across the room to one of the side exits. Outside, Chris squinted in the brightness. She started to search her handbag, then remembered that she had left her sunglasses beside the pool.

Hank pulled her along, rushing her farther away from the hotel. People were wandering around. There were a lot of cars. She realized that she was on the main parking lot behind the complex.

So disoriented, she thought. Gotta pull myself together.

They stopped.

'My car,' Hank said. 'Want to get in?'

She shook her head.

'Wait here, Chris. I'll check around. Maybe someone has a car phone or CB.'

He hurried away. Chris, watching him, leaned back against the side of the car. And lurched off it, gasping, as the sunheated metal seared her buttocks through the thin fabric of her swimsuit.

She rubbed herself.

She realized what she was wearing.

Swell, she thought. My clothes are in the room.

She looked at the hotel. From out here, no one would ever guess the conflagration inside. The only sign that anything might be wrong was a thin screen of grey smoke rising into the sky on the far side – probably pouring out the lobby door that Mordock had smashed.

Chris wondered if she could get to her room.

I'm not going back in there.

Besides, the corridors might be filled with smoke.

No great loss, she told herself. My clothes, but . . . oh, Darcy. Darcy had a whole steamer trunk full of things.

As long as *she's* all right . . .

Chris remembered seeing the stuffed kitten, Snow, on Darcy's bed that morning. Snow. Santa had given her Snow when she was four.

Tears suddenly flooded Chris's eyes. She lowered her face into her hands and wept.

A family outing. A goddamn parade. Daddy held the little kid on his shoulders for a better view.

'You got a car phone?' Hank asked the man.

The man glanced at him, said, 'Sorry,' and pointed. 'See there, Andy? See the fire in the window?'

Hank hurried on. A few of the tourists were in their cars and driving slowly through the lot, trying to leave. But most were standing around to watch the fire.

Hank flinched as something burst. He looked at the hotel. Black smoke was rolling through a second floor window near the middle, probably just above the lobby. The noise he'd heard must have been the window pane exploding.

He glimpsed claws of flame in the smoke. They curled up the outside wall.

Someone squeezed Hank's wrist. An old woman in round spectacles smiled up at him. Her thick lenses were like magnifying glasses; made her eyes huge. The whites were yellow and webbed with red. 'How did it start, duke? Y'see how it started?'

He shook his head.

'My land, ain't this the berries?' Her hand shook his wrist as if she were demanding an answer.

'Yeah,' Hank said. 'The berries.'

'She's goin' up in smoke. Wouldn't you say so, duke? Goin' up in smoke.'

'Right. Excuse me.' He freed himself from the

woman's bony grip and hurried away.

Not far ahead, a young man and woman were sitting on the hood of a Jeep Wagoneer. They both wore cowboy hats. They both had bottles of beer. Clamped between the knees of the woman was an open bag of potato chips.

'Have you got a car phone?' Hank asked. 'A transmitter of some . . .'

'Nope,' the guy said. 'What's the trouble?'

'We've got to report the fire.'

'It hasn't been *reported*?'

'I don't think so. We tried to call right after it broke out, but the phones were dead.'

'Shit, that fucker's gonna burn to the ground.'

As he said that, his eyes went wide. Hank whirled around in time to see a section of the roof cave in. Seconds after the crash, a galaxy of glowing embers floated up through the smoke. Flames began to chew the ragged edges of the crater.

'Take this, pal.' The man gave his beer to Hank. 'Come on, Luce,' he said, and leaped off the hood.

'What?'

'We're gonna lay rubber outa here and report this bitch before the whole fuckin' place goes up.'

Hank clapped him on the shoulder, then waved some bystanders out of the way to make room for the Jeep to back out of its parking space.

Once out of the lot, it picked up speed.

No matter how fast it goes, Hank thought, it couldn't reach town in much less than twenty minutes. Then it might be another twenty minutes before the first fire truck could arrive. At best.

Maybe, somehow, the fire's already been reported.

But Hank doubted it.

He continued his search for someone with a car phone or radio transmitter.

Standing on the bumper of Hank's car, Chris spotted him near the far side of the lot. He was wandering among the spectators, stopping briefly and moving on.

'Looking for someone, honey?'

She nodded, and glanced down at the man. He wore a blue T-shirt and jeans. His T-shirt read, 'Save a Tree, Eat a Beaver.' His eyes were inspecting the merchandise.

Chris realized her shirt was open. She started to button it.

'Aw, now.'

'Don't bug me, okay?'

'I happen to have a fully equipped bar over in my trailer. You look like a martini might do you a world of good.'

'No, thank you.'

'Some fire, isn't it? I hear a couple of folks got cooked. They say there's more than a hundred trapped in the cave.'

'Including my daughter. Get outa here.'

'Well, excuuuuuuse me.' He turned away. As he walked off, Chris heard him mutter something that sounded like, 'Tightass cunt.'

She flinched at the roar as another section of roof collapsed. The fire was spreading more rapidly to the right – to the east . . . in the direction of the cave elevators.

A man with a home video camera crossed the driveway at the front of the parking lot. He stepped over the curb and made his way closer to the burning complex.

A young woman in a guide uniform rushed up behind him.

Thick, reddish-brown hair. She had to be Lynn, Darcy's room-mate.

She grabbed the man by the arm, spoke to him, turned him around and walked him back into the lot.

Chris leaped down from the bumper. She hurried forward, weaving between parked cars and spectators, scanning the area ahead, trying to spot Lynn.

And found her near the front.

'Lynn!'

The girl turned to her. For a moment, she looked confused. Then she raised her thick eyebrows. 'Oh, Darcy's mom, right? Hey, you know, I'm sure Darcy's just fine. I mean, there's no way in the world the fire's going to get down in the cavern. She's totally safe, you know?'

'I have to talk to you.'

'Sure. Shoot. You got any idea where Mordock is? He ought to be helping with the crowds, you know?'

'He's dead.'

Lynn's eyes went wide. She didn't appear bothered by the news, just surprised. 'No fooling? Dead? Ethan? The owner?'

'That's right. He's been dead from the start. You've got to help me, Lynn.'

'Sure. Just name it.'

'Darcy's trapped.'

'Yeah, I know. The pits, but like I say . . . I mean, I wouldn't wanta be stuck down there myself, but it's safe, you know?'

'How is she going to get out?'

101

Lynn shrugged. 'I guess the elevators.'

'The place is burning to the ground,' Chris pointed out, trying to keep her patience. This girl seemed incredibly dense. How could she be a guide, like Darcy? 'In a little while, there won't *be* any elevators.'

'Well, yeah, I guess not. But the shafts, they'll be there. They aren't going anyplace. So the fire department can maybe lower ropes or a basket or something.' As if reciting, Lynn added, 'The shafts are a hundred and fifty-three feet deep.'

'That's pretty goddamn deep.'

'I'm sure the fire department will have a way to get to them. Don't you think so?'

'I suppose.'

After the fire's cold, Chris thought. After the rubble has been cleared from the shafts. 'Are there supplies down there?' Chris asked.

'You mean like food? Nothing like that. There's plenty of water, though. You shouldn't worry about it, really. I mean, I can't imagine they won't be out in a few hours. By tomorrow, anyhow.'

'I took the tour, yesterday,' Chris said. 'Darcy talked about a natural opening to the cavern.'

'Yeah, but that's all blocked off.'

'With a rock wall like the one on the inside?'

'I guess. I've never seen it up close.'

'Do you know where it is?'

'Kind of.' She pointed to the east.

'Come with me.'

'You've been there?' Hank asked.

The girl shrugged. 'Well, see, I wasn't what you might say actually *there*.' A voluptuous ditz, Hank thought. 'I

102

mean, I saw it from the other side of the valley. Tom – that's the guy who helps with the boats down in the cavern – he's down there, too, you know.'

'What about him?' Hank asked.

'Well, it's just that Tom's the one that showed it to me. We were on this dirt road over across from it. So I couldn't see it too well.'

'But you know where to find it?'

'I think so.'

Hank opened the passenger door of his rental car. 'How about climbing in. I'll drive us over there.'

'Gee, I don't know. I'm sort of like on duty, you know, and I really don't know . . .'

'Is something more important,' Chris asked, 'than getting those people out of the cave?'

'Well, I guess not. But you can't get in. Like I was saying, it's all walled up.'

'We'd better take some tools along,' Chris said. 'A pick or something.'

'You'd need lights, too,' Lynn told them. 'Really, you oughta just wait for the fire department. They'll get everybody out.'

'Eventually,' Chris said. She looked at Hank. 'What do you think?'

Hank gazed past her at the blazing hotel. The entire east wing was now engulfed, so the area housing the elevators was already being consumed.

'The fire department isn't even *here* yet,' he said. 'By the time they get this thing out, there might be a ton of rubble covering the elevator shafts. They'll have to bring in heavy equipment to clear all that away.' He turned to Lynn. 'How far is it through the closed part of the cave to that other wall?'

'About half a mile. But it's dark and there aren't any walkways or anything. I mean, it'd be the pits, you know? And there's that chasm somebody might fall into like Elizabeth Mordock. I don't think . . .'

'We could probably get to them in a couple of hours,' Chris said.

'Depending on the walls,' said Hank.

'Really, you two, I don't see what the big hurry is. The fire department can take care of it. They'll get 'em out.'

'It's our daughters down there,' Hank said.

'But they're safer staying where they are until the fire department can . . .'

'How do you know that?' Chris asked her.

'Well . . .'

'What if something's gone wrong down there?'

Hank felt a sudden tug of fear. 'What do you mean?'

Frowning, Chris shook her head. 'Maybe somebody's been hurt. If they don't already know they're trapped, they'll find out pretty soon. People might panic. There might be arguments, fights. God only knows. I just think, the faster they're out of there, the better.'

'Same here,' Hank said. 'Let's go for it.'

8

'On the bright side,' Greg said, 'we've got light and heat.'

After the initial confusion, nearly everyone had stood up and approached the blazing remains of the elevators. Darcy stood with the others in a semi-circle, Greg at her side. Some held out their hands as if to warm them at a bonfire.

A man said, 'Who's got the marshmallows?'

His little girl frowned up at him. 'You're not funny, Daddy.'

'How in God's name do we get out of here, now?' a woman asked.

Darcy didn't care about that. Not at the moment. Staring into the flames, she could only think about her mother.

Something awful had happened up top. A fire, maybe an explosion. Maybe a nuclear blast like the man had suggested so long ago.

Mom's all right, she told herself. Please. She has to be.

Greg put his arm around her. 'Don't worry,' he said.

'My mother.'

'I'm sure she's fine. She probably had plenty of time to get away.'

'What do you mean?'

'It wasn't anything sudden,' he said. 'Whatever happened, it must have started when the lights went off. It took all this time before the elevators dropped, so the whole place didn't go up at once.'

Darcy thought about that. Greg was right. Obviously, the entire complex hadn't been destroyed in some terrible cataclysm. The fire must have started a distance away and spread until it consumed the elevator housings. So people had time to get away. Maybe Mom was okay. Maybe she wasn't even in the hotel when it happened.

Darcy looked at Greg. 'Thanks,' she said.

He nodded. His broad face was ruddy in the firelight, his eyes shining. Steam was rising off the front of his sweatshirt. Darcy rested her head against his shoulder.

The heat from the fires was almost too much. She had thought for a time that she would never be warm again. But now her face felt as if it were being seared. Her skin was stinging under the snug heat of her trousers. The touch of the windbreaker against her breasts was painful. Sweat trickled down her sides.

She turned around, and sighed with relief as the hurt faded and her back began to warm up.

Someone sidestepped through the fluttering light and moved in front of her. The man in the Peterbilt hat. 'You're supposed to be in charge here,' he said. 'What are you gonna do now?'

'Just take it easy,' Greg told him.

'I'll get us out of here,' Darcy said.

Those nearby, who heard her over the other voices and the windy noise and snapping sounds of the fire, stepped in closer and looked at her.

'Gonna get us out, are you? How do you figure that?'

He spoke to Darcy as if this were all her fault.

'Cool down, slick.'

'Butt out,' he snapped.

The old man's head moved forward on his long neck. His scalp was hairless except for a white fringe over his ears. His eyes were small and squinty, his nose a beak. He looked to Darcy like a bald eagle about to rip off the bastard's face.

'Don't let him rile you, Calvin,' said the buxom woman at the old man's side – maybe his daughter. She tugged his arm. He pulled it free.

'Yeah, Callllllvin,' mocked the man in the truck hat. 'Don't want you having a heart attack.'

'Low-life son of a whore, you best start minding your manners, or . . .'

'Or what, Callllllvin?'

'All right, now!' Greg's voice shot out. 'We've got enough trouble without fighting among ourselves. Darcy said she's going to get us out, so why don't we listen to her?'

Those nearby gathered in closer. Others, farther off, continued to talk among themselves.

'LISTEN UP!' It was the fat boy.

The voices went silent. Darcy stepped past the scowling man, patted the shoulder of his son, and made her way into the cool shadows a distance from the fires. Turning around, she found that Greg had stayed with her. She held up her arms.

The people faced her, their backs to the blazing elevators.

'Obviously,' she said in a firm voice, 'it's a lot worse than we thought. The area above us is burning.'

'Tell us something we don't know.'

'Would you *please* hush?' A woman's voice.

'What'll we do?' Another woman.

'We're going to die.' More of a whiny squeal than a voice.

'Nobody's going to die,' Darcy said. 'I still think that rescue is possible from the elevator shafts, but that'll take a lot longer than we imagined. And since we don't know what's going on up there, I think it would be foolish to do nothing but wait. There is another way out.'

'The natural opening.' It was the fat boy's knowing voice.

'That's right,' Darcy said. 'Just before the lights went out, I was showing you Ely's Wall and telling about how he closed off the other half of the cavern. There's a pick axe near the dock area. With that, I'm sure we'll be able to break through the wall. From there, it's only about half a mile to the natural opening. We'll take the pick axe with us, and knock out the wall at that end. Then we'll be home free.'

'Fuck. Should've done that in the first place.'

'Yeah, we'd be out by now.'

'Let's do it!'

Back-lit by the fires, the group seemed to Darcy like a band of villagers eager to begin a foolhardy errand. Movie extras. Faceless dark forms gesturing and mouthing brave words. A hunting party, a lynch mob, peasants working themselves up to go chasing the Frankenstein monster.

'What're we waiting for?'

'Let's haul ass!'

'EVERYBODY SHUT UP!' Darcy shouted.

The noise faded to mutters.

'It won't be a picnic. We've got one good flashlight and one that's nearly dead. Beyond Ely's Wall, there will be no walkways. There is also the chasm that Elizabeth Mordock fell into. In other words, the terrain will be rugged and dangerous. If we all try to go trooping through there, most of you will be doing it in darkness.

'Here's my suggestion. I think that no more than six of us should try to go out that way. One flashlight should be enough for a group that small, and we'd be able to keep track of each other. Everyone else can wait here, where there's warmth and light. Once we're out, we'll make sure the rest of you are rescued as quickly as possible. You'll either be lifted out through the elevator shafts or a rescue party with plenty of good lights will come in from the natural opening and guide you out. Either way, you won't be in here much longer than those who go in the first group with me. But you'll be able to leave in a lot more safety.

'I'll give you a while to think about it. Decide whether you want to stay here or go with the escape party. I recommend you choose to stay here unless you've got a very good reason not to. After you've had a chance to make up your minds, I'll pick my group from those of you who want to leave with me.'

'Guess that leaves *me* out,' muttered the Peterbilt man.

'That's right,' Darcy said. Raising her voice, she announced. 'You've got five minutes.'

'I absolutely must be one of the six,' Helen said to Carol.

'I'll stick with you.'

Helen shook her head. The lenses of her glasses reflected fire. She lifted a hand to Carol's cheek. 'You're so sweet. But there's no need for you to risk life and limb. Besides, look how you're dressed.'

'I know how I'm dressed,' Carol said. The heat from the burning elevators felt wonderful, and she knew she would regret leaving the warmth. 'Hell, the fires aren't going to last forever.'

'I'll leave you my sweater.'

'I'm going with you. If they'll let me.'

'Stay. I'd stay, myself, if it weren't for this damned diabetes. I just can't take the risk of waiting any longer than necessary. The hotel must have burnt.' She shook her head. 'I'll have to go into town, I suppose.'

'We'll both go, Helen.'

'It might be terribly dangerous. You heard what the guide said. There won't be a walkway. And that chasm. It sounds just horrendous. I wouldn't be able to forgive myself if you came along on my account and . . . something happened to you.'

'Nothing will happen. Besides, what makes you think I'd want to stay behind? I don't know any of these people. You're my best friend. Even if you are a pain in the ass sometimes.'

Helen made a sound that was more like a sob than a laugh, and embraced her.

'I'd sure like to see what's on the other side of that wall,' Wayne said.

'Don't be ridiculous,' Jean told him. 'It wouldn't be any different than what's on this side.'

'Except it's been closed up for about sixty years. And it's where Elizabeth Mordock died.'

'Daddy, don't be so disgusting.'

'Might be haunted,' he said.

110

'There's no such things as ghosts,' Katie told him.

'Who says so?'

She slapped his arm.

'You hit me one more time, young lady, I'll knock your block off.'

'Mommy.'

'Don't speak to her that way, Wayne. It's not funny.'

'That's right.'

'She shouldn't go around hitting me all the time.'

'You shouldn't tease her about ghosts.'

'Who's teasing?'

'If you really thought Elizabeth Mordock's ghost might be lurking in the other side of the cave, they couldn't *drag* you there. You're the biggest chicken I know.'

Wayne laughed. She was right, of course. 'Well,' he said, 'it's quite obvious that I can't go with the first group and leave you two alone. We'll get to see the other end of the cave sooner or later, anyway.'

'I don't want to,' Katie said.

'It's either that, or we'll have to be lifted out with ropes or something. Personally, I'd rather take my chances with Elizabeth's ghost than get dropped.'

'Goddamn it, Wayne!'

'I reckon you'd rather stay here by the fire,' Calvin said, smiling and patting Mavis's considerable backside.

'Don't tell me *you* want to go.'

'I don't aim to leave you behind, that's for sure. Minute I'm gone, old slick'd take it into his head to give your ass a poking.'

'Calvin!'

He laughed.

111

'It's not at all funny.'

'Don't fret. It ain't about to happen. I'll be right here and see to it. 'Sides, I reckon his pecker's so teeny he'd never find it in the dark.'

'Why don't you quit harping about him? Honestly, Calvin, you act like such a baby sometimes.'

'Which is it, a baby or a chauvinist?'

'Both.'

'You sure do take pleasure in insulting a man. Not that I hold it against you. It's just the way you gals are. No sooner you get married than you turn into a shrew.'

He saw the corners of her mouth turn down. Now I've gone and done it, he thought. 'Shitfire,' he said, 'don't take it personal.'

'How am I supposed to take it? You as much as said you wished you hadn't married me.'

'I said no such thing, May. You're just fine, you're just fine.'

'You called me a shrew.'

'Well, you *are* a shrew. But like I say, it ain't your fault. You're just a woman, and that's a natural part of the equipment. It comes with the wedding band.'

Now, she was weeping. In the firelight, Calvin saw shiny tears rolling down her cheeks.

'Oh, damnation,' he muttered. He clamped his cane between his knees, and put his arms around her. 'I'm sorry, sweetie-pie.'

'You should be.' She squeezed him tightly. He felt the cane move. 'Is that *you*, Calvin?'

'If I go,' Paula asked, 'will you come, too?'

Kyle went tight and cold inside. 'You don't want to go, do you?'

'My dad . . . I'm scared he might've gotten hurt. And even if he's okay, he must be awfully worried about me. I've just got to get out of here as fast as I can.'

'If your father were here,' Kyle said, 'I bet he'd want you to stay and wait for a real rescue.'

'Why?' .

'Because he wouldn't want you to take a chance like that. It'll be . . . really bad on the other side.'

He wished he could tell her how bad. He wished he could tell *Darcy* how bad, and talk her out of breaking through the wall.

At first, after the elevators fell, Kyle had been stunned to realize that the trouble was more than a simple power failure. The whole complex up top must be burning down: the hotel, the tourist area with its gift shop and snack bar, his own room – and worst of all, room 115.

The loss of 115 *hurt*. To think that it was gone before he'd even gotten another chance to use it.

He told himself, Dad'll rebuild the place. He'll make another room just like 115. It will be the same, and some day I'll be running the new hotel and I'll pick who I want to put in there.

The thoughts of rebuilding made him feel a lot better, but then Darcy started talking about escape through the other end of the cavern, and Kyle felt a rush of dread that turned his legs soft and he'd held onto Paula to keep himself steady.

He couldn't let them do it!

If they broke through Ely's Wall . . .

How could he stop them?

Warn Darcy. But what could he tell her without revealing the truth?

There had to be another way.

Get rid of the pick axe. Without that, they wouldn't be able to smash through the barrier.

The pick axe must be in the grotto where Darcy had changed clothes. Kyle hadn't seen it there, but his eyes had never left Darcy. Still, that's where it probably was. Cubby Wales had been working to enlarge the grotto and must've left his tools behind.

While Darcy continued speaking to the group, Kyle imagined himself finding the pick axe and hurling it into the Lake of Charon. They'd never find it there.

He would have to sneak away. Maybe whisper to Paula that he had to take a leak, then hurry to the grotto. Without any light. (Follow the railing.) But it would take so damn long. They were bound to notice he was gone. When they got to the grotto and the pick axe wasn't there, Darcy would know he was the one who took it. Then, after they found the pick axe (they'd make him show where he threw it), they'd break through the wall anyway.

They'd find what was there.

Maybe not.

But if they did, they'd realize that Kyle knew about it – otherwise, why did he ditch the pick axe?

I can't do anything, he finally decided. I can't let on that I know. Then, whatever happens, I won't get the blame.

If there was some way to stop just Darcy . . .

Don't think about it, he told himself. You can't do anything. Maybe she'll be all right.

But now Paula wanted to go along, too.

Kyle took Paula by the hand and led her away from the others. 'I have to tell you something,' he said. They walked towards the darkness. The heat from the fires faded. 'I don't want anyone else to know this, so you've got to promise you won't say anything.'

'What is it?'

'Do you promise?'

'Sure,' she said. Her voice trembled slightly.

'It's who I am.' He stopped. He looked back. They were far from the rest of the group. He put his hands on Paula's shoulders. 'I'm Kyle Mordock.'

'You mean like Mordock Cavern?'

He nodded. 'My family owns all this. My dad, actually.'

'Oh Kyle, I'm sorry. Maybe it's . . . just a small fire.'

He shrugged. 'Doesn't matter. It's all insured. Dad has lots of insurance. We'll rebuild. But the thing is, it has to be a secret that my dad's the owner. If the others find out, they might . . . you know, cause trouble. They might blame me.'

'Doesn't Darcy know?'

'Yeah, but that's different. And I don't think she's told anyone. Do you know what a scapegoat is?'

'Sure.'

'I'd be the scapegoat if it got around. That's why Darcy's keeping it a secret. The thing is, I've lived here all my life. My dad and I, we've got rooms in the hotel. So I know a lot about the cavern – maybe more than anyone. I know some things the guides don't know.' He eased Paula closer to him. He felt the soft push of her breasts against his chest. 'The other part of the cave . . . a certain area behind Ely's wall . . . used to be an Indian burial place. I've read Ely's diary. When he closed it up, all the bodies were still there. A whole lot of them. And he even wrote that he thought it was spirits of the dead Indians that pushed his wife into the chasm. That's stupid, of course. I mean, I don't believe that, myself. But the corpses of all those Indians . . .' He shook his head. 'I get the creeps, just thinking about it.'

'Aren't they buried?' Paula whispered.

'They're just . . . like lying around. Some are sitting up, some leaning against the walls. At least that's what Ely wrote.'

'Jesus.'

'That's how come I don't think you really want to go along with the others. Me, I don't want to set foot on the other side of Ely's Wall. I don't want to see those things.'

'Me neither,' Paula said.

'You'll stay, then?'

She nodded, her hair tickling Kyle's cheek.

'If we're lucky,' he said, 'we'll get rescued through the elevator shafts. Then we won't have to go through that place at all.'

'Oh, I hope so. Jesus. Shouldn't we tell the others?'

'We can't. They'd find out who I am, and . . .'

'Okay,' Darcy called, 'those of you who want to go along with me, step forward and I'll make the final selection.'

Paula looked over her shoulder at the others. Then her arms tightened around Kyle.

Darcy was glad to see that there weren't many volunteers. For most of the people, remaining here with the light and heat of the elevator fires was apparently far more attractive than venturing into the chilly darkness, into an unknown and dangerous section of the cavern.

Greg volunteered, as she expected he would.

So did Jim and Beth Donner.

Tom.

A young man and woman who were holding hands. The woman wore a maternity dress in the style of a sailor suit.

A white-haired, obese man who was smoking a cigar and appeared to be at least sixty years old.

A pair of lean, matching men in plaid shirts and goatees.. They appeared to be about forty.

A couple of women, one rather stiff looking in a sweater, blue slacks and glasses, the other looking innocent and vulnerable and wearing a sleeveless sundress that must have kept her in shivers until the fires came down.

No Kyle. That was a nice surprise. Maybe he'd dumped Darcy for that girl – Paula. She felt a small stir of guilt, once again, for pairing Paula with Kyle.

Might not be such a good idea, she thought, leaving them here together.

Hell, I'm not a chaperone.

She looked at the people gathered in front of her. 'I'm afraid I won't be very democratic about this. Tom, I want you staying here. For one thing, you shouldn't be exerting yourself. For another, I want you to take charge of the group that stays behind.'

'Either way's fine with me,' he said.

Darcy turned to the pregnant woman. 'There may be a lot of rock climbing in the darkness. I don't want to worry about you falling.'

'I'm perfectly capable of . . .'

'I'm sure you are. But you're staying unless you've got some kind of overwhelming reason to get out fast.'

'You're not being fair.'

'I'm being practical. You're staying here.' She turned

to the heavy man with the cigar. 'You, too.'

'You're the captain,' he said.

Darcy smiled. 'Thanks.' She scanned the others. 'Greg, I want you to come. Jim and Beth – you've both been a lot of help, so you're welcome to join us . . . though God knows why you'd want to.'

'I miss the sunlight,' Beth said.

'And we have dinner plans,' said Jim.

'Well, you're in.' Darcy looked at the remaining four. 'I only want to take two more, and I think men . . .'

'I have to go with you,' said the woman with the glasses. 'I'm a diabetic. I left my insulin in the hotel. I need to follow a special diet and I didn't expect to miss lunch. I'm afraid that if . . .'

'Okay. You're in. Both of you.' She turned to the matching men. 'Sorry, fellows.'

'It's quite all right with me,' said one. 'It was all Brian's idea, and I'm sure I would much prefer to stay cozy and snug by the fire.'

'You're such a sissy,' said Brian.

'You wouldn't have me any other way.'

Darcy raised her voice. 'Okay, my group is ready to go. I'll be leaving Tom in charge here with one of the flashlights. We'll be as quick as possible. For all I know, you people might be out before we are. In any case, you won't be in here for more than a few hours.

'Any questions before we go?'

There were no questions. A few people wished them good luck. Someone said, 'Break a leg.'

'We'll try to avoid that,' Darcy said.

Crouching, she rushed to one of the blazing elevators. The heat pressed against her. She squinted into the debris, then grabbed a broken length of plank. She backed up, pulling it out. Its end was burning. It would make a fine torch for as long as it lasted, and postpone the time when she would need to use the flashlight.

Greg, hurrying past her, found a fiery brand for himself.

Jim did the same.

Those staying behind stood in silence as Darcy, her torch held high, led her small group into the darkness.

9

'You don't get me going in there,' Lynn said as Hank pulled out of the parking lot. He glimpsed the burning hotel in the rear-view mirror. 'I mean, Elizabeth Mordock's *body* is in there.'

Chris looked over her shoulder. 'You don't have to go in. All we want you to do is show us where the place is.'

'You won't be able to get in.'

'We'll get in,' Hank said. He glanced at Chris. 'We have to make a detour into town, first. There's a shopping centre. Paula and I stopped for doughnuts this morning. I think it had a hardware store.'

'Yeah,' Lynn said. 'Andy's. I've been there a few times. They've got all kinds of stuff.'

Hank slowed the car to round a bend, then picked up speed again. The trees along the roadside flashed by in a blur of green.

Where the hell are the fire trucks? he wondered. Then he thought, who needs them? If they'd shown up in time to save the elevator area . . . The way it's going, we'll reach the girls before the fire even gets knocked down. That's if the fire department shows up at all.

Maybe they were busy at another call.

121

Maybe that guy in the Jeep changed his mind about reporting it.

Doesn't matter any more. We'll get the girls out.

Hank shuddered.

I can't go into that cavern.

He imagined the darkness, the walls closing in on him, suffocating him.

I can do it, he told himself. I'll have to do it. I can't send Chris in alone.

'Are you okay?' Chris asked.

'Does it show?'

'I'm just worried about Paula.'

'I've told you,' Lynn said from the back seat. 'Everybody's safe down there. What won't be safe is leading that whole bunch out through the bad end of the cave. I mean, I don't think you know what you're doing.'

Hank sped around a curve, saw a stop sign ahead, and hit the brakes. As the car slowed, he checked the main road. Nothing in sight. He rolled past the sign, swung onto the road and floored the accelerator. The car shot forward, pressing him into the seat.

'What do you suppose that was all about?' Chris asked.

'Back in the lobby.'

'And Mordock being dead?' Lynn wanted to know.

'A guy came in with buckets of gasoline and a cigar,' Hank said. 'He was upset about some woman he thought had been a guest at the hotel. Apparently, he thought Mordock had done something to her. He doused Mordock with gasoline, and Mordock suddenly started busting caps.'

'Started what?' Lynn asked.

'Shooting at him. The guy tossed his cigar, and *poof*.'

'Man,' Lynn murmured.

'What did he think Mordock did to her?' Chris asked.

'Made her disappear. I guess this guy had talked to Mordock about it before. He seemed sure that the gal had checked in, but Mordock must've shown him the registration cards to prove that she hadn't. Her card wasn't there. That's what convinced the guy that Mordock was behind her disappearance.'

'He must've been crazy,' Chris said.

'The gal was probably his sister or wife or something.'

'I wonder what Mordock did with her.'

'Who says he did anything?' Lynn argued. 'Just because some guy accuses him . . .'

'The man seemed absolutely certain she checked in. She'd probably phoned him from the hotel.'

'I had Mordock figured for a sleaze,' Chris said. 'But it's hard to imagine he actually . . . do you suppose he killed her?'

'I bet the guy with the gas thought so.'

'Ethan wouldn't do that,' Lynn said. 'He was a nice guy.'

'I got the feeling he was *too* nice,' Chris told her. 'At least as far as pretty women were concerned. I noticed you didn't seem very upset when I told you he was dead.'

'I don't care about him one way or the other. I mean, it's too bad he got killed and everything. But I don't think he was some kind of a lunatic going around murdering his guests like that guy in *Psycho*. That's nutty. And I don't think it's nice to dump on him now that he's crumped.'

'Somebody got rid of that woman's registration card,' Chris pointed out.

'Assuming she did check in,' Hank said.

'I have a feeling she did.'

'So do I.'

'That doesn't mean Ethan had something to do with it,' Lynn persisted.

She sure is sticking up for him, Hank thought. Maybe she'd been involved with him. Possible. It couldn't have been a very serious relationship, though, or she'd be more upset about his death.

None of my business, he decided.

As his car bore down on the rear of a station wagon, Hank swerved across the centre line. In an instant, he passed the station wagon. He swung back into his lane. The wagon shrank in the rear-view mirror.

'If anybody was nuts around there,' Lynn said, 'it was that kid Kyle.'

'Who's he?' Chris asked.

'Ethan's kid. Wouldn't surprise me much if *he* tried messing around with a guest. I wouldn't put anything past him. Spooky kid. He *really* had Darcy going crazy.'

'He'd have access to the registration cards,' Hank said.

Chris turned around on her seat and looked back at Lynn. Her left knee touched the side of Hank's leg. He glanced at her smooth thigh. It was draped by a corner of her shirt. The bottom of the shirt was open. Between her legs, the swimsuit was narrow and tight. Hank didn't allow himself more than a glimpse before forcing his eyes back to the road.

'What did he do to Darcy?' Chris asked.

'Not much. I mean, he had a . . . he was interested in her. He kept going on her tours and staring at her. You'd be surprised how many guys on those tours get *very* interested in us. I don't know, maybe it's the uniform. These teenage guys, you can almost see their mouths watering. You just . . . it's flattering, you know, and nothing much ever . . . they take the tour and go away, you never see them again. But not Kyle. He's always around. And he's Ethan's son, so Darcy wasn't real eager to tell him to fff . . . bug off.'

'This Kyle . . .' Chris's voice stopped. Her head snapped towards the front.

'It's about time,' Hank said, hearing the sirens. Slowing down only slightly, he eased the car to the right. The side tyres rumbled on the gravel at the edge of the road.

The sirens blared louder, louder, and a police car shot around the bend and flashed past, lights whirling. Next came the red car of the fire chief. Then an emergency rescue van, a pumper truck, a hook and ladder. They roared by and the noise faded. Hank swung back onto the road and pressed the accelerator down. 'Nothing that'll get our kids out,' he said. 'They'll need a bulldozer, probably. Maybe a crane.'

Chris nodded. Her face was grim. She turned her head to look at Lynn in the back seat.

Hank glanced again at her inner thigh, the clinging swimsuit. He felt a warm rush of arousal and guilt.

Keep your damned eyes on the road, he told himself.

'You said this kid, Kyle, went on her tours.'

'Yeah, and he'd just gaze at her. It was like he had a crush on Darcy. Only with him, "crush" doesn't seem like the right way to put it. It seems too . . . I don't know.'

'Innocent?' Chris asked.

'Yeah. I mean, he's only like fifteen but he doesn't

come across as innocent. He's pretty spooky for a kid.'

'Was he on the tour this morning?' Chris asked.

'Yeah, he was. We passed, you know? Darcy's was taking her bunch in, and mine was on the way out. Yeah, Kyle was right behind her.'

'Great,' Chris muttered.

She looked at Hank. He met her worried gaze, shook his head, and put his hand on her leg. He felt guilty about that. I'm just comforting her, he told himself, and kept his hand there. 'I'm sure it's all right,' he said.

She put her hand over his.

'Yeah,' Lynn said. 'He's not gonna . . .'

'You just told me you wouldn't put anything past him,' Chris reminded the girl.

'Well . . .'

'Chris,' Hank said, 'there are over thirty people down there.' Including Paula, he thought. Paula. The same age as the kid, and alone.

Kyle had access to the registration cards.

Kyle could have made that other girl disappear.

Paula's trapped down there with him.

But it's Darcy he's got the hots for. And there are all those other people. He wouldn't try anything.

'Darcy can take care of herself,' Chris muttered as if trying to reassure herself.

Ahead was a traffic light. It was red. As Hank slowed down, he saw the shopping centre beyond the intersection. The sight of it should have been a relief. Instead, Hank felt his stomach knot.

We're that much closer.

When we leave, we'll be heading for the cavern.

I'll be okay, he told himself.

Like hell.

126

As long as Paula's okay, that's all that counts. And Darcy. If that fucker's messed with them, he'll pay.

The light turned green.

'You two go on ahead,' Chris said as they walked across the parking lot. 'I'll go to the sporting goods store and meet you back at the car.'

'They've probably got flashlights at Andy's,' Hank said.

'I need clothes. If they have a Coleman lantern, I'll pick up one of those and some flashlights.'

'If you really plan on going into the cavern,' Lynn said to Hank, 'you should have a sweatshirt or something. You'll be cold in that.' She fingered the front of his knit shirt.

'I'll pick up something warm for you,' Chris told him. 'I'd already planned on it.'

He reached into the back pocket of his shorts and took out his wallet.

'Forget it,' Chris told him. 'You take care of the pick or whatever.'

Lynn went along with Hank, which suited Chris fine. She hadn't cared much for Lynn from the moment Darcy introduced her yesterday. The girl had struck her as being not only a little vague, but irresponsible. And back in the car, the way she'd taken Mordock's side when anyone could see that the guy was a creep – he's dead, Chris reminded herself.

And maybe his son's as bad as he was, or worse. The kid had a lech for Darcy.

I can thank Lynn for that cheerful information.

The girl had seemed to savour telling her about it. A juicy bit of gossip.

Hey, guess what. You think Ethan was a creep, you should get a load of his son. Oh, and by the way, he's hot for your daughter and he's in the cave with her. God only knows what he might be up to. I tell you, I wouldn't put anything past him.

Just what I wanted to hear.

Then she's running her fingers down Hank's chest.

Not only a twit, but a flirt.

Chris entered the sporting goods store. The air inside was cool on her bare legs.

A man standing in the checkout line stared at them.

Big deal. Hasn't he seen legs before?

She grabbed a shopping cart and rolled it through the aisles until she came to the sportswear section. She found warm-up suits in her size, picked a blue one and dropped it into the cart. She found a plain grey sweatshirt for Hank, then changed her mind and chose a warm-up suit for him. After all, she thought, he's not only wearing the shirt Lynn seemed so fond of touching, but shorts. Surprising that Lynn didn't give those a stroke, while she was at it.

Remembering the stares of the man in the checkout line, Chris picked up a pair of jogging shorts for herself. Then she headed for the shoe department, and threw some white socks into her cart.

As she scanned the shoe display, a young man with a moustache and the heavily muscled body of a weight lifter approached her. 'Can I help you with something?'

'I'd like a pair of running shoes. White. Size six.'

'Have a seat. I'd better measure. It's very important, particularly with athletic shoes, to have a perfect fit.'

'I'm in a hurry. Size six will be fine. Regular width.'

'If you say so.' He sounded slightly reproachful. 'Any particular style or brand?'

'Something like this,' she said, pointing out a white Reebok on the display wall.

'Excellent choice.' He lifted the sample and inspected it.

'May I help you?' asked an older man approaching from the side.

The one with the muscles held the shoe towards him. 'We'd like a pair of these in size six, regular width.'

'Certainly.' He disappeared into the storeroom.

'You don't work here,' Chris said.

'I hope you won't hold it against me. My name's Brad.' He made a smile which he obviously considered charming.

'You have a foot fetish?'

'Legs, and so on. Oh, don't look so annoyed. You're flattered, and you know it.'

'Give me a break.'

He arched an eyebrow. 'You're a very beautiful woman.'

'Thanks. But I'm also very busy.'

'Are you alone?'

'Not as alone as I'd like to be.'

'Ha! I like a woman with a good sense of humour.'

The batwing doors swung open and the salesman came out with two shoeboxes in his arms. 'You might want to try these, first.' He gave her the box on top. 'They're six and a half. Reebok sizes run fairly small.'

Chris sat down. She felt the chair's vinyl upholstery against the backs of her legs. Both men stood in front of her, watching as she bent over and slipped into one of the shoes. 'Feels fine,' she said, and took it off.

'You'd better try it with a sock on,' Brad suggested. He stepped to her shopping cart, took out the athletic socks, and handed them to her.

'Thanks,' she said, wishing he would disappear.

She pulled a sock on, then stepped into the shoe again.

'How's that?' asked the salesman.

'Good.'

Squatting, he began to lace the shoe. The bald top of his head was sunburned and peeling. He tied a bow, then squeezed the sides of the shoe, its toe. He nodded. He murmured, 'Mmm-hmm, mmm-hmm.' Chris couldn't see his eyes. But she thought she could feel their gaze like oiled fingers sliding up her thighs.

I never should've come in here dressed this way, she thought.

The salesman tipped his head back and smiled up at her. 'They seem all right to me,' he said.

'Maybe you should try walking in them,' Brad suggested.

Right. Let's have a parade! 'These fit fine. I'll take them.'

'Would you like to wear them now, or . . .'

'No.' As the salesman reached down to remove the shoe, she brought her foot up. She propped it on her knee and quickly removed the shoe and sock. While the shoe was being boxed, she slipped into her sandal and stood up. She was glad to be standing, glad to have the shirt draping her thighs.

'Will there be anything else?' the salesman asked.

'I'll just look around, thanks.' She put the socks and shoebox into the shopping cart, and headed away.

Brad stayed at her side.

'Don't you have something better to do?' she asked.

He grinned. 'If I did, I'd be doing it.'

Chris steered the cart into an aisle between displays

of camping equipment. She found a Coleman lantern and lifted its box into the cart. Brad lifted a one-gallon tin of fuel.

'Want this?' he asked.

'Thanks,' she muttered.

'Going on a camping trip?'

'Something like that.' Beyond the end of the aisle, backpacks were hanging on the wall. She chose a small red one.

'That won't hold much,' Brad informed her.

Ignoring the comment, she added it to her collection.

She came to the flashlights. Some were as long as her forearm, others no larger than a pencil. Some had casings of ribbed metal, some of rubber, others of red plastic. She decided the plastic ones would do fine. She counted them as she placed them into her shopping cart.

'Going out with a girl scout troop?' Brad asked.

Eight. That was all they had, but there were metal ones the same size so she began putting those into her cart.

'That's a lot of flashlights.'

She looked at Brad.

He raised his eyebrows.

'There are about forty people trapped in Mordock Cavern. I'm going in with a friend to get them out.'

He looked her in the eyes. 'You're shitting me.'

'Right. I figure I need twenty lights.'

'I'll get the batteries for you.' He checked a flashlight package. 'Size D,' he muttered, then sidestepped, bent over, and began picking up Everready twin-packs. 'How did it happen?'

'A fire in the main complex. The elevators are gone.'

'So how're you planning to get in?'

'The natural opening.'

'That's blocked off.' He dumped a handful of batteries into the cart, and crouched to get more.

'My friend's buying some tools.'

Brad whistled softly. 'Going into Lizzy's Tomb,' he muttered.

'Is that what they call it?'

'Around here. Wow. How come you're doing it?'

'My daughter's trapped.'

'Jesus.' He added more batteries to the growing pile. 'Isn't that a job for the police?'

'Probably. But we're doing it.'

'You and who else?'

'Hank. His daughter's trapped, too. There's a guide, Lynn. She's going to show us . . .'

'Lynn Maxwell?'

Small world, Chris thought. But it didn't come as much of a surprise to learn that a girl like Lynn was known by a pushy young man like Brad. 'You know her,' she said.

'A friend of a friend. If Lynn's showing you the way, who's the guide in the cave?' He frowned. 'It isn't Darcy Raines?'

Chris's heart thumped, and she felt heat rise to her face. 'Yeah, Darcy.'

'Shit. Better her than Lynn, though.'

Chris stared at him. 'What the hell do you mean by that?'

'She's got it all over Lynn. She's really got her act together, you know? If I had to get trapped in that damn cave, I'd want her to be the one in charge. I don't want to insult anyone, but Lynn's a flake.'

I'm starting to like this guy, Chris thought.

He dropped another handful of battery packs into the cart. 'Okay, that makes twenty pairs. Have you got twenty flashlights?'

She nodded. 'How do you know Darcy?'

'Seen her around. I took her tour. We've had drinks together a couple of times. I take it you know her.'

'I know her.'

'Look, if she's stuck in the cave . . . Could you people use an extra hand?'

'You want to come along?'

'I'd like to help.'

Chris stared him in the eyes. He met her gaze for a moment, then looked away.

'Hey, I'm aware I was acting like a creep a little earlier. I was just fooling around. I'm not always like that.'

'God, I hope not.'

He let out a short laugh.

'Yeah, you can come with us. An extra body might come in handy.' Chris picked up a plastic lantern. 'Want to get me a six volt battery for this?'

'Sure. Hey, since we're going to be partners in this adventure, how about telling me your name?'

'Chris Raines.'

Smiling, he held out his hand. As Chris shook it, he frowned. 'Raines?'

'Darcy's old lady.'

'Now I *know* you're shitting me.'

Lynn folded her arms across the back of the passenger seat, and said, 'It's sure taking her a long time.'

'She had more to buy.'

'You interested in her?'

133

'We just met,' he said.

'So? You are, aren't you? Interested in her.'

'Some reason I shouldn't be?'

'No, I'm not saying that. Just curious. She's not too bad looking for a woman her age. She must be up there pushing forty, don't you think? I mean, Darcy's twenty-one, so . . .'

'You're so interested, why don't you ask her?'

'None of my business.'

That's right, Hank thought, and wondered what was going on with Lynn. She'd started acting pretty chummy while they were in the hardware store. When they'd returned to the car, Lynn had waited by the passenger door and given him a sharp glance when he opened the door to the back seat for her. Now, she was trying to run down Chris.

He supposed it was nothing more than Lynn feeling like a third wheel and wanting to usurp Chris's position.

Too bad Lynn's necessary at all, he thought.

Well, she'd claimed she wouldn't go into the cavern. If she didn't change her mind about that, she'd be out of the way before much longer.

'About time,' Lynn said.

Hank looked through the side window and saw Chris leave the sporting goods store. A man in jeans and plaid shirt walked beside her, pushing a loaded cart. Just outside the store, Chris stopped and spoke to the man. She reached into the cart, took out a pair of red shorts, and stepped into them.

'Miss Modesty,' Lynn muttered.

Hank felt a small pull of guilt, wondering if he was the reason she'd bought the shorts.

Once the pants were on, Chris scanned the parking

lot, spotted the car, and started forward. The man with the cart stayed with her.

'Gee, that's Brad what's-his-face. God's gift to women. Too bad, Hank.'

Ignoring the remark, he climbed out and went to the rear of the car. He had the truck open before they arrived.

'Hank,' Chris said, 'this is Brad.' As they shook hands, she explained, 'We met in the store. He knows Darcy.'

'I'd like to come along and help, if it's okay with you.'

'Fine.'

Quickly, they put the warm-up suits, lantern and fuel, and a bag that was heavy with Tropical Chocolate bars into the trunk. The flashlights and batteries were dumped onto the back seat next to Lynn. Chris took her shoes and socks into the car with her.

Brad got into the back with Lynn. As they greeted each other, Hank drove out of the parking lot. Chris slipped her sandals off and started to put on her socks.

'I figured it couldn't hurt,' she said, 'having another man along. Especially when it comes to breaking through those walls.'

'Yeah. It'll help.'

When her shoes were on, Chris turned around. 'Hand up some of those batteries and flashlights,' she said.

Chris, Lynn and Brad loaded the flashlights while Hank drove as fast as he dared towards Mordock Cavern.

10

'I wonder if they're at the wall, yet,' Paula said.

'It's too soon,' Kyle told her. He wished she hadn't mentioned the wall. He didn't want to think about that.

Darcy's group had no sooner started off than Kyle began to regret his decision not to sneak away while he had the chance and dispose of the pick axe. So what if they figured out he'd been the one who got rid of it? No big deal. They weren't crazy, they wouldn't do something like torture him to make him tell where he'd put it. They'd be pissed, but so what? If they couldn't find the pick, they'd have no way to get through the wall.

It's too late for that, now.

But not too late to stop them.

If Dad was here, *he'd* stop them. No way would Dad let them break in there.

I'm just a kid.

If I try to stop them and they go in anyway, they'll know I'm involved.

Just forget it, he told himself. Play dumb. Dad'll catch the blame. Nobody's going to think I had anything to do with it. I'm just a kid.

With Dad out of the room, Amy changed. She stopped

struggling against the ropes binding her to the bedframe. Some of the terror seemed to fade from her eyes. They met Kyle's eyes and seemed to plead with him. The noises coming from her taped mouth were no longer frantic grunts and moans; they were soft sounds, each rising at the end like a question.

Naked, Kyle stepped to the end of the bed.

He saw Amy glance at his erect penis, then lift her gaze to his eyes. Shaking her head slowly from side to side, she made humming noises. There were no words, but Kyle knew that she was trying to talk him out of it.

It would be interesting, he thought, to find out what she has to say.

Interesting to hear her beg.

He crawled up the bed. Her legs were wide apart and he could put it right into her – just get a little lower and it'll run right in. But there was plenty of time for that, for everything, and he wanted to hear what she had to say.

He climbed over her thighs and sat down. He felt her pubic mound pushing against his rump, felt a moist pad of hair against his skin. Her torso gleamed. Her breasts rose and fell as she panted for air.

Amy was holding her head up, staring at him and humming, 'Mmmm. Mm? Mmmmm?'

Kyle leaned forward. The head of his penis prodded him above his navel. He reached towards Amy's breasts, realized the feel of them would probably make him lose control, and placed his hands on the slick hot skin above them.

You could fingerpaint on her sweat, he thought.

He looked into her eyes. 'You want to say something?'

Her head jerked up and down.

138

'I'll take the tape off your mouth,' he said. 'But if you scream or make any loud noises, you'll be sorry. Real sorry.'

Amy nodded some more.

'Besides,' he added, 'it won't do you any good. The room's soundproof.' He didn't know that, but it wouldn't surprise him. Dad had gone to a lot of trouble fixing up this room. 'Nobody'd hear you but me, and I'll hurt you bad.'

Kyle slid a fingernail under a corner of the tape, picked, caught the tape between his thumb and forefinger and ripped it from her face. She winced and flinched. The flinch felt good for Kyle.

'Let me go, okay?' she whispered. 'You're just a kid. You don't want to . . .' Her chin started to shake. Tears made her eyes shine. 'That man hurt me a lot. He . . . he did bad things to me.'

'He's my dad.'

'But you're not like him. I can see that. You're a good boy. You don't want to get into something like this. Untie me, okay? Untie me and help me get away. I'll give you anything you want, and I'll never tell on your father. I promise. Okay?'

'What'll you give me?'

'Anything.'

'I want to fuck you.'

'Okay. That's okay. That's fine. Untie me, and I'll make it real good for you. It'll be the best, okay?'

This is terrific, Kyle thought. She'll make it good for me. She wouldn't give me the fucking time of day if I didn't have her like this, if we met on the street or something.

She'd been nice to him at the restaurant.

But he could just imagine the look of scorn in her eyes if he had dared to ask her for a date.

Don't be ridiculous. Get lost.

They were all like that – all the pretty ones, anyway. School was full of them. Lovely, slender, laughing girls you could never have. They looked right through you. You were a sub-species, a lower form of life, best ignored. Don't feed it, maybe it'll go away.

'If I let you go,' Kyle said, 'will you marry me?'

That one threw Amy. For a moment, she looked confused. 'Sure. Of course I will. I was engaged, but I broke it off. You're a handsome young man. I . . . I'd love to be your wife.'

'Will you let me kiss you?'

She nodded.

Kyle put his hands on the mattress and bent down. He felt her nipples touch his chest. He kissed her mouth. At first, it was shut tight. Then, as if she decided she'd better make this good, she opened her mouth. Her lips writhed against his. She sucked on his mouth and moaned as if consumed with passion.

Kyle caught her lower lip between his teeth, bit into it and sat up fast, tearing it off. Amy's eyes bulged. Blood gushed over her teeth. Kyle slapped a hand across her mouth in time to muffle the scream.

He blew out the lip. It shot onto her face and stuck beneath her left eye, clinging there like a fat slug.

Keeping her mouth covered with his left hand, he used his right to punch the side of her head. His pounding fist crashed against her cheek, her temple, her eye, then her cheek again. When he took his hand off her mouth, she didn't try to scream. She just coughed, spraying up blood.

He grabbed the pillow case and shook it until the pillow dropped out. Then he stuffed an end of the cloth into her mouth. He crammed more and more in until her mouth was full. He flapped the rest of the case up so it hid her face.

She kept coughing, but the sound was quiet. Each cough made her body jerk under Kyle, made her breasts jump and sway. He scooted backwards and pressed his face between her breasts, smelled her sweet rose perfume and her sweat, felt her breasts patting his cheeks as she squirmed and coughed.

It was too much. He wasn't even in her yet, and it was too much. One knee was between her legs but the other was still outside and he wanted to be *in* her but her breasts were buffeting his face, whapping his cheeks, and he grabbed them and squeezed and she squealed into the cloth and he clamped himself to her thigh and slid against it, gasping and pumping.

When he had his breath back, Kyle got to his hands and knees. He looked at the clock on the nightstand.

He'd been with Amy less than fifteen minutes.

Plenty of time left, he thought.

Time for everything.

But it went by so terribly fast.

Kyle heard a soft whistle. He looked over his shoulder. Dad was standing near the wall. Apparently, he had entered the same way as before, through the space left by the mirror. He was shaking his head, grinning. 'Guess it *does* run in the family.'

'Do I have to stop?' Kyle asked.

'There'll be other nights. Right now, we've got to clean up and take care of business.'

Kyle crawled off the bed. He stood and looked down

at himself. Most of his skin was smeared with blood.

'You really did a number on her,' Dad said.

'Yeah.' He wasn't embarrassed by the remark. He felt as if he'd been expected to do a number on her, and had fulfilled some kind of unspoken obligation.

'I'd ask if you enjoyed it,' Dad said, 'but I guess that goes without saying.'

'When can I do it again?'

'We'll discuss that later.' He came over to the bed and gazed down at Amy's sprawled body. 'What'd you cut the ropes for?'

Kyle shrugged. 'She was out cold.' Or dead, he thought. 'I didn't see any harm.'

'Was she unconscious before you took the tape off her mouth?'

'Well, no. But she didn't scream or . . .'

'Did she have anything interesting to say?'

Kyle grinned. 'She said she'd marry me if I let her go.'

Dad snorted. 'That's a good one. Amazing what they'll come up with.'

'You talk to them sometimes?'

'Not so much anymore. After a while, they all sound pretty much the same. They beg and whine. They offer you money, sex – which is a yuck considering you're going to get that anyway.' He reached down and pressed fingertips to her wrist. 'Still has a pulse,' he said after a few moments.

'Really?' Kyle was surprised.

'That's all right. It's better not to kill them.' He looked at Kyle and raised an eyebrow. 'You're a lot like your grandfather. He always left a real mess. I'm not that much into savaging the bitches. Just use enough force to subdue them, you know?'

Kyle felt heat rush to his face. 'I'm sorry. I just . . .'

'No, it's all right. If you like it that way, fine. It's a matter of personal taste. But you're going to have to replace the sheets and things out of your own pocket.'

'Okay.'

Dad nodded toward the bathroom. 'Now get in there and take a shower, son. Make it quick, but get all the blood off. Be sure to get it out from under your nails.'

'What are we going to do with her?'

'Nurse her back to health and give her a bus ticket to Omaha.'

'What?'

'You'll find out. Take your shower.'

Kyle stepped into the bathroom. On the metal shelf over the sink were Amy's toothbrush, a small tube of Crest, a bottle of roll-on deodorant, a hairbrush with a clear pink plastic handle and quite a lot of wispy brown hair tangled in its bristles.

What are we going to do with all this stuff? he wondered.

What are we going to do with *her*?

She isn't even dead. Weird. He'd felt sure she was dead before he even took the pillow case out of her mouth.

Dad says it's all right, though. Dad knows what he's doing. He's done all this before, plenty of times – enough times to get tired of listening to them.

Kyle leaned forward and studied his face in the mirror above the sink. He looked for a difference in his eyes. They seemed pretty much the same as usual. He wiggled his eyebrows. The skin on his forehead felt stiff because of the partly dried blood. He smiled. His whole face felt stiff. A single, short curl of hair clung to the blood near the corner of his mouth. He left it there, and turned away from the mirror.

A bath-towel was hanging on a bar to dry, but a clean one remained neatly folded, clamped in place on the wire rack. The bath-mat was draped over the side of the tub. He spread it onto the floor and stepped on it. It felt damp and cool.

A wash-cloth had been left hanging over the cold water nozzle. A small, plastic bottle of shampoo stood on an edge of the tub. In the soap dish was one of the tiny white bars provided by the hotel.

Kyle picked up the wash-cloth.

Amy had used it, rubbed herself all over with it.

He pressed the thin, damp cloth to his face, breathed through it, sniffed it. It smelled faintly of soap, nothing more.

But he was flooded with memories of his last time in Darcy's room, the feel and aroma of her wash-cloth, the cool dampness of her bath-towel against his bare skin.

He turned on the water, washed his hands under the spout, then pulled the knob to make the shower come on. He stepped into the tub and pulled the curtain shut.

The heavy, hot spray of water felt good. The blood seemed to melt off his skin. It slid down him, turned pink around his feet and ran towards the drain.

As he soaped himself, he imagined Darcy tied to the bed in the other room. If it had been Darcy instead of Amy tonight, it would've been even more incredible. In a way, it *had* been Darcy. Once the pillow case hid Amy's face, he'd been able to fill his mind with the slender, beautiful guide. That made it better, but he'd known all along he was just pretending.

If it had been Darcy tonight, he thought, it'd all be over now.

I don't want it to be just an hour with her.

Days, weeks.

It'll never happen, he realized, sinking inside. But getting her for a while, maybe for a whole night . . . that could happen.

Something to shoot for.

Wearing soap lather like a suit of white foam, Kyle shampooed his hair. He rinsed, then checked his fingernails. They looked clean.

He turned off the water, slid back the curtain, and stepped onto the bath-mat. He pulled the clean white towel off the wire rack. He dried himself. When he was done, he held the towel open in front of him and checked both sides. It was still white.

His clothes were in the other room. He wrapped the towel around his waist. It was just large enough to meet at the hip. When he tucked the corners together, the side of his leg was left bare.

When I run this place, he thought, the guests will get bigger towels. No wonder we get rated so low.

He stepped out of the bathroom.

The bundle on the bed looked like a cocoon. Amy had been rolled up in the sheets, which were tied around her with ropes. The white sheets were soaked through with blood.

Dad, standing at the foot of the bed, was shaking open a plastic garbage bag.

'What should I do?' Kyle asked.

'Just watch. I'll show you everything. Next time, you'll do it all and I'll supervise. You'll be doing it by yourself one of these days.'

Kyle stepped over to his pile of clothes. The towel came loose as he walked, and he held it up, wondering why he bothered; he'd been naked in front of his father only a little while ago. It seemed different, now. He tucked the towel together and it stayed in place until he had his briefs on. Then he let it fall. He watched his father and continued to get dressed.

With the plastic bag open, Dad crawled onto the bed. He started to slip it around Amy's wrapped feet. 'All you missed,' he said, 'was tying the sheets around her. I already checked the bedspread and blanket. They're all right. They were off the bed before you started working on her.' He lifted the bundle, pulled the bag up to Amy's waist, then went for another bag. He put that one over Amy's head, drew it down so it overlapped the top of the other bag, then started binding them together with duct tape. Before climbing off the bed, he slapped the plastic mattress cover. 'This saves our mattress. We'll come back afterwards, mop it off, do a final clean-up.'

He went into the bathroom. Kyle watched him wash his hands, then gather up everything Amy had left behind, including the small bottle of shampoo on the edge of the tub. He brought her belongings out, and put them into her suitcase. 'One rule,' he said. 'We don't keep anything except cash. Nothing that can connect us to her.'

He wandered the room, collecting all of Amy's possessions and adding them to the suitcase. When he found her handbag, he took out the wallet and removed a handful of bills. He stuffed them into his pocket. Then he took out a key case.

'She drove in, so we've got a car to deal with. First

thing in the morning, Ralph Dexter'll take it off our hands. He's been taking care of the cars for years, never asks any questions. He's got a garage, paints 'em, changes licence plates, does the whole nine yards, has some kind of connections so they end up being sold out of state. We've never had any trouble with the things getting traced back to us.'

Kyle shook his head, amazed. 'You've really got it . . . set up.'

'Had a lot of practice,' Dad said. He shut the suitcase and snapped its latches. 'It started with Ely, and we've been doing it ever since.'

'And getting away with it,' Kyle said.

'We've had a few close calls. Your grandfather got busted once, but they dropped the charges. No evidence. That's part of the trick, don't leave any evidence. But the main trick is this: don't arouse suspicion.'

Dad wandered the room, making a final inspection, then picked up an ashtray, sat on a corner of the bed and lit a cigarette. 'I've been averaging about one a month for almost twenty years, now. I did it sometimes before then, but when your grandfather had his stroke, I took over the whole thing from him. Do you know how many women that makes?'

Kyle shook his head. He felt tired, excited, too dazed by it all to fool with maths.

'It makes about two hundred forty. That's give or take maybe a dozen. And I've never been busted. It's because I'm careful, and you've got to be careful too. You'll be doing all this by yourself, some day. For the time being, I'll show you the ropes, we'll share, take turns, that kind of thing.'

Kyle nodded.

Dad blew twin streams of pale smoke out his nose. 'It all comes down,' he said, 'to who you put in this room. You want them to be young and good looking, right? Where's the thrill of doing a gal looks like she's been whapped with an ugly stick? But there's a lot more to it than that.

'You're working the registration desk, a gal comes in. If she's not alone, obviously you forget it. The nice thing is, the cavern's an attraction that pulls in all kinds, and we get some women who are travelling alone. Not a whole lot of them, but enough so you can pick and choose.

'Okay, she's someone you wouldn't mind putting it to and she's alone. Is she married? Check her rings. If she's married, forget it. She fills out the registration card. Does she live nearby? Normally, they don't, or they wouldn't be checking into the hotel. But pay attention to where they live. Go for the ones who live out of state.'

Dad crushed out his cigarette. 'Take Amy. She comes in alone, she's a little hefty but cute. No wedding or engagement ring, and she's from Ohio. I talk to her a little bit, just acting friendly. Find out she's had a falling-out with her financee, a guy who's a little nuts and likes to knock her around. She's on her way to Manhattan, planning to start a new life without him. Saw the hotel sign as she was driving by, decided to spend the night and see the cavern tomorrow. Probably hoping to run into a nice young man in the process.' Dad grinned. 'And she did, huh? Two nice young men.'

Kyle chuckled.

'The point is, I got to know her some. Enough to find out nobody has an idea she's stopping here for the night.

That means, when she turns up missing, nobody is going to come around here asking questions. She's perfect. So I check her into 115. See this?' He took a folded card out of his shirt pocket. 'It's her registration card. I burn it, no record she was ever here.'

Dad stood up. He set the ashtray on the bureau, and turned to Kyle. 'That's how it's done. You want to find a gal who can't be traced to the hotel. That's ninety-nine per cent of the trick. The other one per cent is making sure you don't get caught in the act. No big problem with that. Grab her suitcase.'

11

Kyle picked up the suitcase. His father lifted Amy's wrapped body off the bed and slung it over his shoulder in a fireman's carry. 'Another rule to remember,' Dad said as he started to walk under the burden. 'Don't bite off more than you can chew. Don't kill more than you can carry. It's not easy, lugging these bitches around.' He stepped through the opening left by the mirror.

Kyle followed him.

'Normally,' Dad said, 'I'd put her down on the chair here while I make sure the coast is clear. You go ahead and check, though.' He nodded towards the storeroom's door. 'Take a peek in the corridor and stairwell. Nobody's going to be wandering around this time of night, but it pays to be careful.'

Kyle set down the suitcase and opened the door. The long, dimly lighted hallway looked deserted. He stepped out and rushed the few feet to the firedoor. He pushed it open, glanced up and down the stairs, listened for a moment, then hurried back to the storeroom. 'It's okay,' he said, picking up the suitcase again.

He held the door open and was surprised by the speed with which his father crossed the open area to the firedoor. Kyle shut the storeroom door, made sure it was locked, then hurried to the stairwell.

Dad was already at the bottom, pushing the exit door.

He's taking the body outside?

He knows what he's doing, Kyle told himself. Must.

Kyle trotted down the four stairs to the bottom, and followed his father through the door.

The Cadillac was there, its trunk already open.

Dad bent over. The body flopped off his shoulder and dropped into the trunk. The car rocked slightly under the impact. He took the suitcase from Kyle and swung it in beside the body. Then, he lowered the trunk lid and pressed it down firmly so it latched with barely a sound.

Leaning back against the trunk, he folded his arms across his chest. 'That wasn't so hard, was it?'

'We're right out in the open,' Kyle whispered.

'Are we? Take a look around.'

Kyle didn't need to take a look around; he'd been here countless times. They'd carried the body out the fire exit at the end of the hotel's east wing. Their car was backed up very close to the door, but . . .

Dad pointed at the hotel. 'No windows on this end,' he said. 'It was planned that way. Hedges over there,' he added, pointing to the other side of the driveway. Then he pointed out the rows of thick, tall bushes on either side of the exit door. 'And these,' he said, 'are in the way of anyone who might happen to wander onto the driveway from either the front or the back. So we may seem to be out in the open, but this particular spot is pretty well sheltered. If you're going to be seen by anyone, he has to be right on top of you.'

'What if that happens?'

'It never has, so far.'

'But . . .'

'I've always figured, if someone saw me, I'd kill him.' Dad reached behind his back, under his hanging shirt-tail, and pulled out a revolver. 'Insurance.' He slipped the gun back into place. 'Come on, let's get going.'

They climbed into the car. Dad started the engine, and drove with the headlights off until they rounded the first bend. There, trees along the roadside stood between them and the hotel. The headlights came on, pushing bright tunnels into the night.

'Where are we going?'

'Not far.'

'Have you got a special place where . . . ?'

'Very special.' Dad pulled onto the dirt road at the cattle crossing. He climbed out, removed the padlock and chain from the gate, swung the gate open, and came back. He drove slowly forward. 'You know the story of Ely's Wall,' he said.

'Sure.'

'Well, it's a pile of horseshit. Elizabeth didn't fall down any chasm. Ely found out she'd been screwing around with their handyman, a guy by the name of Arnold Winston. So after the elevators were installed, he blocked off the natural opening and took her into the cavern. He tied her up down there. *Then*, he built Ely's Wall. Sealed her right up in that section of the cave, alive and well.'

'Holy shit,' Kyle muttered.

'Ever read *The Cask of Amontillado*?'

'Sure,' Kyle said.

'Well, Ely was a big fan of Mr Poe. It just tickled the hell out of him, walling up that hot-pants bitch of his.'

The car stopped in the middle of a stand of trees. Dad

153

killed the headlights, then pressed the button on the dashboard that released the trunk latch. 'Come on,' he said.

They went to the trunk. Dad handed the suitcase to Kyle. He lifted the body out, swinging it over his shoulder.

Side by side, they walked through the trees. Kyle heard the far-off hoot of an owl. The only other sounds were their footsteps crunching over the forest floor, their breathing. The trees blocked out most of the moonlight. Except for a few speckles and patches of brightness, they walked in darkness.

Finally, Dad stopped near a cluster of rocks. He leaned forward. Amy's body dropped to the ground. Dad leaned back against a boulder, and sighed. 'Put down the suitcase and come here,' he said.

Kyle set it down. As he approached the vague shape of his father, he saw the man swing an arm out, thumb pointing behind him as if he were hitching a ride. 'Take a look back there, but watch your step.'

Kyle moved carefully around the side of the boulder. He saw a narrow patch of black on the dark ground. 'I don't . . . what's there?'

'The chute, son, the chute.'

Kyle shook his head.

'What it is, it's a sinkhole. It's like a natural chimney, drops right down into the closed part of the cave. What Ely did, once he had Elizabeth sealed up down there, he tricked Arnold into coming out here, banged him one on the head, and dropped him down the chute. Ely's idea of justice. His wife wanted Arnold, now she could have him. Forever.'

'Wow,' Kyle said. 'Fixed them, didn't he.'

'Maybe a little better than he ever expected.'

'What do you mean?'

Quiet laughter came from Kyle's father. Strange laughter. It made a chill crawl up Kyle's back.

'They didn't die. Neither one of them. That chute, it goes all the way down, but not *straight* down or the fall would've killed him. It's like a slide – part of the way, at least. Ely, he comes back a few days after he dropped Arnold down, and he yells into the hole just on the chance Elizabeth's close enough to hear. And she answers. They both do. They shout up to him, begging for him to let them out. So what does Ely do? He starts bringing them food and throwing it down the chute. Not much. Just enough so they don't starve. He wants them to stay alive, you see. Alive, but trapped forever down there. In the darkness. In the cold. Together.' Again, Dad let out that weird, crazy laugh.

'He brought them real delicacies. Table scraps, at first. Bones. Raw meat, sometimes. Whenever he showed up, they'd be waiting at the bottom of the chute. He'd tease them. He'd call, "Hungry down there?" And they'd beg him for food, and he'd make them say, "Pretty-please." He really put them through a routine. I'll show you his diary. It's pretty amusing stuff.

'Anyway, he was out driving one day and found a cat that'd been hit by a car. So he scooped it off the road and took *that* to them. He knew they'd eat it. They'd *have* to eat it, or starve. When they found out what he'd tossed down for them, they shrieked and yelled curses. Well, that really tickled Ely. So he started to bring them every kind of disgusting thing. He got hold of snakes and lizards and tossed them down the hole. He trapped rats for their supper. Sometimes, he'd throw them a loaf of bread, but he'd piss on it first. He even shot dogs and waited for them to get ripe before throwing them in.'

'He really did all that?' Kyle asked. He felt a little sick, but at the same time he admired the lengths that Ely had gone to for his revenge.

'Sure did,' Dad said. 'And enjoyed every minute of it. After a while, though, Elizabeth and Arnold changed their tune. They stopped saying "pretty-please." ' Dad started laughing. Kyle, unable to stop himself, joined in.

Finally, Dad wiped his eyes and sighed. 'Anyway, it started getting a little spooky. He'd hear them laughing down there. And they'd call up, asking him to come a little closer. They'd say they had something for him.'

'Wanted him to fall in the hole?' Kyle asked.

'Sure.'

'Sounds like they went nuts.'

'Totally bonkers. But Ely kept coming around and bringing them stuff. Then one day, a pretty young gal showed up at the hotel. She'd been on the road, didn't have any money, asked for a place to stay the night. Ely'd been without his wife for a couple of months, by then, and he was feeling pretty horny. So he used his pass key on the gal's room that night, let himself in, and had at her. She tried to fight him off. He ended up strangling her. When he was done, he brought her out here and gave her a ride on the chute.'

'And they ate her?' Kyle asked. 'That's how it started?'

'Yep. Ely got into the habit. And when his son, your grandfather, got old enough to appreciate the situation, he got initiated and kept the practice up, and passed it onto me.'

Kyle shook his head. 'But they must've died. Elizabeth and Arnold. I mean, that was like sixty years ago, or . . .'

'I imagine they did,' Dad said. He stood up and stepped around the rock. He got on his hands and knees at the edge of the hole. 'Soup's on!' he called. 'Hello! Room service!'

Quiet sounds floated up. Moans, giggles, voices.

Kyle cringed. He felt as if he had spiders in his hair.

The voices, barely audible, made no sense. But they sounded gleeful.

Kyle looked at his father and shook his head.

'I come out here a couple times a week,' Dad said. 'Bring them a little something. And I listen. I figure there's six or eight of them down there. Sometimes, I've heard babies crying.'

Kyle crawled backwards away from the hole and couldn't hear the sounds anymore.

Dad stood up. He brushed off his knees. 'Come on, let's give Amy a ride.'

He picked her up, carried her to the black opening, and dropped her in. The garbage bags hissed and crackled. There were quiet bumps and thuds. Then silence.

'Suitcase, too,' Dad said. 'Keep the folk well-dressed.'

Kyle dropped the suitcase into the hole and listened as it skidded down.

Crouching, Dad cupped his hands to his mouth and called into the blackness, 'Dig in, folks! Get it while it's hot!'

12

Jim's torch died. When Darcy's dwindled to glowing embers, she dropped the smoking remains of the board to the walkway. The middle of Greg's plank still burned. He held it low in front of him so the fire could climb the wood towards his hands.

The flames wobbled and flapped like a bright flag.

'They should give torchlight tours,' said Carol, who was walking just behind her. 'It's a lot more . . . interesting this way.'

' "May you live in interesting times," ' Helen said. 'An old Chinese curse.'

'I think it's nice.'

'You won't think it's so nice,' Helen told her, 'when that one goes out.'

'Greg's won't go out,' Darcy said. 'He's bearing the magic torch.'

'Right,' Greg said.

She put an arm across his back. His sweatshirt was cool and damp under her hand, but she felt his warmth beneath it. She moved closer to him, walking with her hip against his hip, the side of her breast pressing his upper arm.

She knew the others were looking at her. But she didn't care.

It's just Carol and Helen and Jim and Beth, she thought. Though Helen seemed a bit stiff, possibly even prudish, Darcy didn't mind showing some affection for Greg in front of these people. They were little more than strangers, but they were special. They were her team.

She had felt good, almost buoyant, ever since leaving the main group at the elevators. It was as if she had been set free. Kyle had been left behind. So had the man in the Peterbilt hat. And more than two dozen strangers who'd been depending on her to keep order and calm their fears and save them. The relief at being away from them all was huge.

It was like starting home after a bad party.

Or, she thought, more to the point, the senior dance. Very much like that. Her final year in high school, she had been class president and in charge of organizing the entire function – decorations, refreshments, entertainment. And when Mike Wakefield spiked the punch, she got plenty of heat from the adults. They'd blamed her, even though she'd had nothing to do with it. The other kids thought the dance was a great success, but Darcy hadn't been able to relax and enjoy a single moment of it, and the evening became a real ordeal after the liquor was discovered in the punch. Then she left with her date and two other couples and the pressure was gone. She went wild. She shouted and twirled around the parking lot like a mad woman. She talked her friends into driving out to the river and they all went skinny-dipping. She'd never felt so carefree, so daring. She swam under a bridge, leaving everyone behind except Steve, her date. They embraced in the warm water. Then she led him ashore and found a moonlit clearing. Though she'd gone steady with Steve for months, though she knew that she loved him, she had never allowed him to go all the way. That night, dripping from the river, she lay down on the cool grass and raised her arms towards him.

Darcy remembered it all as she walked alongside Greg in the fluttering glow of his torch. Always before, her memories of that night had been tainted by thoughts of their break-up, the letter Steve sent during her first spring at Princeton. Now, she felt none of the usual pain. Steve was part of the past, and Greg was with her and she felt the same sense of relief and daring that had possessed her after escaping from the senior dance.

The springy feel of wood under her shoes pulled Darcy out of her revery. She was on the dock. She stopped. 'I forgot the pick,' she said. 'Do you want to go back with me and get it?' she asked Greg. She wondered if he could hear the tremor in her voice.

'Sure.'

She unhooked the flashlight from her belt and turned it on. 'We'll be back in a few minutes,' she told the others.

Greg gave his torch to Jim. Beth, Carol and Helen formed a circle around the small flame as if it were a campfire.

Back on the concrete walkway, Darcy said, 'We walked right past it. Stupid. I was daydreaming.'

'About getting out of here?' Greg asked.

'Not exactly.' She played her flashlight beam over the shiny limestone wall to the right, and spotted the grotto entrance. Taking Greg's hand, she walked closer. Her mouth was dry. Her heart beat fast. Though her mind flashed a reminder of her earlier encounter with Kyle at the grotto, she wasn't bothered by it. What happened with Kyle didn't matter. Not at the moment.

Greg, at her side, she climbed the stone stairs.

They entered the grotto. The pale beam of the flash-light illuminated the wheelbarrow, the pickaxe leaning against its side, her blouse and bra draped over one of its handles.

'This is where I changed,' she explained.

'And became what?'

She turned to Greg. Smiling, she shook her head. Then she looked down and began to hook the flashlight to her belt. As the metal clip slipped into place, Greg put his hands on her shoulders. He eased her forward, and she wrapped her arms around him and tipped back her head. He kissed her. It was a gentle, tentative kiss at first. Then his lips parted and Darcy stroked them with her tongue and their mouths joined, pressing hard and sucking. His hands roamed her back.

This is crazy, she thought. The others are waiting.

Let them wait.

Her hands went under Greg's sweatshirt. His skin was damp, but warm. His tongue filled her mouth. She squirmed against him, rubbing herself on his firm body. His hands moved up and down her sides, caressing her through the thin fabric of the windbreaker. She wanted them inside, wanted them on her skin.

His mouth pulled away from hers. 'We'd better get back,' he muttered.

'I know.'

'The others.'

Nodding, she dropped her hands to her sides. He was right. No matter how much she wanted this time with Greg to last, it wouldn't be fair to make the others wait. 'Duty,' she muttered.

'After we get out of here . . . maybe we can spend some time together.'

'That would be nice.'

'A lot of time.'

'I think I'd like that.' She put her hands on Greg's hips. 'I think I'd like that very much.'

He lifted a hand to the side of her head, he fingered her hair, her ear, her cheek. 'I want to be with you in the sunlight.'

She kissed his palm. Then Greg drew her to him and for a moment their mouths met.

His breath was warm on her lips when he said, 'Let's bust outa here.'

'As fast as we can,' Darcy said.

They turned away from each other and went to the wheelbarrow. Greg hefted the pickaxe and swung it onto his shoulder. Darcy touched her blouse and bra. They were wet, very cold. She considered putting them on, not because she saw any use for them, but because she was tempted by the idea of taking off her windbreaker in front of Greg. Even if she kept her back to him . . . She imagined him stepping up behind her and putting his arms around her, his big hands closing over her breasts. She felt warm and snug in the windbreaker. The bra and blouse would feel awful. Worth the discomfort, though. Worth it to stand in front of him, bare to the waist, and have him touch her. She would turn to him, and he would gaze at her, and then he would bring her up against him . . .

Greg reached out and squeezed a sleeve of the blouse. 'Yuck,' he said. 'You're not thinking about putting these on, are you?'

She shrugged. She blushed, but her face was in

shadow so she was sure he didn't notice.

'You'd freeze. You'd better forget it.'

And she blushed even more as she plucked the front of the windbreaker away from her belly and said, 'It's just that I feel so naked in this.'

'You're not. It's perfectly circumspect.'

'I bounce when I walk.'

'Not much,' he said, 'and very nicely. You don't want to put those things on. Come on, let's go.'

They turned toward the opening, and Darcy unclipped the flashlight from her belt. 'You've been watching me bounce.'

He laughed softly. He patted her rump. He said nothing.

They trotted down the stone stairs. Darcy saw the others waiting on the dock, still clustered around the tiny fire of the torch in Jim's hands.

It's over, she thought. And it's their fault.

Don't blame them, she told herself. They're simply part of this, the same way Greg is part of this.

And this is just fine.

Though Darcy ached with a mild feeling of loss because she could no longer be alone with Greg, the ache was mixed with a sense of fullness, of wonder.

She felt *so* close to him.

It's almost as if we made love, she thought.

We *did* make love. That's exactly what we were doing in there. Just didn't have time to finish.

We'll finish when we get out of here.

After I find out about Mom. Mom's all right. She has to be.

Entering the glow of the torch, Darcy switched off the flashlight and put it on her belt. 'All set?' she asked.

'That ought to do the job,' Jim said, nodding towards the pickaxe.

'It will,' Greg said.

Darcy led the way past the first boat and stopped beside the other. 'Okay, everybody in.'

Greg lowered the pickaxe carefully into the boat. He and Darcy held onto the gunnel while the others climbed in. Carol and Helen took seats in the middle. Jim stood near the bow so the torch would be at the front. Beth sat down behind him.

'Go on and get in,' Greg said. 'I'll tow it to the wall.'

'Maybe I should try pulling it along on the spikes.'

Greg shook his head. 'If it was too dangerous before, it's too dangerous now. I don't want you catching one of those things in the face.'

'I could try,' she said, though she knew he was right. Even under normal conditions with the lights on, the method of propelling the boats forward by grabbing the spikes along the cavern wall was hazardous. It required a firm stance, good balance, and frequent ducking to save your head from jutting rocks. Attempting it by torchlight, or even with the flashlight, would be foolish. But she hated the idea of Greg going into the water.

'I'll have to get wet again, anyway,' he said, 'when we reach the wall.'

'But . . .'

'You can just enjoy the ride, this time.' He stepped out of his shoes. Putting a hand on Darcy's shoulder to steady himself, he peeled off his socks. 'I'm not going to get my clothes wet, this time,' he said. He pulled the sweatshirt over his head and gave it to her. Then he opened his pants, pulled them down his legs and shook them off. He was wearing white briefs.

Darcy looked at the women in the boat. Only Carol was watching Greg.

Darcy stepped forward to block her view.

Greg gave the pants to Darcy, then squatted and put his shoes on his bare feet. While he was retying them, Darcy crouched and picked up his socks. She pressed the bundle of clothes to her chest, and put a hand on his back. He was shaking. 'Are you sure . . . ?'

'No problem.' He stood up. He grinned at Darcy in the faint, shimmering light, then clapped his hands once, pivoted away from her, and trotted up the dock. Just past the bow of the boat, he dived.

He sprang off the dock, stretched his arms out beyond his head, and the dim shape of his body flew low over the Lake of Charon. He hit the surface almost flat. Water splashed up, droplets glinting in the torchlight.

Darcy shuddered. She could *feel* the terrible shock of cold.

Greg came up, swam in a circle, and stopped in front of the boat. 'Are you all right?' Darcy asked.

'It's . . . invigorating.'

'I'll bet.'

'Nice dive,' Jim said.

As fast as she could, Darcy untied the boat. She climbed in next to Jim and knelt, looking down at Greg. The boat began gliding forward.

His arms and shoulders were shiny in the torchlight. His hair, flat against his head, looked oiled down. His face was beaded with water. His eyes were fixed on Darcy. His lips were peeled back, showing his teeth in a rigid grimace.

Darcy covered his hands with hers. They felt as if they'd been dipped in ice water.

He winked at her. 'Don't look so miserable,' he said. 'It's not bad. Doesn't even feel as cold as before.'

'When we get to the wall,' Jim said, 'it'll be my turn. You've done enough already. I'll knock the hole through that wall.'

'Well, don't try and deprive me of my chance to warm up swinging the pick. I'm looking forward to it.'

'We can all take turns,' Beth said.

'But me first,' Greg insisted.

'It's a man's job,' Jim said. From the tone of his voice, Darcy knew he'd made the remark to tease Beth.

Beth rose to the occasion. 'Oh yeah, bub? How'd you like a fat lip?'

'Apologize, Jim,' Greg said as he pulled the boat along. 'Don't get us in trouble with the broads. We're outnumbered.'

'Broads?' Darcy asked. She grinned.

'We can take 'em,' Jim said.

'Maybe in a fair fight,' Greg told him. 'But dames don't fight fair. They bite, pull hair . . .'

'Do this,' Darcy added, and leaned out over the bow and pressed a hand down on top of Greg's head. His head went under. The cold water wrapped Darcy's hand to the wrist. Immediately, she felt bad. Her throat tightened.

Stupid! Not funny at all!

'That wasn't necessary,' Helen said.

'Score one for the females,' Beth said.

Jim was laughing.

'Is he all right?' Carol asked, worry in her voice.

Greg was still under. Then his head bobbed to the surface. His eyes crossed and he spouted water from his mouth. The thin stream arched over the front of the boat, splashed Darcy's chin and ran down her neck. Yelping, she clutched her throat, but not before a few drops made their way inside the windbreaker. They slid like melted snow down her warm skin, and she slapped a hand between her breasts to snuff the drops as if they were burning embers.

Greg looked up at her, a silly grin on his face.

Darcy leaned out over the water, the metal gunnel pressing into her ribs. She took Greg by the ears and pulled him gently closer and kissed him on the mouth. 'That's for dunking you,' she whispered. 'Forgive me?'

'No need to forgive you – I got even.'

She settled back, holding his hands again.

The boat moved along, silent except for occasional murmurs of water lapping the hull. Jim held the torch low. Its charred end almost touching the water beside Greg. The broken plank burned near its middle, the flames clinging to one edge like fingers trying to hold on. The light given off wavered, faded and grew and dimmed again as the flames struggled. Surrounding the fire was a faint golden aura that shimmered on Greg's wet skin, spread a dim layer of brightness on the water beside him, and hung in the air like a mist. Darcy could barely make out the wall of the cavern to her right, almost beyond the reach of the glow. Though she thought she knew every inch of that wall, the squirming light and shadows gave it an alien appearance that she found somewhat unnerving.

Don't let it get to you, she told herself. Just the same old wall.

It looked *alive*.

Goosebumps crawled over her skin.

This is ridiculous. Your mind's doing a number on

168

you. She reminded herself of other times she had felt this way: getting into the car after a scary movie and feeling that someone might be crouched on the back floor; reading late at night and suddenly afraid to look at the window, certain a face is pressed against it; taking a bath and hearing a faint noise somewhere in the house; getting out of bed and walking to the bathroom and suspecting that one of the shadows along the way might lurch out and rush at her. Nothing more than the mind playing tricks, teasing, making shivers.

Darcy wanted to force her gaze away from the wall, but she was afraid *not* to watch it.

'I think this little lake has grown since the last time,' Greg said.

His voice erased Darcy's anxiety.

She looked down at him. She slipped her fingers around his wrists. 'We must be almost . . .'

Black descended. Someone behind her gasped. Jim muttered, 'Shit.'

Where the torch had been, there was a vague patch of red. It moved upward. Darcy heard a puffing sound. The red brightened. A tiny flame licked the darkness, then sank. The puffing sounds went on – Jim blowing on the embers. The crimson glow swelled and faded, but with each breath it weakened.

'For Godsake,' Helen whispered. 'Darcy, don't you have a flashlight?'

'It's all right,' she said. She plucked the flashlight off her belt and turned it on. The beam shot into the blackness, pale and cold after the mellow light of the torch. The bright disk at its centre caught the edge of Satan's Buoy, no more than two yards behind Greg's back.

'You'd better watch where you're going,' she said.

He glanced over his shoulder. 'Woops.' He side-stepped, turning the boat so it would pass between the small jagged island and the side of the cavern.

'That's where Tom fell,' Beth said.

'Yeah, that's the place.' Darcy raised the flashlight. It made a tunnel of brightness through the black, and stopped at the barrier of Ely's Wall.

Today, it seemed more like a door than a wall – a door of rocks and conrete.

Darcy supposed that Ely had chosen this particular spot for his barrier because nature had nearly done the job for him. The cavern seemed to end here except for the fissure that would have provided a passageway before it was closed off. The gap must have been no more than a yard in width.

There had been no Lake of Charon before the wall. The river had probably been a shallow stream here, just as it still was on the other side of the dock where the cavern was higher. Darcy imagined that the water had not even reached the tops of Ely's shoes as he crouched and cemented the first rocks into place.

Though he'd left a narrow gap at the bottom, the wall had restricted the natural flow of the River Styx. About four feet of his handiwork was now below the water. The visible portion looked like a three-foot square.

That's where we'll break through, Darcy thought. Don't want to mess with what's below the water line, or we'll have the lake pouring into the other side.

'Where do you want me to park this thing?' Greg asked.

'Might as well put it all the way up,' she told him.

He stepped out of the way, held onto the port gunnel, and eased the boat forward until it gently bumped to a stop.

'Okay,' Darcy said. 'I'll secure it.' She asked Jim to move back, then picked up the bow line, stepped in front of him, and tied the rope around a spike jutting out of the water at her shoulder level.

– The spike she'd been holding while she delivered her story about the origin of Ely's Wall to the tourists.

It seemed like days ago.

She remembered being annoyed by Kyle's lecherous gaze.

Wonder how Paula's getting along with him, she thought.

'How about some light?' Greg asked.

She turned around, keeping one hand on the spike, and aimed the flashlight high so it wouldn't shine in Greg's eyes as he reached up and accepted the pickaxe from Carol.

With the pick held overhead like a soldier's rifle, he waded alongside the boat, past Darcy, and took a few steps to the left. He stopped in front of Ely's Wall and looked back. 'This'll just take a minute,' he said, smiling.

'Hope so,' she told him. 'Try not to smash things up below the water.'

'Aye-aye.' He faced the wall, lowered the pick, lifted it over one shoulder and swung. The blade struck with a deafening metalic clamour that made Darcy flinch. A knob of rock flew off the wall and splashed in front of Greg. Darcy's ears were still ringing when he slammed the pick into the wall a second time.

'*Jesus.*' Carol's voice.

'Loud enough to wake the dead,' Beth muttered.

Greg pounded the wall again and again, striking it high near the area where Ely's rocks met the cavern's smooth, ancient limestone. Chips flew. Chunks fell and thumped the water. Most of his blows seemed directed at the mortar filling the spaces between the rocks. Sometimes, entire blocks came off, hitting the water with such force that Greg's face was sprayed.

As the opening grew, Darcy expected to see the darkness of the cavern on the other side. Instead, she saw another layer of rock. Greg kept hacking and prying at the outer wall until the opening was large enough to crawl through – if there hadn't been the second layer.

Breathing heavily, he rested the pick on his shoulder. He shook his head and turned around. 'That Ely . . . didn't fool around. Wonder how thick he *made* the damn thing.'

'Why don't you climb aboard and rest up?' Jim suggested. 'I'll take over for a while.'

'Think I'll take you up on that.'

As he returned to the boat, Jim began to undress.

Darcy took the pick from Greg. It was warm where his hands had been clutching the haft. The boat wobbled as he climbed over its side. He stood up straight and folded his hands behind his head and panted for air.

Jim, stripped down to his boxer shorts and shoes, sat down on the gunnel and lowered himself into the water. 'Whoa! Damn!'

'Start swinging that sucker,' Greg told him, 'and you'll be toasty in no time.'

Darcy handed the pick down to Jim. He carried it to the wall. Beth holding the light on him, he began to smash at the inner layer of rock.

Darcy turned to Greg. Helen had apparently given her sweater to him. He was using it like a towel. Picking up his bundle of clothes, Darcy stepped over a seat. She stood at his side, facing him, watching as he bent over and ran the sweater down his legs. When he swung the sweater behind him to dry his back, Darcy set his clothes down. 'I'll get your back,' she offered, speaking loudly to be heard over the clank of the pick.

He gave the damp sweater to her, and turned around. She mopped his back. Crouching, she rubbed his buttocks, then his legs.

'What do you know!' Jim called.

Looking over her shoulder, Darcy saw a patch of blackness in the wall. He'd broken through.

'Thank God,' Helen muttered.

The clamour started again.

'Won't be long, now,' Beth announced over the noise.

'Then the *real* fun will start,' Greg said.

Darcy patted his rump. 'You mean this isn't the real fun?'

Though she was still drying his legs, he turned around. His groin was at her eye level. She glanced at the bulging front of his briefs, then lowered her eyes and began to rub the sweater on his thighs. He put a hand on her head, he knew, just as she did, that he had already dried the fronts of his legs.

She looked at Carol. The woman's head was turned. Her eyes were on Jim.

Darcy slid the sweater up one of Greg's legs and, as if by accident, touched the back of her hand to the damp underside of his pouch. He flinched slightly.

'Your shorts are sopping,' she said.

'Is that so?'

She rubbed them gently, a single layer of the sweater between her open hand and his briefs. She curled a hand under his scrotum, slid her palm up the underside of thick, rigid penis, then stood up, smiled at him and said, 'All done.'

'Glad it's dark in here,' he said close to her ear.

'Something you wouldn't want the others to see?'

'How about handing me my pants?'

'Don't you think you should get out of those yucky, wet shorts?'

'Oh, I don't think so. Maybe some other time. My pants, please.'

'I like you better without them.'

'This is a hell of a time for you to get horny.'

'Me?' Darcy asked. 'You're the one with the . . .'

'All right!' Jim called. 'That should do it!'

Darcy looked around. He was holding the pick at his side, stepping close to the wall.

The hole in front of him was about two feet across and nearly a yard high – plenty large enough for them to crawl through.

The bottom edge of the gap was just above the surface of the lake. Jim's chest pushed against it as he leaned forward to peer into the darkness.

'What do you see?' Beth asked.

'Surely you jest.'

The flashlight's beam was at such an angle that, even had Jim not been in the way, it wouldn't have penetrated the opening.

Jim said, 'It's just as black as . . .' He staggered backwards a step and Darcy glimpsed a thick, pale shaft protruding from his mouth. It came out and Jim started to slump.

An arm darted through the hole, clutched his hair, and yanked him forward. His head went into the darkness.

Beth started to scream.

Darcy gazed, stunned, as Jim's body slid up out of the water and disappeared through the opening in Ely's Wall.

13

When the sound of the first clank reached them, Kyle heard snatches of conversation from those gathered in front of the elevators.

'All *right*.'

'They made it.'

'They're starting in.'

Kyle felt a shiver of dread, and pressed Paula more tightly against his side.

The sounds went on. Nobody spoke now. Everyone seemed to be listening to the quiet metallic clanking that came ringing up the tunnel of the cavern from Ely's Wall. The distant clamour, though faint, was distinct through the soft crackle and pop of the elevator fires.

Maybe something will happen, Kyle told himself. Maybe the pick handle will break and they'll have to quit and come back. Maybe the wall's just too hard, and they won't be able to break through it.

He couldn't convince himself.

He remembered the giggles, the moans, the mad hushed voices he'd heard coming up from the chute. Six or eight people down there, Dad had told him.

Crazy people. Living in the blackness, nothing to eat except what was dropped down the chute to them.

Amy Lawson. They *ate* her.

And now, no matter where those crazies might be within their sealed length of cavern, they had to be hearing the pick as it clashed against the wall.

He could see them moving blindly towards the noise.

Maybe they won't go towards it, he thought. They might not understand what's going on. Maybe they'll be frightened, and hide. Maybe they'll stay hidden the whole time, and Darcy and her bunch will never even guess they're around.

It could happen that way.

Soon, the far-off pounding ceased.

Paula turned her head and looked up at Kyle, the firelight flashing on her glasses. 'They must've gotten through,' she said.

Kyle heard others.

'They did it.'

'Didn't take long.'

'The thing was probably old and falling apart, anyway.'

Kyle, feeling as if his bowels were being squeezed, let go of Paula and sank to a crouch.

Then the pounding came again.

'Damn.'

'They were probably just taking a rest.'

'Maybe they busted through, but only just decided they oughta make the hole bigger.'

'Whatever, it won't be long now.'

'Shhh. I can't hear.'

'Who gives a hot fuck if you can hear?'

'Cool out, Slick.'

'Up yours, Callllvin.'

The pounding stopped again. So did the voices of those clustered with Kyle around the elevator fires.

Kyle's guts felt knotted. Paula, standing beside him, brushed her hand through his hair. And suddenly clenched his hair as the shrill of a scream floated in from the distance.

Heart slamming, he sprang to his feet. Paula released his hair. He gaped at her. She looked stunned.

The scream went on and on.

Nearby, a girl made terrified whiny sounds.

'It's all right, honey.'

'Jesus H. Christ,' someone muttered.

'What'n hell's going on?'

Kyle *knew* what was going on. The crazies beyond the wall hadn't hidden, they'd attacked. He felt as if snakes were squirming up and down his back.

The screaming stopped.

Though no one had moved from in front of the fire, nearly every head was turned, facing the darkness. The whining kid, a girl of about seven, was clutching her mother.

Tom said, 'I'm sure everything's all right.'

'Like hell it is.'

A man who stood with his hands on the shoulders of the frightened girl said, 'Maybe we'd better . . . some of us should go and find out what happened. They might need help.'

'I'm with you, pardner,' said the old cowboy, Calvin.

'Sure does sound like they might've run into a spot of trouble.' That was the fat old guy who'd volunteered to go with Darcy in the first place.

'Count me in,' said the man with the pregnant wife.

'Oh, no you don't,' she protested. 'You're not going anywhere.'

'But . . .'

'I think we should all stay here,' Tom told them. He fingered the bandaged side of his head. 'A bunch of you go running off into the dark . . . I don't know. I think we should stay together. Since we don't know what happened . . .'

'One of the gals probably just got spooked.' That was the guy Calvin always called Slick. 'Saw a bat or something.'

'There aren't any bats,' Tom pointed out.

'Could've been anything. These bitches'll shriek their heads off at the drop of a hat.'

One of the thin men in the matching goatees said, 'I think we should go and investigate, nonetheless.'

'Well just go ahead,' Slick said. 'Swish on down there.'

'Redneck trash.'

'I'll "redneck" you, you goddamn butt-fucker.'

'Dad, you shouldn't . . .'

Slick backhanded his son across the face. The kid stumbled backward. The father of the little girl caught him before he fell.

'Hey, buddy, that's no way to act.'

'Wanta make something of it?' He brought up his fists.

The other guy rubbed his hands on his jeans and lumbered toward him.

'Wayne, don't!'

'C'mon, c'mon.' Slick flapped a hand, beckoning to him.

'He's mine,' said the goateed man, stepping in the way of Wayne.

'I'll take y'both. C'mon, c'mon.'

'Stop this!' Tom shouted. 'I'm in charge here, and I won't have you people . . .'

'Shut the fuck up.'

The gay guy pushed Wayne back, then turned to face Slick, who grinned and kissed the knuckles of his right fist, then cocked the fist back, ready to smash the man.

And didn't see Calvin beside him.

'Hey there, you son of a whore. Didn't I warn you?'

Slick whirled to face Calvin.

He was still whirling when the wiry old cowboy jabbed with his walking stick. The brass end of the cane flashed golden in the firelight. It sank into Slick's belly. Whoofing, Slick started to double. Calvin let go of the cane with one hand, took a single step forward as Slick was buckling, and smashed a fist into the side of the man's face. Spittle flew from Slick's mouth and his head snapped sideways. The blow sent him stumbling towards an elevator. People gasped. He fell inside the car, and yelled as he crashed down on burning debris. Sparks flew up around him.

The two men with goatees rushed in, grabbed him up by his jacket, and dragged him out.

His hat was gone, his hair on fire.

The man he'd called a 'butt-fucker' slapped his head and snuffed the flames.

They let go of him. He dropped to his knees, sobbing, and clutched his smoking scalp.

'Should've let the low-lifer burn,' Calvin said.

Slick's son threw himself down and hugged the whimpering man. 'Dad?' he asked. 'Are you okay? Dad?'

Slick shoved the boy away.

'You're some kinda work,' Calvin said, and bashed the guy's head with his cane.

Slick crumbled and lay still.

'You old fool, you've killed him!'

'Don't get yourself all riled up, May. I didn't kill the sidewinder, though it might've been a boon to humanity if I had.'

A few people applauded.

Calvin tipped his Stetson to them.

The guy who'd put out Slick's burning hair crouched down, felt his pulse, and nodded. 'He's not dead.'

'Ah,' said his friend, 'but I should think he'll have a frightful headache.'

'His brains needed a good scrambling,' Calvin said. 'I reckon he'll be better off for it.'

The old fat guy handed Calvin a cigar.

'Much obliged.'

'Fellow's nothing short of a bum,' the fat man said, turning away from Calvin and addressing the whole group. 'He had a good point, though, about the scream. Could've been pretty much anything made one of those ladies haul off and scream her head off like that.'

'You're right,' Tom said. 'I think we ought to just stay here. It might've been nothing, so we shouldn't get upset and go off on a wild-goose chase. If they've had a real emergency and they need help, I'm sure they'll send someone back here to let us know.'

If anyone's left alive, Kyle thought.

What *did* happen? he wondered. There were four women in Darcy's group, but the screaming had all been done by just one. Maybe it had nothing to do, after all, with the crazies behind the wall.

Maybe they got through to the other side without being attacked.

Or maybe the others didn't get a chance to scream.

Or they might have all gone silent, hoping to hide in the darkness as the crazies came scurrying through the hole. Even now, a mad hunt and struggle could be going on in the Lake of Charon.

When it's over . . .

The crazies won't go back into their side of the cave. They'll head this way.

Kyle led Paula aside. He felt the heat from the fires fade, the cool air seep through his clothes. Standing in the shadows, he whispered, 'I want to sneak away from this bunch. They're going weird, you know?'

'Just that creepy guy.'

'But look what Calvin did to him. He could've killed the guy. Everyone's real nervous, starting to act crazy. I think we'd be a lot safer if we made ourselves scarce until help gets here. Who knows what they might do next, do you know what I mean?'

Paula nodded. 'You think someone else might start trouble?'

'Yeah, I do, and the longer we're trapped down here, the more likely it'll get. The fires are going down. Before long, they'll be out. It'll be dark again, and cold. Everyone's already nervous, but pretty soon some of them are going to start panicking. When that happens, there might be some *real* trouble.'

'So you want us get away from them and hide?'

Kyle took both her hands in his, and stared into her eyes. He realized that his fear of those from the other side of Ely's Wall had been pushed aside by feelings of eagerness, almost excitement.

They won't get me, he thought. Not a chance. This'll be good, really good.

Hiding with Paula. Away from the others. In the dark.

'I'm just thinking about you,' he said. 'I probably wouldn't bother, just for myself, but . . . Another thing is, I don't like the way some of these guys have been looking at you.'

'What do you mean?'

'Like they might want to . . . I don't know, maybe I just worry too much. But when it's dark again and no one can see what anybody else is doing, people might try things. Stuff they wouldn't normally do. I'd try my best to protect you, but . . . I just think we shouldn't stick around. It'll be better for both of us if they don't know where to find you.'

Frowning, she shook her head. 'You're afraid someone might want to . . . molest me?'

She's buying it, Kyle realized. She believes me.

'Maybe I shouldn't have brought it up,' he continued, 'but yeah, that's crossed my mind. Nothing would surprise me.'

'Who?'

'The one that got knocked out was giving you funny looks.'

'Yug.'

'Both those guys with the goatees, they've been checking you out, too.'

'But they're homos, aren't they?'

'If they're homos, why have they been staring at your breasts?'

'Have they?' She wrinkled her nose.

'Yeah. And the old guy that gave the cigar to Calvin.'

'You're kidding,' Paula whispered.

'But the one I'm really worried about, it's that gal with Calvin.' Kyle wrinkled his own nose and made himself sound disgusted. 'I can almost see her drooling when she looks at you.'

'Oh God. A lizzie?'

'Haven't you seen any of these creeps giving you the eye?'

She shook her head.

'I'm not saying they'll actually try something, but once it's dark . . .'

'So you think we should hide,' Paula said.

'Yeah.'

'Where'll we go?'

He nodded toward the darkness. 'Over there. On the other side of the River Styx. They'll never find us over there.'

Neither will the crazies, he thought. That was the main thing. He wanted to get alone with Paula, but more than that, he wanted to be hidden if those from behind the wall should come. He was sure they'd take the walkway if they left the Lake of Charon. The walkway followed this side of the stream, and would lead them straight to those waiting near the elevators. With or without Paula, he intended to be hiding on the other side of the stream when they arrived.

But with her would be so much better.

'Okay?' he asked.

'Okay.'

Taking his time, he led Paula around the outer rim of the group. No one seemed to notice. Most were facing the fires, as if they feared the darkness and hoped to deny its existence by keeping it behind them.

But there were about thirty of them. For a while, Kyle hovered at the rear of the group, trying to make sure that no one was watching. Then he stepped backwards drawing Paula along with him.

After four silent steps, they were well into the darkness. Even if someone should look now, eyes accustomed to the brightness of the firelight probably wouldn't be able to spot them.

Kyle turned around. Paula stayed at his side. Arms around each other, they moved quietly away, deeper into the dark.

'Can we stay in sight of the fires?' Paula whispered.

'Sure.' He'd already planned on that. He hoped to see what would happen when the crazies showed up. Though he'd warned Paula that the fires would soon burn out, there was enough broken wood inside the elevators to keep the flames going for quite a while yet. With any luck, the fires would last long enough for him to watch the mayhem.

From a safe distance.

Kyle stopped and looked over his shoulder. The clustered people were dark silhouettes against the light of twin fires, forty or fifty feet from where he stood. Taking that distance into account, Kyle figured he must be very close to the railing that bordered this side of the stream.

He led Paula slowly forward, reaching out with one hand until he touched the cold, moist metal of the railing. 'Here we are,' he whispered. 'I'll go first.'

He squatted low and ducked beneath the railing. When he was clear, he turned around and felt for Paula. He found her shoulder. She rose up in front of him.

'This is so weird,' she whispered. He saw the vague shape of her head turn, and he guessed that she needed to comfort herself by looking back at the firelight. 'What if they find out we're gone?'

'Big deal. You think they'll come looking?'

'I just wonder if we should be doing this.'

'Do you want to go back?'

She was silent.

She's not going back.

'I guess not,' she finally said.

Kyle took her hand. 'Well, if you change your mind, fine. Just tell me. I'm not forcing you into anything.'

'I know.'

'I'll go first. Stay in back of me, and hold on.' He turned around. Paula curled her fingers over his shoulders, and he began making his way down the embankment, knees bent, arms out for balance. He could see nothing in front of him. The rock slope felt smooth and somewhat slippery under his shoes. Instead of taking steps, he scooted without lifting his feet.

When he judged that he must be near the stream, he stopped. He slid a foot forward and tapped a few times with his toe. Hearing no splashes, he moved ahead a little farther and tried again. This time, he heard a soft liquid patter when he tapped.

'We have to wade across,' he whispered. 'It's only a few inches deep, but out feet'll get wet. I'm going to take off my shoes and socks.'

'Okay,' Paula said. 'Me, too.'

They sat down beside each other on the slope. Kyle pulled off his running shoes, peeled his socks off his feet and stuffed them inside the shoes. Paula, he remembered, wore a kilt and knee socks. Without the socks, her legs would be bare.

Bare all the way up to the panties she must have on beneath the kilt.

He suddenly pictured Darcy in the grotto, naked except for her panties, clutching her trousers to her breasts. The panties were wet. They were glued to her.

The memories made him hard.

Then came a hollow ache as he realized he would

probably never see Darcy alive again, never get a chance to touch her or squeeze her or taste her, never ram her with his cock or make her bleed and squirm and cry out like Amy Lawson.

Others might get to do it. The ones who dwelled beyond the wall. But not Kyle.

They'll cheat me out of it, he thought.

But I've got Paula.

'Okay,' Paula said.

Holding both his shoes in one hand, Kyle stood. He took her arm, and helped her stand up. She stayed at his side as they eased forward and entered the water.

She made a hissing sound. 'Christ, it's cold.'

'Yeah.' His feet felt numb to the ankles. The stream-bed was gritty as if a thin layer of sand and gravel had been sprinkled over its rock floor. He lifted a foot out of the water, took a small step and set it down carefully. Then he did the same with his other foot.

What if I make her fall? Kyle asked himself. So it looks like an accident. Then her clothes will be all wet and I can get her to take them off when we reach the other side. I'll tell her she can wear my pants, and . . .

If she falls, she might yell. The others will hear her, and come looking.

Forget it.

There'll be plenty of time to work on her. He'd had her blouse open just before the elevators fell, it shouldn't take much to get her bra off, and after that, who knows?

His foot came down, finding rock instead of water. 'Here's the shore,' he whispered. 'I'll go first. Get behind me and hang onto my belt.' He released her arm and her fingers pushed under the back of his belt. Crouching, he felt the rocks ahead and began to move forward up the embankment. His shoulder bumped something, probably one of the stalagmites he'd often noticed along this side of the stream. He stepped around it.

He'd looked across the River Styx countless times, and had even explored over here on several occasions. He knew that the area was cluttered with speleothems that would provide wonderful hiding places, but he couldn't recall the exact details and the dark was disorienting.

He felt his way along like a blind man stumbling through a maze.

And stepped on something soft.

He crouched, stroked the cool cloth surface, and realized what he was touching. 'There's a blanket here,' he said.

'Geez.'

Kneeling, he crawled on the blanket. It was doubled over, giving it a double thickness. It seemed to be about a yard wide and six feet long. When he reached its far end, his sweeping hand crushed a slick, springy mound that he guessed might be a pillow. He explored it with his fingers – and realized it must be a sleeping bag in a stuff sack. He picked it up and heard a muffled clank of glass. Reaching down, he found a bottle. It was heavy. Liquid sloshed inside. He twisted off the cap and sniffed. There was a pungent odour of alcohol. Though he didn't know much about such things, he guessed that it must be a bottle of Scotch or Bourbon.

'Pretty neat,' Paula whispered from behind him.

'There's a sleeping bag.'

'You're kidding.'

'And a bottle of booze.'

'Really?'

He turned around on his knees and eased the bottle in her direction.

'I can smell it,' Paula said.

'Take a sip. It'll warm you up.'

'I don't know.'

'I won't tell.'

'Where'd it come from?'

'Right here.'

'Is this stuff yours?'

'Sure isn't.'

'You took us right to it.'

'Glad I did, too. But it isn't mine. I didn't even know anything was here.'

'If it isn't yours, where'd it come from?'

'God, I don't know. Somebody must've . . . maybe it's a make-out place.' Turning his head, he saw only black. He reached out. Just past the edge of the blanket was a barrier of rock. Rising, he saw the distant shapes backlit by the elevator fires. 'This is great,' he said. He sat down again. 'Think I'll give it a taste.'

'Maybe you shouldn't. If you don't know whose it is . . .'

'Must belong to somebody who works here. Maybe Tom. Maybe he comes over here with one of the guides.' Darcy? he wondered. Had she spent time here with Tom, hidden among the rocks, drinking and fucking?

He imagined her naked inside the sleeping bag, writhing and gasping, but not with Tom. It was Kyle in the bag with her, squeezing her breasts, thrusting deep into her wet heat.

Maybe they would sneak down here at night. Or even hide here during the day, out of sight as tours went by.

Not Darcy, though.

Probably Lynn. Lynn and Tom.

Lynn was such a slut, he wouldn't put anything past her.

'You think it's sanitary?' Paula asked.

'Sure.' He lifted the bottle to his lips, and tilted it up. The liquid took a moment to reach his mouth, so he figured the bottle was about three-quarters full. He sipped. Some kind of whisky, all right. He swallowed and the heat rushed through him. Shuddering slightly, he said, 'Good. Try some.'

He held the bottle out and felt it being taken from his hand. There came a quiet sloshing sound, then 'Whoo.'

'Like it?'

'It's all right.'

'Want to get in the sleeping bag?'

She was silent for a few seconds. 'I don't know. I don't think so.'

'I'll get it out, anyway. We can sit on it.'

'Okay.'

He opened the drawstring, pulled out the sleeping bag, and spread it over the blanket.

They sat on it, side by side in the darkness. Kyle wrapped an arm around Paula's back. She snuggled against him. He heard her take another drink. Then she nudged his chest with the bottle. He found it, and drank.

'Wouldn't it be something,' Paula whispered, 'if we both got smashed? We'd go staggering out of here, blasted out of our gourds.'

'Sounds like a good idea.'

'I was just kidding.'

'Have you ever been drunk?'

'No. How about you?'

'Me neither,' Kyle said. 'But this seems like a good time to try it.'

'I don't know. You wouldn't try any funny stuff, would you?'

'No. Promise. No funny stuff. Cross my heart and hope to die.'

14

Beth, screaming, had leaped off the boat while her husband's legs were still in the air. The soles of his shoes vanished through the hole at the same instant water flew up from Beth's splash.

'No!' Greg shouted at her.

She lunged through the chest-high water, left hand swiping the air in front of her, right hand waving the flashlight. The beam jerked and jumped over the cavern wall, jittering all around the hole.

She hadn't taken two steps before Greg swung Darcy out of his way and threw himself off the boat. Darcy staggered. The edge of the seat caught her behind the knees. She dropped backwards, grabbed a gunnel, pulled herself up and twisted onto her side in time to see Greg hook an arm around Beth. His other arm reached out. He grabbed her forearm as if he feared she might lose the flashlight. The woman struggled against him, trying to pull free.

'Jim! Jim! Come back!'

'Stop it!' Greg snapped. 'Beth, he's gone. Let's . . .'

The back of her head struck Greg's chin. Darcy heard the thud, heard his teeth clash together, saw his head jerk. He dropped backwards. As he went under, Darcy pushed herself up and crouched to dive and glimpsed something off to the side.

Pale movement.

She looked and saw Beth wading. The flashlight beam skittered all over the wall, not settling on the hole but flicking across it. And as it skimmed past the hole, Darcy glimpsed someone coming out head first.

For an instant, she thought it was Jim coming back. (Just an hallucination, seeing him stabbed through the mouth and yanked into the hole.) He was okay after all. Now, he was coming back.

It wasn't Jim.

No *way* was that hairy, bearded thing Jim!

Seeing Greg come to the surface, she dived. In mid-air, she heard Helen squeal and Carol say, 'Oh Jesus God!' Then she hit the water. The cold swarmed around her, but it didn't matter. She was still underwater when her hand pushed against Greg. His hip. She stood and grabbed his arm as he began to wade towards Beth. He was shaking his head, apparently still dazed from the blow.

She turned and moved with him.

Beth, a yard in front of them, made a *whoof* and began to double over. Then she was hurled up. One of her kicking feet brushed Darcy's forehead. She was hoisted above the lake, writhing and flapping, a dim bearded shape rising up beneath her. Not touching her. Throwing her high and over his head with something knobbed at the end like the handle of a baseball bat (a bone?). As she tumbled over him, he jerked the weapon out. The flashlight, still in Beth's hand as she somersaulted, lit the weapon – a bone, more than a foot long, sharp at one end, ashimmer with blood.

Beth hit the water behind the man.

The flashlight went down with her. It stayed on, but the cavern suddenly fell dark. As dark as a moonless night, but not black. Darcy could almost see Greg blend with the man. She heard grunts, growls, splashes, and felt the water churning against her body. She was knocked aside as Greg stumbled backward. The two men went under.

She waded toward the flashlight. It lay on the bottom of the lake, its beam pushing a short tunnel through the water. Ducking down she grabbed the cylinder. She brought the flashlight up in time to see a person crouched on the edge of the hole in Ely's Wall.

Another one?

Her stomach went cold and tight.

The stranger's arms were out against the sides of the hole. Darcy's eyes were drawn to the thin bone it held in one hand. Something shiny at its end.

Scissors.

Toe-nail scissors?

They were somehow fixed to the end of the bone, their tiny blades forming a point for the bizarre weapon.

Long hair hung over the stranger's face. The face looked dead white. The teeth were bared with a snarl. Pointed teeth. In the instant before it sprang at Darcy, she saw that it wore a blood-smeared white turtleneck sweater. Jeans.

Large breasts swayed inside the sweater as the woman leaped from her perch.

Darcy swung the flashlight.

A jolt went up her arm as the head of the cylinder smashed against the woman's face.

The light went out.

The body hit her, driving Darcy backwards and down. The water closed over her. Though she expected a savage assault, no hands clutched at her, no scissor points dug into her flesh. She realized, vaguely, that the blow from the flashlight must've stunned the woman. She rolled out from under her. Wrapped an arm around the head. Got to her feet and pulled the head up out of the water and, hugging the wet face to her cheek, hammered the head with the flashlight. With each impact, the face jerked against her.

She heard the sounds of Greg's struggle off to her side.

One last blow.

Five.

Then a sixth for good measure. Then she let go of the woman's head. The body slid down against her. She kneed it away, turned sluggishly in the water and waded toward the gasping, choking, splashing noises.

Heard quick whispers to her left. Helen and Carol.

A heavy thud and spatter in the lake behind her.

A *third* invader from behind Ely's Wall?

She heard herself whimper. Don't worry about more, she told herself. Worry about the one Greg's fighting. Thank God they're still at it.

She neared the turmoil.

Heard splashes off to the side. Had Carol and Helen left the boat?

Something rammed her thigh. She reached down into the water and grabbed an ankle. She felt a sock under her fingers. Greg wasn't wearing socks. The foot kicked out of her grip.

Not wanting to lose the flashlight, she stuffed it under the elastic bottom of her windbreaker, then reached

194

down again. She clutched a trouser cuff. (Greg was in his briefs.) Face in the water, she climbed her hands up the leg to the inseam. Drove an arm deep between the legs and rammed it up hard into the crotch. The legs clamped on her arm. She felt the body shudder. Pulling her arm free, she clawed at the man's rump, hooked her fingers into the back pockets of his pants, and tugged, trying to get him off Greg.

The flopping, bucking body came with her as she stumbled backward.

She heard a swoosh of water. Coughing. Greg must have come up.

'Got him,' she whispered.

Greg didn't answer. He kept coughing.

'Where *are* you?' Carol's voice.

'Go for the dock!' Darcy yelled. 'Get out of here!'

'Which way?'

How can I answer that?

'Just go! And be quiet! There's more of them!'

The body jerked forward. Darcy yanked the pants pockets, trying to keep it back, then realized that the sudden movement hadn't been the attacker's doing. Greg must be pulling on him. So she relaxed her grip and felt the body dart forward and up. Her fingers slipped out of the pockets.

There was another thumping splash behind her.

Another savage entering the lake?

Soft swashing sounds of someone wading or swimming back there.

Other such sounds ahead of her.

A yelp of fright from the front.

'It's me, just me.' Helen's voice.

'Thank God.'

195

Reaching out, she clutched thick, oily hair. She fumbled under her windbreaker for the flashlight, planning to beat the man with it. But the head rammed violently back against her hand, then went down.

'Okay,' Greg gasped. 'Okay.'

Darcy moved towards the sound of his voice, so close in the blackness. The submerged body was in the way. It sank lower and slipped away as she walked over it with her knees. Then her arms were around Greg. She pressed herself against him, felt his heaving chest, his wet cheek, his warm breath brushing her ear.

There were soft liquid swooshing sounds behind her, in front of her. And breathing sounds. Whimpers nearby, probably from Carol or Helen.

Darcy, herself, was shaking violently.

She flinched rigid as she realized that someone was very near, approaching her back.

'Hold your breath,' Greg whispered.

He pulled her down.

She crouched. The water closed over her head. Greg eased her away, but held onto her arm. He turned her, pulled her. She left her feet and he towed her along. She felt the chill water streaming over her body. He couldn't be doing this and swimming. She supposed he was wading, squatted low to stay beneath the surface.

This will work, she thought. We're leaving them behind.

As long as we stay under, they won't find us. They can only go by what they hear.

We should've told the women to do it.

Darcy began to need air. She fought the need, but soon her lungs ached. Then they burned. She wondered if Greg was going up for breaths, if he'd forgotten about her.

Then he pulled her to a stop. She felt a hand press her mouth. He raised her slowly. When her face was out of the water, he removed his hand. She sucked air into her lungs, but tried to do it quietly.

She expected Greg to submerge her again quickly. He didn't, though.

They stood motionless, holding each other.

Darcy heard her own breathing and the quick thumping of her heart. She heard Greg's too. And a few quiet patters as drops of water fell from them. Nothing else.

It was as if all movement in the Lake of Charon had ceased.

It was as if they were alone in the lake.

What's going on?

She wished she could hear the others.

Maybe Carol and Helen are swimming underwater, she thought. Maybe everyone is.

Or maybe they're all standing motionless, just like us. Carol and Helen hoping their silence will save them. The others hoping for a sound that'll give us away so they can home in on us and nail us.

Suppose the attackers have left? Went back through their hole to the other end of the cavern?

We got two of them. Maybe didn't kill them, maybe did, but that might've taken the starch out of the rest.

No. We weren't under long enough. They wouldn't have had time to get back through the hole.

Greg touched her chin, which she took as a signal to submerge again. She filled her lungs. His fingers were still on her chin, so he knew when she nodded.

They went down slowly, silently.

Greg towed her through the water, just like before.

She sensed that they were moving toward the dock.

That had to be, or they would've run into one of the cavern's walls before now.

If we can just get to the dock!

With just a little headstart on the pursuers, they'd be all right. From the dock, they could find the walkway and follow its railing back to the main group. They'd be safe there. Those horrible things wouldn't dare . . .

Things? People.

But they looked and acted like mindless savages, seemed less than human.

What the hell were they doing behind Ely's Wall? Did they *live* there?

That's crazy. Nobody could survive in . . .

Unless there's an opening somewhere. If they had a way in and out. Not supposed to be an opening, but maybe. Who knows?

Killed Jim and Beth.

Hope Carol and Helen are okay.

We're okay, that's the main thing.

Darcy felt a nudge of guilt and she wondered if she might be punished for her selfishness and she thought, Please God, let Carol and Helen be all right.

Greg's hand covered her eyes, then slid lower and pressed her mouth. She nodded. She put her feet down and let him guide her to the surface.

The cavern was no longer silent.

Loud splashing. But far away. Behind them.

And suddenly a high terrified voice whining, 'No! No! Leave me be! *Please!* MY GOD!'

It was Helen. Her voice went silent. The splashing continued, but with less frenzy.

They got Helen, Darcy thought. Oh Christ, they got her.

198

Feeling Greg's hand on her cheek, she took a deep breath and nodded. They went down again.

Greg's grip on her arm was tighter than before and he seemed to be towing her faster.

Because of what happened to Helen, she thought.

Why are they killing us?

We broke through Ely's Wall. If we'd stayed at the elevators . . . It's my fault. Jim and Beth and Helen, they'd be alive if . . .

Shit, I had no way of knowing. Who could have known we'd be *murdered*?

They must have heard us pounding, and gathered on their side of the wall, just waiting.

Thank God it was Jim who broke through. Jim, and not Greg. It would've been Greg if there hadn't been a second layer of rocks.

Poor Jim, though. *Jesus*. That bone. Right into his mouth. And Beth. In the stomach.

The water carried a hollow, ringing thump to her ears. It came from beside her. From Greg's side. Though alarmed and puzzled for a moment, she quickly understood the meaning of the sound: Greg had gone up for air and struck his head on the hull of the boat that was tied at the dock.

It better be that boat he hit, she thought. If it's the *other* boat, we're in deep shit.

Her grim humour surprised Darcy. It came from relief, she supposed, from knowing that they had found the dock.

Greg pulled her forward, then lifted her.

Before, when they came up for air, they had both remained crouched so that only their heads were exposed. Now, Darcy stood up straight. The water was as high as the undersides of her breasts. She put a hand on Greg's shoulder. He released her other arm, and she reached out to her left. As she expected, her fingertips found the metal side of the boat. The boat, she knew, had been moored snugly against the dock. Raising her arm, she felt the rough wooden planks above her head.

They'll never find us here, she thought. We're under the dock with the boat blocking the way. If they get this far, they'll go around the boat. They'll run into the dock, and they'd be more likely to climb onto it than to search beneath it. If we're quiet, they'll never find us.

You brought me here, Greg. Somehow, you got us here.

We'll be all right, now.

She knew they were coming, could hear the soft liquid sounds of their approach. But they were still some distance away.

She slipped both arms around Greg and hugged him tightly.

They stood in the blackness, embracing. They were both trembling and breathing hard, and she could feel the thud of his heartbeat through his chest. The barrel of the flashlight was pressed between their bellies. After their breathing calmed, he slipped a hand under Darcy's windbreaker and pulled the flashlight out. He gave it to her. She clipped it to her belt, out of the way. For a moment, she considered opening the zipper and spreading the front of the windbreaker. It would be so good, so comforting, to feel him against her bare skin. But she didn't do it. Because those from beyond Ely's Wall were wading nearer and nearer. She pressed herself against Greg, and listened.

And heard a slurp behind her.

Jesus no!

Greg went rigid.

He stopped breathing. So did Darcy.

Someone was under the dock. It seemed impossible, but Darcy had heard the slosh. So close behind her! And it wasn't her imagination. Greg had heard it, too.

If we don't make a sound . . .

Something touched her right shoulder. Flinching, she pushed her mouth against Greg's shoulder to stifle a gasp.

Her shoulder was patted, squeezed. Her hair was stroked.

She heard a faint sigh.

Carol?

Darcy let go of Greg. His arms loosened around her. He, too, must've guessed the intruder's identity. Darcy turned slowly, careful not to disturb the water. Her hands, below the surface, found fabric. She remembered the sundress Carol had been wearing, and moved her hands higher and felt the armholes. She touched an armpit, a breast, the low neckline of the dress. She slid her hand up the side of the neck, and stroked the woman's wet cheek. She felt eager nodding.

And heard a quiet sob.

Curling a hand behind the neck, she drew Carol against her. The woman hugged her. Greg, moving silently to Darcy's side, put his arms around them both.

Carol shook as she wept, and her breath made hitching sounds.

The others were very near. They seemed to be in front of Darcy and over to the right, approaching the dock – probably somewhere just beyond the bow of the boat.

Fearing they might hear Carol, Darcy brought a hand up and pressed the woman's face against the side of her neck to muffle the ragged breathing sounds.

She heard a soft bump, followed by an 'Uh!' Someone must have bumped the edge of the dock.

'What?' A whisper. A woman's voice.

'Hit something.' A man.

Christ, Darcy thought, they can talk.

Patting sounds on the wood. 'I know what this is. It's the pier where they keep the touring boats.' That was a woman. She had to be one of those from the other side of the wall, but she was familiar with this side.

Who the hell *are* these people?

There came a whush of spilling water. A sudden thud as if a heavy object (a person) had been thrown onto the dock. Darcy flinched. Carol jerked rigid and sucked hard on the side of her neck. Darcy felt Greg's grip tighten on her shoulder.

Then there were sloshing sounds, dribbles, thumps and scurrying sounds.

They're climbing onto the dock, Darcy thought. Thank God. They're not going to search under it.

She listened carefully. From the sounds they made boosting themselves up and clambering onto the platform, she guessed that there were at least four of them. Maybe five.

They didn't leave.

Darcy wanted to hear them walk way, but they seemed to be going nowhere. She guessed that they were sitting down. They'd left the water about six feet ahead of her, and had come no closer. She heard water dribbling onto the surface of the lake, probably spilling off their bodies and falling through the cracks between the planks.

They're so damn close, she thought. But not so close that she could hear their breathing. And they can't hear ours, she told herself.

'Let's we leave her for later,' the woman whispered, 'and go after the others.'

Someone laughed as if it were a stupid suggestion.

'I mean it. If they reach the elevators, they'll go up and tell about us. They'll tell what we did. People will come down with guns, and . . .'

A smack. A whimper.

'Okay,' the woman muttered.

Darcy heard quick, soft popping sounds. Things clicked on the wood, skittered along. Something plipped into the water.

Buttons, she thought.

Leave her for later. They weren't leaving her for later. Somebody had just ripped open her blouse, making buttons fly.

That first loud thud before the others climbed onto the dock. It *had* been a body hitting onto the dock. Beth or Helen, more likely Helen since she was the one who'd been caught a few minutes ago.

Carol, apparently coming to the same conclusion, squeezed herself more tightly against Darcy.

The sounds continued. Darcy wished she could cover her ears and free herself from the knowledge of what was happening above. But she heard thumps as limbs were lifted and dropped, the rasps of fabric, the tinkle of a buckle, the skid of a zipper and she could *see* them up there in the black, kneeling in a circle around the body, stripping off its clothes.

They're going to rape her, she thought.

She wondered if Helen was dead.

She heard sighs and moans, quiet chuckles. She

wondered if any of the moans came from Helen.

No, Helen's dead. Must be.

If she isn't, how can we just stand down here, hiding, while they rape her?

What if Greg decides to go to the rescue?

The way he was clutching Darcy's shoulder, she guessed that he might be considering it.

Then came a wet, ripping sound.

Another and another.

Something began to patter the water in front of Darcy.

Blood?

Then came rhythmic squishes, moans, moist sucking – the sounds that people might make with mouths full of meat.

Chewing.

15

With the rubble cleared away, Hank crawled over the rock slab. The water running around his hands and knees, though less than an inch deep, felt like ice. Cool air blew softly against him as if the small hole in the hillside was the open door of a refrigerator. He was bare to the waist, sweaty from wielding the sledge hammer under the hot sun, and the breath of the cavern chilled his wet skin.

Goosebumps scurried up his back as he put his head into the cave.

His body blocked out most of the sunlight. All he could see in the dim shadows was more of the shallow, narrow stream.

He crawled farther, until he was completely inside the cave. The cold wrapped around him. The dark pressed in on him. His heartbeat quickened. Though he couldn't see the walls or ceiling of the cavern, much less *feel* them, he sensed them shrinking, closing in on him, suffocating him. The air was being squeezed from his lungs.

Water swirled around his hands as he rubbed the stream-bed. That's solid rock, he told himself. It felt like concrete. This cave's been here thousands of years, maybe millions. It isn't about to fall in on you.

It's solid rock. It's a cavern. It's safe.

'Yoo-hoo, Hank,' Lynn called from behind him in a sing-song. 'What are you doing in there?'

What *am* I doing in here? he wondered.

Testing myself? Giving it a little try to see if I can take it?

I'll take it, no matter what. Paula's at the other end of this darkness, and I'm going to get her out.

'Is everything okay?' Chris asked.

It was good to hear her voice.

'Fine.'

Fine, like having a pillow pressed against your face by someone trying to cancel your ticket.

Hank began crawling backwards. He wanted to rush, to free himself from the oppressive tightness, but forced himself to move slowly.

Then he was free. He filled his lungs. He sniffed the piney air of the hillside. The sunlight clothed him with wonderful heat.

As he stood in the water, gasping, the others stared at him. He saw concern on Chris's face, confusion on Brad's, and a strange, rather leering smile on Lynn's as her gaze roamed down his body.

'What's wrong with you?' Brad asked.

'Closed-in places. I don't like them.'

'You've got claustrophobia?'

'But only a touch of leprosy.'

'Well,' Lynn said, 'what do you know about that?'

Brad arched an eyebrow and rubbed one of his bulging pecs. Like Hank, he had stripped off his shirt during their labours to smash through the wall. He had the body of a Mr Universe contestant, and his sweaty skin gleamed in the sunlight as if slicked with oil. Hank

206

suspected the man's chest didn't itch, that he was rubbing it simply to draw Chris's attention to his amazing proportions. But she was looking at Hank, not Brad.

'Maybe you should wait here,' Brad told him, and Lynn nodded in agreement.

'I'll be all right.'

'What if you're not? Suppose we get in there and you have some kind of panic attack?'

'Don't worry about it.'

'I think you should stay here,' Lynn said.

Of course you do, Hank thought. You'd like nothing better than to get me alone.

He suspected that the girl was less interested in seducing him than in defeating Chris. Some kind of a competitive thing that had little to do with desire, a lot to do with ego.

Earlier, when they parked the car on the dirt road across the small valley, she had climbed out and tied her jacket around her waist and proceeded to unbutton her uniform blouse. There was nothing under it but skin. She didn't take the blouse off. Instead, she lifted its front and knotted the tails just under her breasts. From the glances she gave Hank, the show was for his benefit, not Brad's.

When it came time to distribute the equipment for the hike to the cavern, she insisted on carrying the backpack full of flashlights and candy bars. She faced Hank while she put it on. Her struggle getting into the straps made her blouse spread apart and one side fell away, baring her left breast for a while before she noticed the problem, said 'Woops', and covered it.

Hank might have been amused by such ploys, but he sensed Lynn's rather malicious intent – and Chris was a witness to every display. Though Chris didn't complain, Hank caught her frowning slightly, sometimes shaking her head, and she'd even rolled her eyes upward as if asking the Lord for mercy when Lynn so accidently exposed the breast.

Chris stayed at his side as they hiked across the narrow valley and up the hillside to the cavern. Lynn, continuing with her tactics, walked a short distance ahead of them, swaggering and waving her rump, often walking backward to give Hank a view of her half-naked, bouncing breasts. Whenever she faced him, she spoke to Hank as if Chris and Brad weren't there. She told him about Tom. 'He's a nice guy,' she said, 'but we weren't, you know, serious. I mean, he's not all that mature.' She asked if Hank was still married. He said, 'No.' She asked, 'So what happened to your wife?' A dark place swelled inside him. 'She died.' And Lynn said, 'Woops.' And he thought, you are a little shit. But Chris looked at him with tenderness in her eyes and said softly, 'I'm sorry.'

Now, Lynn wanted him to stay behind with her while Chris and Brad went into the cavern.

Not a chance, he thought.

Even if he didn't need to go in for Paula, it would take more than claustrophobia to make him remain behind with Lynn. He wanted nothing to do with her.

And he didn't want Chris and Brad to be thrown together.

Though Brad was more subtle than Lynn, he'd obviously taken a fancy to Chris. He would be very glad to have Hank stay with Lynn. Then, he'd have Chris all to himself in the dark cavern.

'Frankly,' Brad said, 'your condition might endanger the rest of us.'

'Frankly, bullshit.'

'Chris, maybe you can talk sense into him.'

Chris glanced at Hank, her brows drawn together. Then she looked at Brad. 'Hank's already talking sense. It's his decision. I'm sure he's aware of his . . . limits. If he thinks he can make it, he should give it a try. I want him with us.'

'So what am I supposed to do?' Lynn asked with a whine in her voice. 'Stay here all by myself?'

'Or go back to the car,' Hank suggested.

That got a quick grin from Chris.

Lynn, pursing her lips in a pout, tipped her head to one side. She folded her arms, squeezing her breasts together and lifting them. 'So I just get left out?'

'Come with us if you prefer,' Chris told her.

'Maybe I just will.'

'It's up to you,' Hank said.

'Come on with us,' Brad urged her. 'Why not?'

She nodded briskly. 'I think I'll do just that.'

Great, Hank thought. Shit.

'That's good,' he told her. 'You can carry the backpack. You've very accomplished at that.'

She wiggled her eyebrows, grinned, and said, 'You bet.'

While Hank and Brad had taken turns smashing through the layers of rock and concrete with the pickaxe, sledge hammer and wedge Hank had bought at the hardware store, Chris had fuelled the Coleman lantern, and lighted it. Now, crouching beside the hissing lantern, she picked up the fuel canister. She slipped it into the backpack and took out four flashlights. Putting them down, she lifted the pack and offered it to Lynn.

Lynn squirmed into the straps. Though she stretched and squirmed more than necessary, her blouse didn't spread open quite as much as before and she failed to expose either of her breasts entirely. When the pack was on, she modestly tightened her blouse's loose half-knot.

A corner of Chris's mouth curved up as she watched the girl. 'Aren't you going to wear your jacket?' she asked.

Lynn patted the sleeves tied at her waist. 'I have it if I need it.'

Chris glanced at Hank. She looked as if she might start laughing. 'Up to you,' she told Lynn.

'That's right. I mean, it's boiling out here. It's going to feel nice in the cavern.'

Even as she spoke, Brad was pulling his knit shirt down over his head.

'Why don't you take my shirt,' Hank told him. 'I won't need it.'

'If it fits,' Brad said.

Hank tossed it to him, and Brad put it on over his own shirt. His arms fit into the short sleeves, but he was unable to button it across his massive chest.

'Nothing a diet wouldn't cure,' Hank said.

Brad whuffed out a laugh.

Sitting down on the hillside near the cave entrance, Hank pushed his feet into the warm-up pants Chris had bought for him. As he drew them up over his shorts, he watched Chris step into her pants. She left her red shorts on. Balancing on one foot, then the other, she pulled the pants up, and her slender bare legs vanished inside the baggy garment. Instead of taking off the oversized white shirt she'd worn as a cover-up, she tucked it in. Her fingertips pinned the cuffs against her palms to keep the sleeves from climbing her arms as she slipped into the warm-up suit's jacket. Like a kid, Hank thought. Just how a kid does it.

She left the front of the jacket open.

Getting to his feet, Hank put his jacket on. It clung to his sweaty skin. He pulled up the zipper, stuffed a flashlight into a side pocket, and lifted the sledge hammer.

'Are we going to take the hammer *and* the pick?' Brad asked. He already had the pickaxe resting on his shoulder.

'I guess just one or the other,' Hank said. 'Might as well make it easy on ourselves.'

They decided to leave the sledge hammer and wedge behind. Brad insisted on being the one to carry the pickaxe. Hank lifted the lantern by its wire handle. 'I guess we're all set,' he said, and a tremor passed through him as he turned toward the dark opening of the cave.

He entered first, on his knees and one hand, the lantern held out before him. The twin mantles glared silvery-white and produced an amazing amount of light. He saw the stream stretching out ahead of him until it was engulfed in darkness. The walls around him formed a low, narrow tunnel. Though the ceiling was several inches above his head, he felt it pressing down on him, squeezing the breath out of his lungs. His heart hammered. He gasped for air. But he kept crawling.

'You all right?' Chris's voice. Close behind him.

'Yeah,' he managed.

He heard a clank, apparently the head of the pickaxe bumping a side of the cave.

They're all behind me, he thought. Blocking the way out. Jesus.

A vice was tightening around his chest. He heard a ringing in his ears. He made high-pitched wheezing sounds each time he sucked air into his shrinking lungs.

A hand rubbed the calf of his right leg. Chris. 'God,'

she said, 'it's really bad for you. Do you want to go back?'

'No,' he gasped.

The hand went away, and he kept crawling. Though the cave seemed to be crushing him, he could see that it was growing larger. A short distance ahead, the walls and ceiling seemed to vanish. He scurried forward, sprang to his feet, and rushed on to make room for the others to come through behind him. Then, stopping, he raised the lantern high.

The ceiling, jagged with stalactites, was probably thirty feet above him. The walls to his right and left were barely visible at the far extremes of the lantern light. Surrounded by columns and stalagmites, he felt as if he were standing in a forest of rock. The formations gleamed and glistened and cast deep shadows.

'How are you doing?' Chris asked.

He turned around and watched her stand up. The legs of her pants were wet from the knees down. She rubbed her hands on her thighs. She looked wonderful.

'Better,' he said. He *was* better, though he hadn't realized it until now. He still felt trapped under the weight of the hill, he still struggled to breathe, but he was no longer wheezing and his heart had slowed down somewhat. It no longer slammed inside his chest as if trying to smash through his ribcage. 'It's not . . . so tight,' he said.

Chris stepped closer, and he swung the lantern out of the way. She put her arms around him, pressed her cool cheek against his. And the vice on his chest loosened just a little more. He curled his free hand over the firm soft mound of her rump. Squeezed it. Then moved his hand up her back as Lynn crawled out of the tunnel's mouth.

The girl stood up and staggered toward them. Her blouse was untied. Her breasts, half covered by the hanging fabric, bobbed and swayed. They stopped moving a moment after she did. Smirking at Hank, she shook her head.

As Brad came up behind her, she fastened a button at her waist, then a second one a few inches higher.

Hank lowered the arm that was wrapped around Chris. She kissed his cheek, then turned around. Hank could still feel the warmth her body had left on him. Too quickly, the cold seeped in.

'How are you doing?' Brad asked.

'Better.'

'You sounded terrible back there.'

'Well, it's not so bad now.' But it seemed to be getting worse now that Chris was no longer holding him.

'Good.' Brad's head tipped back and swivelled. 'This is incredible,' he said. 'You realize, we're the first people to set foot in here since . . .'

'1923,' Lynn supplied, and looked pleased with herself.

'Man,' Brad went on. 'Just think of it. It's awe-inspiring. I've been hearing about this end of the cave all my life. To think that nobody but us . . . *nobody* . . . has set foot in here during all that time. Hell, my grandfather was a *kid* in 1923. Incredible.'

'Incredibly creepy is what it is,' Lynn said. She looked around. Her lip was curled up. 'I mean, this is where Elizabeth Mordock bit the big one.'

Chris, who'd stepped around behind Hank while the others were talking, took hold of his left hand. The tightness in his chest eased slightly. He looked at her and smiled.

He gulped a few quick breaths, then said, 'We might as well get going.'

She kept her grip on his hand as they turned around.

'Up the middle of the stream?' Chris asked.

'The River Styx,' Lynn informed them.

Scanning the lighted area in front of him, Hank saw that the stream itself was lower than its banks and free of obstructions. All the stalagmites and columns and other rock formations, which seemed to surround him, were actually off to the sides of the narrow waterway.

'It'll be a lot easier if we stick to the stream,' he said, and began walking, Chris at his side.

'I wouldn't mind getting my feet out of the water,' Lynn said. The beam of her flashlight poked in among the cones and pillars on the high ground to the right. Hank glimpsed the far wall of the cave, probably thirty feet beyond the shore of the stream. Lynn's light swept to the other side. More of the same. 'Forget it,' she muttered.

Prefers wet feet, Hank thought, to climbing around in all those shadows.

Can't blame her.

'Creepy as shit,' she said.

'I'd thought you might be used to the cavern,' Brad told her.

'Yeah, right. The *lighted* side. Where there's for christsake a *sidewalk*. And where there isn't any goddamn *stiff*.'

'I don't think we'll run into the stiff,' Brad said. 'It's supposed to be at the bottom of a chasm.'

'Yeah, well, it's here just the same. I don't have to *see* it to know it's here.' She splashed up behind Hank, appeared at his side, and wrapped her fingers around his upper arm. The arm carrying the lantern.

'I need this for myself,' he said.

'Sure.' She let go, but stayed beside him.

The stream was really too narrow, Hank soon realized, for the three of them to walk side by side. Though Lynn often nudged him, he refused to give ground and force Chris over. Let Lynn be the one crowded against the bank. Maybe she'll get tired of it.

When they came to a thick truck of rock on the stream's edge, Lynn turned sideways to squeeze by. Her backpack hissed against it. Her left breast rubbed against Hank's upper arm. 'Excuse me,' she said, and edged out in front of him. The rubbing had brushed the blouse off her breast. Her nipple, jutting out like a fingertip, nearly touched the lantern's glass chimney. Hank quickly swung the lantern out of her way, though it crossed his mind that he might've let her get burnt as a lesson.

Saying 'Woops,' she covered herself.

'Maybe you should stay up in front of us,' Hank said. 'Or go back with Brad.'

'Yeah,' came Brad's voice. 'I'm all alone.'

'Too bad, so sad.' Sidestepping, she grinned at Hank. Her pack hit another stalagmite. Yelping, she twisted around and flopped facedown into the water.

Chris groaned. Brad started to laugh.

Hank, pleased but worried, said, 'Are you okay?'

Gasping, 'Oh shit, shit, *shit*!' she pushed herself up to her hands and knees. Chris hurried forward, clutched her arm, and helped her up. 'God *damn*!'

Lynn turned around. Hunching over and shivering, she looked down at herself and shook her head.

'Did you hurt yourself?' Chris asked.

'Yes! No.' With a whine in her voice, she added, 'Shit, I'm soaked.'

Her dark hair was matted across her forehead. Her

face dripped. Her blouse was dark and clinging to her chest and belly. The front of her pants hugged her legs.

'Let me carry the backpack,' Chris offered. She held it while Lynn squirmed out of the straps.

Brad came forward and stopped beside Hank. He was still chuckling. 'Fall down go boom?' he asked.

'Eat my shorts.' She plucked the blouse away from her skin as if its touch were repulsive. Then she opened the two lower buttons and took it off.

Brad whistled.

'You don't have to watch,' she said. She used the dry back of her blouse to wipe her face, her arms, her chest and large pale breasts, her belly and sides.

Though Hank watched, the sight of her stirred no desire. She had a fine body, he couldn't deny that. But he felt embarrassed that she had stripped like this in front of Chris. He was annoyed, too. Her fooling around, acting the tease, had led to an accident that might've been serious, an accident that *was* delaying their progress through the cavern, postponing the moment when he would reach Paula.

'Hold this,' Lynn said, and handed her blouse to Chris. Making no attempt to cover herself, she staggered toward Hank. 'The lantern,' she muttered. Hank was holding it down at his side. He raised it as she approached with outstretched arms.

'Careful,' he warned her.

She stepped close to it, and looked as if she might hug the glowing lamp to her chest. She sighed. 'Ah. Ah, that feels good.' Her head tipped back. She shut her eyes. Her mouth hung open. She might have been standing under a shower, luxuriating in its hot spray. She took long, deep breaths. She began to rub her breasts.

'For the love of Christ,' Hank snapped.

Her eyes shot open.

'Put on your jacket and let's get going.'

She gave him a hurt look. 'I was just trying to get warm.'

'You're getting me downright hot,' Brad said.

She scowled at Brad, then pulled apart the sleeves of the jacket tied at her waist. Backing away from the lantern, she put the jacket on. She tugged its zipper up to her throat and said to Hank, 'There, are you happy now?'

'Can we go?'

Chris, coming up behind the girl, met Hank's eyes. She shook her head, grinned, and tapped Lynn on the shoulder.

Lynn took the wet blouse from her. 'What are you smiling about? You think this is real funny?'

'I'm just happy for your boobs,' Chris said. 'I'm sure they're a lot warmer now.'

'Hardy har.' Lynn tied the sleeves of the blouse at her waist. 'You're a real laugh riot. I don't know what I'm doing here anyway.'

'You don't have to stay,' Chris told her.

'Oh, you'd like that, wouldn't you.'

'You're holding us up,' Hank said.

'I *fell*! Or doesn't that mean anything to you?'

'I'm sorry you fell, but . . .'

'Do *you* want me to leave?'

Here's my big chance, Hank thought. Say yes, and she'll probably go.

To his amazement, he realized that he felt sorry for her. She was somehow like a kid, a troublesome brat, but a brat who was starved for attention, approval, even love.

Don't go soft, he told himself. She's a pain in the ass,

and this won't be the end of it unless you get rid of her.

'Well?' she asked. 'Just say the word, and I'm out of here.'

'I don't know. Will you behave?'

'Behave? Are you shitting me? You sound like my old man.'

'I believe,' Brad explained, 'that Hank is asking you to stop acting like a bitch in heat.'

'Spare me, huh?'

Chris put a hand on Lynn's shoulder. 'You don't want to go back alone,' she said.

Lynn stared at her. No smart remark came out.

'Let's get moving,' Hank said. 'Take the lantern, Lynn. You can lead the way, and the thing'll help warm you up.'

Nodding, she took the lantern from him. She turned around and began walking upstream, her shoes making soft splashes. Brad followed, the pickaxe resting on one shoulder. Chris put her hand in Hank's. They walked up the stream behind Brad.

They were in shadows. Though Hank could see the brightness ahead, the dark seemed to be pressing in on him. Sometimes, when Lynn passed a bend in the stream and high rocks blocked the light, he felt the cavern shrinking. His heart hammered. He struggled to breathe. When the brightness bloomed ahead of him again, the pressure receded slightly.

He wished he hadn't given the lantern to Lynn.

At least she's out of our hair, now, he told himself. Then he realized her annoying antics had been such a distraction that, for a while, he'd forgotten he was in the cave.

I ought to thank her, he thought.

Ought to hurry on ahead and catch up with the little twit and encourage her to start flaunting herself again.

'Do you smell that?' Chris whispered.

He sniffed the dank air. Though he'd been inhaling it, often frantically, from the moment he crawled into the cave, he hadn't given any thought to its smell. Now, he did. And detected faint odours he hadn't noticed before. 'My God,' he muttered.

'It smells like . . . faeces. And rotten meat.'

'Must be . . .' He fought for breath. 'Animals. Must live in here. And die.'

The hooch was suddenly on top of him, crushing him. Not just the hooch, but his gunner, Willy Jones. Blackness. A stench of shit. He knew Willy was hurt, felt the blood running all over him. It didn't take long to realize Willy was dead. But he couldn't move, couldn't get out of the blackness, couldn't get out from under the body. Which started to rot.

'Hank? Hank!'

Chris was in front of him, shaking him, then clutching him tight to her body as he shuddered and wheezed.

Light came. As he began to recover, he saw Brad and Lynn in front of him, staring with alarm.

'I'm okay,' he gasped.

'You're in no shape to go on with this,' Brad said.

'Maybe we'd better all turn back,' said Lynn.

'No. Got to . . .'

'It's all right,' Chris whispered close to his ear. 'You're all right, now.'

'What set him off?' Brad asked.

'We were talking about that odd smell.'

'Yeah, what *is* that smell?' Brad asked. 'I just started noticing it, myself.'

219

'Death,' Hank muttered.

Chris rubbed his back.

'Can't be nothing dead in here,' Lynn said, sniffing the air. 'It's all closed up.'

'So what's the stink?' Brad asked her.

She shrugged. 'Does smell a little like shit, I guess. But that's impossible.'

'Not just shit,' Brad said. 'It's like there's a rotting carcass.'

'Elizabeth Mordock? Maybe we're close to that chasm.' Lynn, still sniffing, started to look around as if searching for it.

'She's been dead sixty years,' Brad said. 'She's got to be nothing but bones by now.'

'Maybe we'd *better* get out of here.'

Brad looked at Hank. 'You going to flip out again?'

Flip out.

Hey, this guy's flipped out.

Well fuck, wouldn't you?

That's what they'd said, the Marines who pulled him out. Pulled him out after an eternity that had actually lasted three days – the time it took to recapture the base camp after it had been shelled by the NVA and over-run.

'I didn't flip out.' Hank told Brad. 'You don't know what the fuck flipping out is.'

He felt Chris go rigid, as if shocked to hear the hard words spew out. He stroked her hair. Some of the tension went out of her body. She ran her hands down to his hips. 'You okay?' she asked.

He nodded. 'Let's keep going.'

They parted, and he saw Lynn shaking her head. 'Not me. No way. This is getting too damn weird. I mean, you're throwing fits and . . . and it *doesn't* smell right in here. It didn't smell like this before, and that means something's up ahead and I mean it must be dead and stinking, whatever it is, and I don't want to find out. No thanks. It's not like they even *need* to get rescued. If you don't get to them, they're just gonna get taken up in the elevator shafts so what's the point anyway? It's stupid. So from here on, you can just count me out.' She thrust the lantern toward Hank. He took its wire handle. 'Adios.' She turned her flashlight on, and step-ped forward as if to pass between Hank and Chris.

'Wait,' Hank said.

'You're not going to talk me out of it, this time. Huh-uh. I'm getting bad vibes about this place, *real* bad. So you guys enjoy yourselves.'

'Hold on. Chris, maybe you'd better go with her. Brad and I can go on ahead, if he's still willing.'

Brad nodded.

'I'm not leaving,' Chris said.

'I don't need an escort,' Lynn said. 'I'm a big girl.'

'I'm staying with you, Hank.'

'Something's very wrong about all this,' he told her.

'I know.'

'This part of the cave is supposed to be closed up. Isn't it, Lynn?'

'It was till we knocked through the wall.'

'No other way in or out?'

'Not supposed to be.'

'Well, something has been decomposing in here.'

'And taking dumps,' Lynn added.

'It's turning nasty,' he said to Chris. 'I've got . . . bad feelings, myself.'

'Well, I'm going with you.'

'Bye.' Lynn stepped between them and started to run.

Looking over his shoulder, Hank saw her dashing down the middle of the stream, the beam of her flashlight jumping around the rocks. Then she disappeared around a bend. The sound of her splashes faded.

'Let's stick close together,' Hank said.

Holding the lantern out ahead of him, very aware of Chris gripping his other hand, he started walking. Brad stayed close behind them.

Though Hank still had some trouble breathing, he felt as if all his senses had been put on alert.

There was danger here.

Danger that he could feel, that he could smell in the subtle foulness of the air.

The cave no longer squeezed him. He wasn't in a cave, he was in the jungle, on patrol. He didn't know what to expect, so he expected anything.

And therefore he didn't gasp, didn't even flinch, at the sight that made Chris suck in a harsh breath and hurl herself against him and clutch him like a thrown cat.

Brad came up beside them, took a step ahead of them. He brought the pickaxe down, holding it level with his chest as if prepared to use it as a weapon. Turning slowly, he looked from side to side. 'Jesus,' he muttered. Hank heard *him* labouring for breath. Then the big man doubled over and vomited.

A stalagmite to the right of the stream had been clothed in a transparent pink nightgown. Arms of bone hung from the sleeve holes. A gleaming white skull was perched on the blunt top of the effigy. The bodice of the nightgown bulged, but not with breasts. Through the sheer fabric, Hank saw a pair of fleshless heads. Someone had stuffed small, human skulls into the gown. Infant skulls.

Chris shook and whimpered against him. He stroked her back with his free hand. Bart was still hunched over, heaving.

Near the effigy, on a lower clump of rock draped with glossy green satin, was a ribcage. A skull inside it seemed to be peering out through bars.

He saw a pelvis beside it with skeleton fingers reaching through its cavity.

He saw fleshless legs, apparently standing on their own, joined at the top to a gape-mouthed skull.

Hank had seen carnage before. He'd seen hideous desecration of corpses. But never anything done with such perverse artistry – the creations of a mad sculptor.

And we're in his gallery, Hank thought.

The glow of the hissing lantern revealed more than a dozen samples of the maniac's work.

And one sculpture, to the left of the stream, far worse than the others.

It wasn't bare bones.

This is the sight, Hank suspected, that had turned Brad's stomach.

A woman. Young. Lashed to a column by a belt around her throat so she appeared to be standing. Long brown hair, neatly brushed, hung to her shoulders. From the look of her face, she'd been beaten, maybe before her death. The body had no arms, no breasts. Most of the skin, from the neck down, was gone. Her torso appeared to have been hollowed out.

She wore blue jeans. From the way they sagged, there was little left of her legs except bones. But the bare feet were intact.

Something about the feet.

Hank realized that they were on the wrong sides of her body. Her legs had been reversed.

'I don't believe this,' Brad muttered. He was facing Hank, but still bent over slightly. 'I don't believe this,' he said again. 'It's . . . it's . . .' He shook his head and squeezed his eyes shut.

'I bet,' Hank said, 'it's Amy Lawson.'

16

The chewing went on. There were sighs, moans, sounds of tearing flesh, crackling gristle. Sometimes, Darcy heard small splashes as if inedible pieces had been tossed into the lake. She wanted to duck below the surface to stop herself from hearing the horrid feast, but she didn't dare move. She stood in the black, hugging Greg and Carol, waiting.

Then came whispers.

'Take her back?'

'Get the others. Take 'em all back. Save 'em up.'

'We don't have to go back.' The woman's voice. The one who had known about the dock and tour boats and elevators. 'We're free. We can get out, maybe.'

'Topside?'

'Yeah, topside.'

'No topside.'

'Where're your balls?'

A sharp smack. The woman gasped.

'Coward,' she said in a shaky voice. 'You're afraid of the Mordock.'

'I fear no one.'

'Then come with me. We'll leave the world. We'll kill the Mordock and live in the sun. It's wonderful up there, you'll see. But we've got to go now. We've killed topside people, and they'll hunt us with guns if we don't get out now.'

There was silence for a few moments. Then the man spoke. 'We go. We kill the others. We take them back to the world, save them up.'

'But you don't under . . .'

Another blow. This one didn't sound like a slap; it might have been a fist striking her face. She grunted. A moment later came a thud as if her head had struck the flooring of the dock. She moaned for a few moments, then squealed from a new silent hurt, and started to whimper. Squealed again. Gasped. 'No, don't. Please. I'm sorry.'

'We go,' the man said.

Darcy heard sounds of movement, then footsteps that passed directly over her head and kept going. The woman still whimpered.

'Lana.'

Moaning, she began to move. There were rubbing sounds, creaking wood, soft bumps. Darcy pictured her rolling over and getting to her knees. Then the woman was up and walking.

Darcy listened to the footfalls on the planking. Soon, she could no longer hear them.

My God, she thought, they've actually left. They're on the walkway now, heading away.

Carol, who had been rigid in Darcy's arms, began to shake and sob. Darcy stroked her hair. She felt Greg's arm loosen its clamp across her back.

'Okay,' he whispered. 'We're all right.'

'Was that Helen?' Carol asked, her voice quiet and trembling. 'Do you . . . think that was Helen?'

'I think so,' Darcy said. 'It could've been Beth, but I don't . . .'

'They ate her. They ate her, didn't they?'

'That's what it sounded like,' Greg admitted.

'Eeeeeeeeee.'

'Carol, stop it.' Darcy shook her.

'Eeeeeee.'

Darcy pinched the ridge of her ear.

She gasped and stopped making that crazed sound.

'Greg, what'll we . . ?'

'She was such a prude,' Carol said. 'Frigid, you know? Wouldn't have anything to do with men. They stripped her. Did you hear them strip her? Boy, would she be pissed. Her stepfather used to fuck her, that's why.' Carol's voice came out in a breathy rush. She sounded as eager as a town gossip. 'Hated men. Thought I was dirty 'cause I liked 'em. Not that I was promiscuous or anything, God knows, but all the time she was warning me, you know? Don't let 'em touch you. Don't let 'em touch you. Boy, she sure got touched. Did you hear them strip her? I bet she didn't like that, not one little bit.'

'Carol.'

'Such a prude. Always changed in the bathroom, you know? And I'd go to change and she'd go away. Like it was a big sin, you know, to take off your clothes? God, and they just stripped her naked, didn't they. Tore her clothes right off.' Carol began to squirm, rubbing her pelvis and breasts against Darcy. 'Bet they felt her up, too. Touched her all over. Didn't fuck her, though, did they. Didn't sound like it. They could've, could've all taken turns, you know, and really . . .'

Darcy thrust the clinging, writhing woman away from

her body and pressed her shoulders down, submerging her for a few seconds. Carol came up coughing, and began to weep.

'I'm sorry. God. I'm . . .'

'Calm down, okay?' Darcy said. 'And be quiet.'

'They ate her. They ate *Helen*.'

'Shhh.'

'What're we gonna *do*?'

'We'd better not stay here,' Greg said, sounding calm. 'They'll probably come back.'

'Oh God.'

'The way they headed,' Darcy said, 'they'll run into the others.'

'Then they'll probably turn back.'

'Do you think so?'

'They aren't about to go up against a group like that. They're only – what, four of them?'

'I'm not sure,' Darcy said. 'Four or five, I think.'

'They wouldn't go up against thirty.'

'I don't know. God knows what they'd do. They might try. If it's dark when they get there, they might try anything. If the fires are out, they could sneak right in. Nobody'd even know what was going on.'

'So what do you want to do?'

'I'm responsible for those people, Greg. I've already lost three, and . . .'

'It's not your fault.'

'If we hadn't tried to go through . . .'

'It's not your fault.'

'I don't want any more to die. We have to do something.'

'Okay.'

'Go after them?'

'No!' Carol cried.

'I guess we'd better. But not . . .'

'No, please! They'll eat us!'

'Wait here,' Greg said.

'What?'

'I'll get the pickaxe. If we catch up to those bastards, I want to have something to use on them.'

'Can you find it in the dark?'

'I hope so. It was right at the wall before the shit hit the fan.'

'Okay. But hurry.'

He let go of Darcy and brushed against her back.

'Don't leave us,' Carol begged.

'It's all right,' Darcy told her. 'He won't be gone long.'

'What if they come back?'

'We'll just be real quiet.' She turned her head toward the sloshing sounds of Greg's movements. 'Be careful.'

There was a quiet slurp, then silence. Darcy guessed that Greg had gone down to pass under the boat. Moments later, she heard him come up. From the quick noisy splashes, she guessed that he was swimming.

'He'll be back pretty soon.'

Darcy felt Carol embrace her. Remembering the way the woman had squirmed against her earlier, she was tempted to push her away. But there was no hint of erotic frenzy this time. Carol simply hugged her like a terrified child. So Darcy held her and listened to Greg splashing through the lake.

If he finds the pickaxe, she thought, he won't be able to swim back with it. He'll have to wade. That would take a while.

The longer it takes, the less chance of catching up

with those savages. They already had a headstart.

Better if we don't.

She felt a stir of guilt. There were kids among the tourists. The little girl, the fat boy, Paula, the son of that creep in the trucker hat. Kyle.

Big loss if they nail Kyle.

That pregnant woman.

Quite a few men, though. Maybe the men would be able to handle the situation. But if the elevator fires are out . . .

Confusion. Nobody knowing what's going on, who to fight. There could be a slaughter in the darkness.

I don't have to wait for Greg, she thought. I could go on ahead and try to warn them.

She imagined herself being grabbed along the walkway, thrown down. She felt hands ripping at her clothes. *Tore her clothes right off . . . Touched her all over*. Felt the hands on her bare skin. Coming from every direction. Clutching, probing. Fingernails digging in. Then teeth. Teeth sinking into her arms and thighs and belly and breasts. Felt them tugging ripping. Heard the wet sounds of chewing.

It happened to Helen, it could happen to me.

Go off by myself, try to warn them, it really might happen.

You owe them a try.

Not my life. God, no.

Enough of a try, waiting for Greg and going after them with the pick. We'd stand a chance that way. Won't help anyone if I run on ahead and get nailed.

'Ugh!' The splashing stopped.

Carol stiffened.

Darcy wanted to call out, but she feared that she

might be heard by the savages. No telling how far they'd gone, and sounds could carry a long way in the cavern.

Then she heard Greg resume swimming.

Maybe he'd run into a body, she thought. A nasty surprise like that could've made him gasp and stop short.

Three bodies in the lake. Maybe. The woman who threw herself at Darcy, the guy who killed Beth, and Beth. All floating around near Ely's Wall.

'He must be just about there,' Darcy whispered.

She felt Carol nod, the woman's face sliding against her cheek.

The sounds of the swimming stopped.

Carol, tight against Darcy, rammed her backwards, breath exploding out, fingers digging into her back. Darcy felt a hot stab. She went down, Carol on top of her, pinned to her. Darcy jammed a hand between their bodies. Felt the slick shaft joining them: it jutted out of Carol and entered Darcy just below her ribcage on the right. As she clutched it, the shaft was driven forward. It started to penetrate deeper. She twisted away, shoving at Carol, and felt the point rip free of its hole and skid across her skin.

Then she was clear. She rolled and rolled through the water, trying to put distance between herself and the attacker.

She burned where the point had entered her. It hadn't gone in very deep, she thought, or it wouldn't have pulled out so easily. Half an inch, maybe less.

A bone weapon like the other guy had used on Beth?

Must've speared Carol through the back.

Darcy's side bumped a wall. Rolling, she pressed herself to the rocks and held herself motionless. Currents stirred against her. She heard splashing nearby, and wondered if the attacker was still with Carol. She needed air. Hoping the sounds of the turmoil would cover any sounds she might make, she eased herself upward until her head broke the surface.

As she took a shallow breath, she heard splashing nearby. Harsh breathing. Grunting sounds. The savage still wasn't approaching her.

More splashing in the distance. Those sounds had to come from Greg. He knew there was trouble, was swimming back.

A sigh under the dock. Then quiet sloshing.

He's coming for me.

Darcy held her breath.

If he can't hear me, he can't find me.

Her heart thudded. Her wound pulsed fire.

He seemed to be heading straight for her.

Maybe he hears my heart.

Smells my blood.

Pressed flat against the wall, she felt the flashlight pushing into her side. Greg, she remembered, had slipped it into the pocket of her windbreaker. She eased it out.

What now? she wondered.

Whirl around and try to bash him with it?

If he's got that pointed bone . . .

Darcy still didn't know what to do, but the wading sounds were little more than a yard behind her, now, she let herself drift backward away from the wall, then brought the flashlight out of the water.

Toss it over to the side, the way guys always did in the movies to mislead the bad guys?

That's the movies.

Might work, though. Might make him think I'm over there.

Not gonna stake my life on a goddamn movie trick.

Darcy spun around, jumped, felt herself rise out of the water to the waist, tucked her chin down hoping her head wouldn't hit the underside of the dock, heard herself growl like a furious dog, and threw the flashlight straight ahead with all her strength. The sound of the impact would've come at once if she'd been on target. It didn't. She twisted her body. As she splashed onto her side, she heard a ringing clamour and realized the flashlight must've struck the side of the moored boat.

Going down, she kicked her way toward the bottom, stroked once hard, then let herself glide forward hoping she was off to his side, hoping to slip past him before he had time to react.

An explosive splash. Something rammed between her legs, searing an inner thigh. She clamped her legs together. Trapped it. Crossed her ankles. Twisted. Felt an instant of resistance. Then it was loose and the momentum of her turn rolled her over. She reached down. Grabbed the pointed end of the bone as her face came out of the water.

She sucked air.

She got her other hand on the shaft.

Then lost hold as her forearm was yanked. She kicked and writhed as the attacker tugged her to him. He jerked her upright. She felt his breath on her face, smelled its fetid stench. She drove a knee up. It struck him, but the blow seemed to have no effect. He clutched the front of her jacket. His other hand hooked her groin. He grunted, and Darcy was hurled upward. The top of her head slammed the floorboards of the dock.

Pain burst through her. She saw bright flashes. Heard ringing in her ears. Smelled the odd, metallic odour she vaguely remembered from times she had bumped her head at the ice skating rink.

Greg, she thought, Maybe Greg . . .

Through her daze, she realized she was soaring again toward the underside of the dock. She flung her arms up. Her fists were battered between her skull and the planks.

He lowered her again.

Darcy opened her numb fingers. Reached out. Grabbed hair. Pulled and drove her head forward. Her wide open mouth found flesh. She bit. Her teeth sank in, and the man bellowed. She bit down as hard as she could. Something came off in her mouth. His nose? He was yelling, staggering backward, still clutching her jacket and crotch. She spit the flesh out.

They both went down.

Darcy squirmed lower, tearing at his hair, forcing his head back. Her mouth found the side of his neck. She burrowed in, biting and ripping, and suddenly felt as if a garden hose had been thrust into her mouth, hot water gushing from its nozzle.

Got him, she thought.

Took out the carotid.

Jesus.

His clutching hands jerked against her, fluttered away.

She shut her mouth, but didn't release him. Still clinging to his hair, she wrapped her legs around him. Together, Darcy and the savage rolled slowly beneath the surface of the lake. She felt his body jump with spastic shudders, felt the warm current throbbing against her face. She needed air. Her lungs ached. But she stayed with him until he went limp.

Then she shoved him away and stood up, gasping.

She heard splashes nearby.

'Greg?'

The splashing stopped. 'Darcy? My God, what's going on?'

'Nothing. Anymore.'

'Are you okay?'

'Not exactly.'

'Oh God. What happened?' From the quiet sloshing sounds, he was wading toward her.

'He got Carol.'

'Oh, no.'

'He . . . stayed behind, I guess. Waited till you were far enough away. Then he . . . I think Carol's dead. Carol?' she called.

No answer. She hadn't expected one.

'What happened to him? Where is he?'

'Around here someplace. Belly up.'

'You killed him?'

'Yeah.'

'I shouldn't have left you two. I shouldn't . . .'

Darcy reached out and touched Greg. He moved in against her. His arms went around her. She squeezed herself tight against him and winced at the pressure against the wound below her ribs.

'Did he hurt you?'

'Here and there. I got . . . poked a couple of times.'

'Stabbed?'

'He had one of those pointed bones. Like the guy who got Beth.'

'Oh Christ. Where'd he get you?'

'It's no big deal,' she said. Her thigh wound didn't hurt much. It felt as if a path had been scraped along her skin. The other wound hurt plenty. It might have had a hot coal stuffed inside it. Her head had a dull ache from striking the dock.

'We'd better get out,' Greg said, 'and patch you up.'

Darcy shook her head. 'We've gotta get moving. Those others . . . they'll reach the group.'

'I didn't bring the pickaxe. I found it, had it in my hands. Then I heard something going on over here. All I could think about was getting to you as fast as I could.'

'As cavalry charging to the rescue,' Darcy said. 'you leave a lot to be desired.'

He laughed softly, then kissed her mouth. 'Thank God you're all right.'

'To the extent that I am.' She eased away from Greg. 'I'll find his weapon. It's down around here someplace.' Holding onto him with one hand, she lifted each of her feet and pulled her shoes off. She gave them to Greg. Then she wandered slowly, searching along the bottom with her feet. She felt sand and gravel through her socks. Stones, slabs of rock.

She heard Greg moving around nearby, and guessed that he had joined in the search.

'A femur?' he asked.

'I didn't see it, but I think so. It was long enough to go through Carol and stab me.'

One of her feet snagged something soft that wrapped around it. Raising her knee, she untangled her foot. The thing was fabric. She explored it with her hands, and moaned.

'What?'

'Carol's dress.' She remembered the splashing she'd heard just after the attack and before the savage came for her. The grunts and hard breathing. He'd stripped the sundress off Carol. What else had he done to her?

'God,' Darcy muttered, and hurled the dress away.

'Maybe we'd better give it . . .' His words broke off with a gasp.

'What?'

'Another . . .' Slurps of water. 'Found your . . . *Jesus!*'

'What is it?'

'His face, it's . . .'

'Yeah.'

'You did that?'

Darcy felt heat rush to her face as if Greg had discovered a nasty secret about her. 'He was trying to kill me,' she said.

'You really . . .'

'Would you stop fooling with him?'

'Sorry. I didn't mean to . . .'

'Just stop, okay?'

'I want to see if he's got anything that might . . . Yeeuh.'

'If that's his throat . . .'

'No.'

'I tore it out, that's what I did. What was I supposed to do?'

'Hey, it's okay. I'm not . . . you did great. I'm just glad you were able to do it.'

'Then it'd be nice if you'd quit going yick and yuck.'

'I got a handful of the guy's dick.'

'What?'

'I was trying to check his pockets. Hasn't got any.'

'He's not wearing pants?'

'Or anything else.'

'God.'

Shouldn't come as any red-hot surprise, she told herself. Not after finding Carol's dress.

He probably stripped off his clothes before he even attacked.

Naked the whole time because he knew he was going after two women.

Naked when he got Carol, naked when he grabbed Darcy and smashed her head against the dock, when she bit his face and neck, when she straddled him and wrapped her legs around him, when he jerked against her in his death throes.

Standing rigid in the water, she wrapped her arms across her breasts and squeezed her legs together tight.

She heard Greg sloshing around nearby, heard his breathing.

She knew she should keep looking for the weapon, but she couldn't force herself to move.

'I think I've found it,' Greg whispered. A moment later, he said, 'Yeah, here it is. Christ, it's a bone, all right. Ball joint at one end. The other end feels like it's been broken off. Pretty sharp. Darcy?' He waded closer. 'Darcy, you okay?'

She shook her head.

'Darcy?'

'I want it to go away.' Her voice sounded strange to her – high and pinched. 'Greg? I can't . . . It's . . . I want it to go away. I want it all to go away.'

17

'Lucky Lynn,' Brad said. 'She got to miss all this.'

'Never seen anything like it,' Hank muttered.

Chris eased away from him, but kept a hand on his arm and stared at his chest. 'Let's get out of here,' she said.

'I'm with you,' Brad told her. He was standing close behind Chris, but she didn't turn around to look at him. If she did that, she would see the sculptures of bone, the ravaged remains of the woman. 'Seemed like a good idea, going through this end, but . . . this is bad shit. We'd be nuts to go on.'

'I didn't mean leave,' Chris said, keeping her eyes on the front of Hank's warm-up jacket. 'I want to keep going, get away from . . . If it stops. Maybe it doesn't stop, but . . .'

'You're kidding, right?'

'I want to get to Ely's Wall.'

'Hank?'

'I'm not turning back. I don't know what's going on down here, but my kid's on the other side.'

'Yeah, okay, but what's on *this* side? That's what I want to know – what I *don't* want to know. I mean, some kind of maniac's been messing around down here.

I don't want to meet him. Hugh-uh. We're talking real sicko. This isn't something you fuck with. You want to end up like these poor stiffs, some kind of cave decorations? Not me.'

'Well, leave me the pickaxe,' Hank said.

'Are you out of your mind? Do you want to get yourself killed? Want to get Chris killed? Come on, man! What about Chris? She won't go on without you.'

'You should go back with Brad,' Hank said. 'He's right. I can go ahead and get to the girls. It doesn't have to be both of us.'

'I'm going with you,' Chris told him. 'And I think we should stop talking about it and get moving.'

'What if I turn back?'

'You won't. But if you do, I'll go on without you.'

'She wouldn't be able to break through the wall by herself,' Brad said.

'Don't count on it,' Chris told him.

'Okay. Well, I'm not going to stand here and argue. You two want to be heroes, fine.'

Chris took the Coleman lantern from Hank. Brad handed the pickaxe to him. 'I'll be waiting outside. Good luck.' He gave Chris's arm a brief squeeze as he stepped past her. She watched him over Hank's shoulder. He was only visible for a moment before vanishing around a bend in the stream. The splashing sounds of his footfalls faded.

'You're sure about this?' Hank asked.

She looked into his eyes, and nodded.

Hank smiled. 'More guts than brains.'

'Goes for both of us.'

Hank lifted the pickaxe. He held it in front of his chest with both hands – as if it were a rifle, Chris thought.

She lowered her gaze to the water in front of her feet, and turned around.

It wasn't good enough. Her peripheral vision picked up the grim sentinals on either side of the stream.

She walked fast. Hank stayed at her side.

'Christ,' Hank muttered. 'They go on.'

She could see that. But the horrors weren't distinct, just vague shapes at the edges of her view.

'Like running a goddamn gauntlet,' Hank said.

'Who could've done this?'

'Nobody in his right mind.'

'Do you think he knows we're here?'

'If he's here, he probably knows. I'm sure he would've heard us pounding to break out the wall. But I can't imagine . . . Nobody could *live* in here. There's got to be a hidden entrance. Whoever it is, he probably brings his victims in, does his thing, and leaves.'

'Ethan Mordock?' Chris said.

'My God, of course. If that . . . mess back there was Amy Lawson . . .'

'Even if it wasn't. Mordock owned the hotel, the cavern. He had access – not just to the cavern, but to guests at his hotel. And its pretty obvious he was involved in making Amy Lawson disappear.'

'The guests check in,' Hank said, 'but they don't check out. Some of them, anyway.'

'Probably young women who check in alone. And they wind up down here.'

'Could've been going on for years.'

'And Mordock's dead!' Chris clutched Hank's arm and turned her face to him. She saw the same knowledge and relief that he was probably seeing in her eyes. And beyond his head, a fleshless skull wearing a green pillbox hat with a ragged red feather.

She winced and lowered her gaze.

They started walking again.

'If it was Mordock,' Hank said, 'we don't have to worry about getting jumped by some lunatic.'

'Thank God. It's bad enough without that.'

'We'd figured it out a little sooner, Brad might've stuck.'

'Who needs him,' Chris said.

They rounded a bend in the stream.

'Mordock was creepy,' she said. 'I could tell, just the way he'd look at me and Darcy, that he wasn't right. But . . . God, I never would've guessed he'd be capable of this kind of madness. It's hard to imagine *anyone* taking bodies and . . .'

'Speaking of which, I don't see any around. I think we left them behind.'

Chris looked up. The pale glow of the lantern revealed a forest of stalagmites and columns on either side of the stream. Rock, clean and glistening, bare of body parts. She sniffed. The foul odours remained, but seemed less oppressive than before. 'Situation's improving,' she said.

'I think we'll have to reach the wall before long. Which brings up another matter. I'm starting to wonder if we should bring the people out this way.'

Chris had seen them lined up to wait for Darcy's tour to begin. She remembered there had been women, several children. 'There were kids,' she said.

'Mine's one of them. I don't want her to see Mordock's handiwork. My God. She can be a pretty gutsy kid, but I wouldn't wish that on anyone. She'd be seeing it the rest of her life.'

'I don't want to see that stuff again, myself.'

'We'd better figure something else.'

'Once we get to them, maybe it won't matter getting them out right away. I mean, the main thing is to get to Darcy and Paula. Once we're with them and know they're all right, maybe we can just wait along with them.'

'Yeah. The fire department'll get everyone out sooner or later.'

'I wouldn't care even if it took a day or two, as long as I'm with Darcy.'

'And we've got the candy bars,' Hank reminded her.

'Yeah. Nobody'll starve.'

Chris suddenly felt as if an awful weight had been lifted.

There was no longer the prospect of the return trip.

She and Hank would stay on the good side of the cavern with their children and the tourists, and eventually be hoisted up the elevator shafts by the fire department or some other rescue agency. She would not have to walk again among Mordock's dead.

'Maybe we can find the other opening,' Hank said. 'The one Mordock used.'

Her relief started to fade.

'I don't want to go exploring, do you?'

'Well . . .'

'I think we should just join up with the others and . . .'

'What's that?' Hank nodded to his right.

Chris wasn't sure she wanted to look.

'Over there by that big clump of rock.'

He sounded curious, not disgusted or wary, so Chris looked. Running along the floor of the cave, almost beyond the glow of the lantern, was a slot of darkness that appeared to run parallel to the stream.

'A crevasse?' Chris asked. 'Maybe it's that chasm Elizabeth Mordock fell into.'

'Want to take a look?'

'No. Let's just keep moving, okay?'

'Maybe the hidden entrance . . .'

'One of us might fall. Besides, I don't care about any hidden entrance. If I see daylight, *then* I'll care. Otherwise, let's not take any detours, okay?'

'I suppose you're right.'

They kept on walking.

'Since when did you become a cave explorer?' Chris asked. 'And what ever happened to your claustrophobia?'

'Thanks for reminding me. I'd forgotten all about it.'

'How can you *forget* to be claustrophobic?'

'I'll ask my shrink if I ever go to one.'

'You're not having any symptoms at all?'

'Very mild, maybe.'

'Must've gotten shocked out of you.'

'Could be.'

'All those awful bodies, and . . .'

She saw daylight.

'Good Lord,' she whispered.

A pale hazy glow far ahead in the blackness beyond the reach of her lantern's illumination.

'What do you know about that?' Hank muttered. 'You said if you saw daylight . . .'

'That's what I said. And I meant it. Geez, this is getting better and better.'

They continued to walk in the stream, but Chris kept her eyes on the distant light. It seemed to fill an opening about the size of a doorway in an area she guessed must be near the right-hand wall of the cavern. Sometimes, it vanished as rock forms blocked her view. Then, it would reappear and look closer then before.

She hoped the stream might lead directly to it.

But when they came abreast of the dim glow, it was still off to the right. They stopped and stared at it.

'Do you want to wait here while I check it out?' Hank asked.

'You've got to be joking.'

'Well, I'd better lead the way.' He lowered the head of the pickaxe into the water and propped its haft against the slope of the embankment.

Chris gave the lantern to him.

He climbed the bank. Chris lifted the pickaxe, swung it over one shoulder, and followed him. When he looked back, he said, 'I thought we'd leave that behind.'

'We might not want to search for it,' she told him. 'Besides . . .'

'What?'

'I just think we should hang onto it. You never know.'

'Want me to carry it?'

'*And* the lantern?'

'Well, we could trade.'

'I'd rather have you go first. I'm all right with this thing.'

Hank shrugged, and resumed walking. Chris stayed close behind him. They took a winding route, skirting rock formations that rose from the cavern floor to block their way. The area of pale light grew. Chris saw that it did come from an opening in the wall of the cavern.

Hank stopped at the opening. As he leaned forward and swung the lantern through it, Chris peered over his shoulder.

The chamber in front of them appeared to be about

twenty feet around. Its floor was heaped with clothing: dresses, blouses, sweaters, undergarments, slacks, night-gowns and robes, even a few jackets and coats. All seemed to be women's clothes. Near one wall, Darcy saw a pile of grooming articles: hair-driers, brushes and combs, curlers, tubes of toothpaste and brushes, sanitary napkins. An open suitcase to the side of the pile was filled with glittering jewellery like a pirate's treasure chest.

'Must be stuff that belonged to his victims,' Hank whispered. 'Makes sense. He'd have to do something with it. Wouldn't want those things lying around the hotel if anyone came snooping.'

He stepped into the chamber. Chris followed. Her feet sank into the heaped clothes.

The clothes of dead people.

She shivered.

Hank's head tilted back. Chris, too, looked up.

The daylight came from above, drifting down like a pale mist through a chimney-like orifice in the ceiling of the chamber. Standing directly beneath the hole, Chris couldn't see the sky. Though the tunnel obviously led to the surface, she guessed that it must curve along the way.

The ceiling of the chamber was at least twice Hank's height.

'You might get in and out this way,' he said, 'but you'd need a rope. Won't do us much good.'

'Do you think this is Mordock's secret opening?'

He shrugged. 'Could be. Maybe if he had a rope ladder.'

'Let's go back to the stream, okay? This place gives me the creeps.'

Hank said, 'Okay,' and stepped backward as if trying to get a better angle on the ceiling hole – and stumbled.

Chris gasped, fearing the lantern might ignite the thick layer of garments on the chamber floor, but Hank landed on his rump and kept the lantern high. 'You all right?' she asked.

He nodded. 'Come here.'

She waded through the clothes.

'Hold this.'

She took the lantern from him. 'What?' she asked.

'Want to see what I tripped on.' He got to his knees and began digging, flinging aside skirts, bathrobes, pantyhose.

'Maybe you'd better not,' Chris said.

He snatched up a wadded blouse, exposing a bare foot and ankle. Chris stiffened. Shivers squirmed like cold worms over her skin.

More bodies, she thought.

Bodies under us. I might be *standing* on one!

Hank touched the ankle, then jerked his hand back fast. He looked up at Chris. His eyes were wide, his mouth hanging open.

'Let's get out of here,' she whispered.

His head shook slowly from side to side, and he began to toss more clothes out of the way. He uncovered another foot. Shins. The legs of the body were side by side, but slightly apart. He exposed the knees.

'Hank. Please. I don't want to see it.'

'This one's alive,' he said.

And it bolted upright through a cascade of clothes, shrieking.

A girl with wild blonde hair. Eyes squeezed shut. Lips curled back, baring pointed teeth. Chris shouted a warning. Even as the word 'Look' burst from her throat, she saw the girl swing a white blade-studded stick at Hank's face, saw his open hand whip sideways at her face, heard a thud and a clash of slamming teeth as the edge of his hand drove beneath the girl's chin. The blow snapped her head back. The scream stopped. Chris's voice, yelling 'Out!' resounded through the silence. She finished her warning while the girl flopped towards the mat of clothes. Hank rammed an open hand against the girl's chest and jerked his other arm up close to his side as if about to blast his knuckles through her throat.

He didn't deliver the blow.

He knelt there, poised for it, and didn't move.

The girl lay motionless.

'Hank?'

He took a deep breath, then reached over the sprawled body and picked up the weapon. He held it up, inspecting it.

Not a stick, Chris realized. A bone. Maybe an arm bone. Its upper half bristled with razor blades that appeared to be imbedded in grooves.

Hank hurled the weapon away. It clattered against a wall of the chamber, and dropped silently onto the floor of clothes. Then, he looked down at the girl. 'What was she doing here?' he muttered. 'And with a thing like that?'

'Maybe . . .' Chris realized she was panting for air. Her heart was slamming. 'We . . . could ask her.'

Hank didn't answer. He began tossing aside more clothes to uncover the girl.

She wore a blue satin negligee with spaghetti straps. One of the straps had fallen, and the white, blue-veined mound of a breast was exposed.

The negligee was taut against her rounded belly.

'Pregnant,' Chris whispered.

The girl looked no older than fourteen or fifteen.

Chris stepped over her and lowered the lantern close to her face. Her eyes were open, but rolled up so that only the whites showed. Her mouth was shut.

Hank opened the girl's mouth and fingered down her lower lip. Her pointed teeth were scarlet with blood from her broken gums. 'Do you believe those teeth?' Hank said.

'I . . . feel like I'm going crazy.'

'We had this thing figured out wrong. There's a lot more to it than Mordock bringing his victims down here for fun and games. Those teeth . . . she's pregnant . . .'

'I don't get it.'

'Neither do I. Let's get going.'

'We can't just leave her. Shouldn't we try to wake her up and . . ?'

Hank gave the girl's chin a small push. Her head flopped toward Chris. Her ear was bathed with blood.

'What?'

'She's dead,' he explained.

Chris felt herself go numb. She heard her voice, distant and strange, say, 'No. She can't be. All you did was hit her once, and . . .'

'Sometimes, it only takes once.'

'But . . .'

'I'm sorry, Chris. I'm sorry you had to see it.' He stood up and faced her. 'She was just a kid, and pregnant, but she was coming at me with a weapon. You don't fool around when that happens. You get just as dead from a kid. Come on, let's get out of here.'

She stood there, staring down at the body.

At the girl's distended belly.

'I killed her, okay? I murdered her and her baby. Those are the breaks. She shouldn't have tried . . .' He suddenly rushed past Chris and the quickness of his movement broke through her daze of shock and regret and she wondered if he'd seen someone *else* rising out of the piled clothes. She twisted around.

Hank, near the wall, snatched up the girl's weapon. He raced back with it, kicking up blouses and skirts.

'What are you . . .?'

'Keep an eye out. God knows, there might be more of them.'

He dropped to his knees between the girl's legs. Clamping the bone in his teeth, he gripped the hem of the negligee and tugged. The fabric split up the middle, baring the dead girl's pubis and belly.

'What are you *doing*?'

He took the bone from his teeth. As he plucked out one of the razor blades, he muttered, 'I don't *know* what I'm doing.' Then he slashed the girl open. Coils of guts spilled out, steaming as they met the chilly air. Hank lifted them out in heaps and dumped them aside.

Chris staggered backward. The pickaxe fell off her shoulder.

She knew, now, what Hank was trying.

No killer.

Wonderful.

And she also knew that her head was spinning and the light from the lantern was dim and she was seeing a blue aura around Hank as he disembowelled the girl and slashed with the razor. She carefully (wobbling) set the lantern down on the soft clothes and stumbled backward away from it before sliding down into darkness.

'Wake up. Come on.'

She opened her eyes.

Hank was kneeling beside her, a bundle in his arm. 'It's a boy,' he said. 'Seems to be all right. She must've been pretty close to . . .'

'You got it out?'

'All yours.' He set the bundle down between her breasts. Chris felt its warmth. It was moving. She parted the sweater that was wrapped around it and saw a pudgy face with half open eyes.

'God,' she whispered.

'You're not much of a midwife,' Hank said, 'but at least you didn't set the place on fire.'

Chris put her arms gently around the baby.

'Come on,' Hank said. 'Let's get going.'

18

'Lemme ha' s'more,' Kyle said, slurring his words as if he were drunk. Paula pressed the bottle against his belly. He took it, raised it to his mouth and upended it. Whisky sloshed against his pinched lips. He made swallowing sounds, then sighed, said, 'Goo' stuff,' and gave the bottle back to her.

'Through the teeth 'n over the gums, watch out, stomach, here it comes.' He heard Paula drink. 'Good for what ails you,' she said. 'That's what my dad says, "Good for what ails you." '

'Your dad drink a lot?'

'Yaaah, he's not a boozer. That what you mean? He's not a boozer, but he drinks. Has a couple 'fore dinner, but just on weekends. *Used* to be a boozer. Cause of Vietnam, Mom said. Then he smashed up the car with me 'n Mom in it. That was the last time he ever got sticko.'

'I'zat when your Mom got killed?' Kyle asked.

'Naw. Nobody got hurt. I was like two years old. I don' even remember the crash. Mom, she had a urinism.'

'A what?'

'A uri . . . *ane*urysm. A blood vessel in her brain. It

just blew and she keeled over.'

'Geez.' Kyle put a hand on her knee. She was sitting beside him on the sleeping bag with her legs crossed. Earlier, he had unzipped the sleeping bag, spread it open and brought its end up to cover their legs. Paula's knee was warm. He slid his hand to the hem of her kilt, and patted her thigh.

He heard Paula take another drink. 'Leas' it was quick, y'know? Better'n cancer or shit like that. Or AIDs. Jesus. Freaks me out, start thinking about shit like AIDs. 'Nough to make you *stay* a virgin.'

'Me, too. It's too damn dangerous.' He realized he had forgotten to slur his speech, but decided it didn't matter. Paula was sounding pretty smashed – probably too smashed to notice. He'd taken a few swallows, at first, but had only pretended to drink once he realized the control he would have over Paula if he could get her sloshed.

'You never . . . did it?' she asked.

'Nope.'

Amy Lawson, he thought, and suddenly felt hot and squirmy inside. What if Amy Lawson had it?

'How'd your mother die?' Paula asked.

'She didn't. She ran off with some guy.'

'Oh yeah, tha's right. Ran off.'

'Bitch.'

'She visit?'

'She doesn't visit, doesn't even send me a fuckin' Christmas card.'

'Tha'sa pits.'

'Haven't heard shit since the day she ran off. Four years. Didn't even say goodbye. Just left a note in the typewriter saying she was sick of wasting her life in

"Hotel Boondocks" and she was going away with some rich guy who'd checked in the day before. Said if she never saw me or Dad again, it'd be too soon. Bitch. Hope *she* got an aneurysm.'

'Oh, Kyle. I'm sorry.'

'Yeah, Well. So much for mothers.'

He heard the bottle clink softly. Then Paula twisted herself towards him, her knee nudging the side of his leg. He slid his hand farther up her thigh, and she didn't protest. He felt the softness of her breast against his upper arm. Her hand found his face and stroked it. The way she leaned on him, he couldn't have stayed sitting if he'd wanted to. He didn't want to. He let himself drop backward onto the sleeping bag and felt her smooth skin slide under his hand as she straightened out her legs. He felt her other thigh on the back of his hand. Felt the slick fabric of her panties. Heat.

I didn't even do this myself, he thought. Just an accident. *She* did it stretching out like that.

God.

A delicious current seemed to surge from her body into his hand and up his arm – sizzling through his whole body, stealing his breath away, making his heart race, swelling his penis to a stout rod.

Then her fingers gently wrapped his wrist and pulled his hand away from the silken fabric, away from the heat, and guided it out from under her skirt.

Okay, he thought. Okay, don't want to spook her.

He put that arm under her head and rolled onto his side. Paula kissed him, but there seemed to be no passion in it. More like a goodnight kiss she might give her father. Then she lay still except for a hand slowly caressing his back.

Kyle slipped his hand under the front of her sweater and cupped her breast through the layers of blouse and brassiere.

'Le's just hug, okay?' she said.

He rubbed her breast.

'C'mon, don't.' Her protest was feeble, lazy. 'Le's just snuggle.'

He'd had her *blouse* open before the elevators fell. Now she didn't even want him touching her through the clothes. The booze was supposed to loosen her inhibitions, maybe even make her horny, but here she was acting as if she didn't want to mess around at all.

Maybe she had too much, Kyle thought.

Maybe she's going to zonk out.

Yeah.

'If that's what you want,' he whispered. He let go. Sitting up, he drew the top of the sleeping bag over Paula. Then he lay down beside her and covered himself. Paula squirmed closer, pressing herself gently against him.

'Cozy,' she whispered.

'Yeah.'

Kyle didn't move again until, from the deep slow sounds of Paula's breathing, he was pretty sure that she was asleep.

She moaned slightly but didn't wake up when his fingers curled over her breast.

He found the top button of her blouse. He was about to unfasten it, but changed his mind. If she woke up and her blouse was unbuttoned, she would know what he'd been up to. He moved his hand down. Her blouse was untucked. He reached beneath it. Her blouse was roomy inside. He fondled both breasts, listening for changes in her breathing.

She's totally out of it, he thought.

Fantastic.

Carefully, he slid a bra strap off her shoulder. His hand fitted easily under the loosened cup. He held her bare breast. The skin was so warm, so smooth. He fingered her nipple. She squirmed a little, but didn't wake up.

'I don't like this,' Katie whispered. 'Not one little bit.'

'There's nothing to be afraid of, honey,' Jean told her.

'Darkness isn't my favourite thing.'

From where Wayne Phillips sat with his family, he could see into both elevators. The flames in the elevator to his left had died out a while ago. Those in the other elevator had burned longer, but the last of them had just fluttered out. Now, there were only red, glowing embers.

Darkness isn't my favourite thing, either, Wayne thought.

The embers gave off some light, but not much. Only enough to see vague shapes.

Pretty soon, he thought, even that will be gone. It'll be black as a pit.

'Look on the bright side,' he said, as much to still his own uneasiness as to comfort Katie. 'I'll make a book out of this and we'll get a lot of money. Then we'll go to Disney World.'

'Oh, sure.'

'Honest. Have I ever lied to you?'

'When you said there was a bone-cruncher living under my bed that was gonna chew off my foot. When you said about the troll under the house. When you said there was Madman Murray sneaking to our front door every night and trying to come in. When . . .'

'Those weren't lies.'

'Don't start, Wayne.'

'They were just stories.'

'A story is a lie,' Katie told him.

'Not exactly.'

'It is, too.'

Wayne sighed. 'Anyway, I'm not lying about Disney World. I'll write a really scary book about all this, and we'll get piles of money and go to Disney World. It's a promise.'

'We'll hold you to it,' Jean said.

'Make sure you take them to the Epcot Center.'

The woman's soft voice didn't startle Wayne, but he was surprised by the discovery that someone was sitting so close to them. Close enough to hear every word. 'Yeah,' he said. 'We'll go there, too.'

'It's not to be missed.'

'I've heard it's very good,' he said.

Right behind me. Christ. I'd better watch my language.

'Does anyone object if I smoke?' she asked.

Several nearby voices urged her to light up at the same time Wayne said, 'No, go ahead.'

He heard quiet sounds, probably the woman searching inside her handbag. Then came a crinkle of cellophane. He looked over his shoulder in time to see a tiny spray of sparks as the match snicked across the striking surface. The matchhead flared. The sudden brightness stabbed Wayne's eyes. He squinted. Around the brilliant flame was a tremulous, yellow-orange aura that illuminated not only the woman with the cigarette in her lips but a few other people seated nearby.

The woman, well over fifty years old and probably tipping the scales at three hundred pounds, wore her grey hair in a Buster Brown cut and glasses as round as her face. She was wrapped in a cable-knit shawl. Her faded dress reached only to her knees. Her calves, the size of hams, were encased in 'knee-high' hose, the tops of which sank into her flesh and were overhung by tyres of blubber.

A real looker, Wayne thought.

Her handbag rested on the tilted platform of the dress stretched taut across her thighs. She dropped the matchbook inside. With a flick of her wrist, she shook out the flame and vanished.

All that remained was the glowing tip of her cigarette.

Wayne thought of the Cheshire Cat. This woman's cigarette was like the cat's smile, staying behind after the rest was gone.

I'll have to use that in my book, he thought. The Cheshire Cat bit.

She would make a good character. A minor character, but sufficiently grotesque to make the readers uneasy. Cook up a nasty ending for her.

Wayne turned away from her and gazed at the embers inside the elevator cars.

What kind of nasty ending? he wondered. You're jumping the gun. Haven't even figured out what's nailing the people. They're trapped in the cave. Something or someone starts ripping them off.

What if that gal has evil powers? She's a sorceress, warps the minds of the people trapped down here, turns them against each other? I can use the bit with Calvin tearing into that asshole. God, I could pretty much use that whole scene just the way it happened.

259

But that's just the start. Really bad shit starts to happen.

Maybe the fat gal's doing it with her magic, or maybe its the evil in all these people coming to the surface because they're tired and frightened. Is it black magic or human nature causing the mayhem? Really play that up, and you'll give the thing some depth, it'll look like more than just a cheap horror novel.

Throw in some scapegoat stuff. They blame the fat gal, call her a witch, burn her at the stake – burn her in one of the elevators.

Shit, this is really shaping up.

Wayne grinned.

'How's it going, Katie?' he asked.

'I'm not having a very good day.'

'Nobody is, honey,' Jean told her.

'Oh, I'm starting to have a pretty good day,' Wayne said. 'I think this little cloud has a silver lining that's going to make us all very happy.'

'Bug squat,' Katie muttered.

'I'm feeling a chill, Calvin.'

'So's everyone else, I suspect. Do you want to move closer to the elevators? They've got good beds of coal built up, probably giving off considerable heat if we hauled ourselves near enough to feel it.'

'Oh, I don't know. It's so dark. We'd trip over people.'

Calvin wondered why she had even bothered to complain about the chill if she wasn't willing to put herself out some to get warm. Just for the sake of hearing herself talk, more than likely. 'Want me to lay on you?' he asked.

'Shhhh. People will hear you.'

'I reckon I could warm you up right quick.'

'*Calvin.*'

Grinning, he patted her thigh. 'Don't you worry, hon, I won't do nothing to embarrass you.'

'A little bit late for that.'

'Shitfire, here we go again.'

'You like to've killed that man.'

'I'd *like* to've killed that man, truth be known.'

'You don't mean that. Calvin, you'd burn in Hell for eternity.'

'Mavis, darling, any God that'd send a man to burn in Hell for eternity 'cause he rid the world of a misbegotten son of a whore like Slick over there – well, I reckon he can just take his Pearly Gates and . . .'

'Don't you dare say such a thing! Lord, you'll get yourself in Dutch for sure.'

''Fraid He'll send down a bolt of lightning to . . . CHRIST!' Calvin blurted as a blast roared in his ears and he thought, *Holy jumping Jesus, I'm a dead man!*

But others were yelling, too, over the deafening noise.

Calvin felt a cold mist on his face. Drops of water pelted him.

The roar seemed to come from the elevator car several yards in front of him. The red glow in its centre was blotted out. Around the blackness, sparks and embers exploded upward and died. In seconds, every trace of light from inside the elevator had been obliterated.

The noise faded, then came again.

A fire hose, Calvin thought. They must've shot a gusher straight down the shaft. Now the fire in the other elevator was being doused.

A few moments later, the roar diminished, then ceased altogether.

'Yuh, I'm drenched!' someone complained.

Another voice muttered, 'All over me.'

The darkness seemed heavy with char-smelling steam. Here and there, people clapped and cheered.

'All *right*!'

'Won't be long, now.'

'Took 'em long enough.'

'Apparently,' someone said, 'there wasn't any Third World War up there.'

'Never thought there was, jerk-off.' That was Slick's voice. Calvin shook his head. The fella'd taken a whooping and got his hair burnt off, but it hadn't straightened out his disposition.

'Can't wait to sink my teeth into a thick, juicy sirloin.'

'I wanta wrap my lips around a bottle of Molsons.'

'I'm gonna reacquaint myself with my old pal Jack Daniels.'

'All I want's a long, hot bath.' That was a woman, of course.

'If I never see another cave, it won't be a moment too soon.'

'Oh, don't be such a downer, Brian. It's been a marvellous adventure.'

'HELLO, THE CAVERN.' The voice boomed through the darkness, silencing everyone.

A bullhorn, Calvin thought.

'This is Chief Richmond of the Pleasant Valley Fire Department. Is anyone there?'

In the quiet following the announcement, Calvin heard footfalls. Then crunching, soggy sounds. Someone, he figured, was stepping into one of the elevators. 'Hello up there!' Sounded like Tom.

The tinny, amplified voice said, 'The fire has been extinguished, and we're making preparations to evacuate you people. Will anyone require medical assistance?'

'We're all okay,' Tom called.

'My ass,' Slick said. 'I been . . .'

'Shut up,' someone told him.

'Who said that?'

'How many are trapped down there with you?' Chief Richmond asked.

'About thirty,' Tom replied. 'How long'll it take to get us out?'

'We'll have you out as soon as possible. Heavy construction equipment has been requested. We need a bulldozer to clear the area up here. Then we'll execute the evacuation by means of a crane. In the meantime, I want you all to adopt a sit-tight policy and stay clear of the elevator shafts. Any questions?'

'How come I don't see any light up there?' Tom called.

'The elevator housing is still intact. It's burnt out, but . . . I've just been informed the equipment is arriving. Again, stay clear of the shafts and wait for further instructions.'

'Ask him to lower us a few flashlights!' someone said.

'Yeah!'

'Chief?' Tom yelled. 'Chief Richmond?'

No answer.

'Shit.'

'No big deal,' Tom said. 'We'll be out of here before long.'

Calvin felt Mavis squeeze his hand. 'Well,' he said, 'I reckon the fun's about over.'

Kyle, squirming and gasping and wanting to roll Paula over and stick it in her (so what if she wakes up), jerked his hand out of her panties when the silence was smashed. Her fingers, curled loosely around his erection where he had put them, wiggled a little. He quickly took her hand away and held it.

Paula sighed and moaned.

The noise faded. So did the voices and shouts of alarm.

Maybe she won't wake up, after all.

Then the roar swelled again.

Paula said, 'Huh?'

'It's all right,' Kyle whispered.

The noise stopped. People spoke, but their words were indistinct.

'What's going on?' she asked.

Did she mean the sounds? Or was she aware of what Kyle had done to her?

She can't know, he told himself.

He'd slipped the bra strap back onto her shoulder before pushing his knee between her legs and lifting the front of her skirt and sliding his hand inside her panties. Nothing had been unfastened or removed.

But maybe she could tell that her clothes had been fooled with.

Could she feel where he had touched her?

Did she know, somehow, that Kyle's hand wasn't what she'd been holding a few seconds ago?

'I don't know what's happening,' he said. 'Some kind of commotion over by the elevators.'

Paula moaned.

Any second, the accusations would start.

'God,' she mumbled. 'My head.'

A hollow, distant voice said, 'Hello the cavern.'

'What's that?'

'I don't know.'

'See what's . . .' She let go of his hand, and moaned as she sat up.

Kyle stayed with her, holding her arm in the darkness. They stood up and turned to the sounds of the voices. As they listened, he touched his penis. It was still big, sticking straight forward, but not as rigid as before so he was able to tuck it back inside his jeans. He left the zipper open. In spite of the voices from the elevator area, Paula might hear if he pulled the zipper up.

Kyle heard Tom call out something about flashlights.

Other people spoke, but their words were too faint to understand.

He and Paula stood silently. The voice of Chief Richmond didn't come again.

'So I guess they're getting us out,' Kyle finally whispered.

'Do you think we should go back now?'

'I bet it'll still be an hour or so before they start taking people out.'

'Yeah?'

'I think we should just wait here.' Kyle told her.

'If we go back now, maybe we can sneak in and nobody'll find out we were gone.'

'Who cares if they find out?' Kyle said.

'Well, yeah. They don't know me.'

'Besides, we haven't done anything wrong.'

Sounding a little bit amused, Paula said, 'They'll probably think we were over here screwing around.'

Man, she doesn't have a hint.

'Well,' he whispered. 'If they're going to *accuse* us of it, maybe . . .'

'Ho ho ho. Right. Want me to barf in your face?'

'Just kidding.'

'God, I never should've drunk all that.'

'Maybe we'd better have some more. They say it's supposed to help.'

'Thanks but no thanks. Maybe someone over there has some aspirin I can borrow.'

Kyle stepped behind Paula and began to rub her neck and shoulders. 'Mom used to do this for me when I had a headache,' he said. Gently, he pulled the sweater down her back. Then he resumed the massage.

She sighed.

'Feel good?'

'Mmmm.'

He kneaded the sides of her neck, moved his hands over her collar and squeezed her shoulders. Her skin felt smooth and warm through her blouse. He wished there was nothing between his hands and her skin.

Just wait, he told himself. Pretty soon.

She began to sway back and forth. As if she were half asleep, or maybe mesmerized.

Kyle continued to hear voices from those near the elevators. He didn't even try to understand what was being said. He didn't care. And Paula seemed oblivious to everything except the rhythmic rub and squeeze of his hands on her neck and shoulders.

He half expected her to slump into his arms.

Leaning forward, he lifted her hair out of the way and kissed the side of her neck. She moaned. She didn't tell him to stop.

Kyle slid a hand over the top of her shoulder and opened the top button of her blouse.

She said nothing.

He unfastened the next button down, feeling her breast under his wrist.

'Hey,' she murmured.

'It'll be better this way,' he said and slipped the blouse clear of her shoulders and went on with the massage. She seemed a little rigid at first, but soon she was limp and swaying again.

Kyle slipped the bra straps out of his way.

Now her shoulders were sleek, warm skin and he knew that the hanging straps left her bra loose and if he wanted he could slide his hands right down into the cups.

His mouth was dry, his heart racing. He lowered a hand, plucked the front of his jeans to free his straining penis, and went back to rubbing her.

He eased forward. The soft wool of her kilt brushed the underside of his shaft.

He slid both hands over the shoulders and down her chest.

Paula flinched and grabbed his wrists, stopping him before he reached her breasts. 'Hey, come on,' she whispered.

'What'll it hurt?'

'Kyle, no. Besides, I'm getting cold.'

'Please?'

'I think it's time we'd better go . . .'

'YEEEEAH!'

It didn't come from Paula. It came from the darkness ahead.

'What the hell . . .?'

'LET GO OF ME!' the woman cried out. 'WHAT DO YOU WANT?'

'What the fuck's going on?'

'Oh sweet Jesus *he's dead*! Somebody . . .'

'HELP! HELP!'

Kyle trembled with terror and joy.

Paula stood rigid, squeezing his wrists. 'God,' she whispered. 'What's happening!'

'Don't know.'

Kyle knew. He knew, all right.

The crazies had arrived.

Those he'd heard mumbling and tittering when he went out in the night with his father to give Amy Lawson a ride down the chute – the wild, demented progeny of Elizabeth Mordock.

They'd poured through the hole in Ely's Wall, just as he'd feared when the earlier scream came floating up the cavern.

They'd probably slaughtered Darcy's group.

Now they were falling upon the others.

He heard shouts of confusion and alarm, shrieks, *laughter*.

He pressed himself against Paula's back. Her body was stiff and trembling. Her hands, still clutching his wrists, shook as if she were seized by a spastic frenzy.

This is it, he thought.

They're here.

The arrival of the crazies meant there was no longer a need to be sneaky, no longer a need to waste time in futile efforts to seduce Paula.

She's mine.

Whatever I want.

Same as if we were in 115.

Do her any way I please.

They'll blame it on the crazies.

'It's all right,' he whispered. 'We're safe over here. We've just got to be quiet till it's over.'

Paula kept on shaking.

'If you make any noise,' he said in her ear, 'they'll come for us.'

She moaned.

'They'll kill us if you make a sound.'

'I . . .'

He wrenched a hand from Paula's grip and pounded it into her belly. Her breath blasted out. She folded. A soft thud. Her head hitting the stalagmite? She stayed bent and didn't fall. Maybe holding onto the rock.

Kyle clawed the blouse down her back. Feeling through the darkness, his left hand found the nape of her neck. He squeezed it, holding her down, and ran his right hand down her back to the bra strap. A quick tug popped the clasps.

Still clamping her neck, he tugged the waistband of her kilt. Something snapped. The kilt loosened. He jerked it down her rump, let go and slid his hand over the slick fabric of her panties. He snatched the panties down. Her buttocks were firm and smooth. He stroked down the centre.

Was blocked by her legs, squeezed tightly shut.

He dug his fingers into the crease between them and brought his knee up against the backs of her thighs to force them apart.

As he pushed and felt them open, his hand at the back of Paula's neck was grabbed, yanked sideways. Taken by surprise, he lost his grip. The clutching hand pulled him forward. He fell against her. She twisted sideways. He slid off her back, onto the blunt top of the rock that scraped his ribcage and rammed his left armpit.

Something pounded the other side of his chest. Though the blow didn't hurt much, it jolted him, started him rolling away from Paula. He raked his right hand through the black, hoping to snag her hair or flesh or clothes, but found only empty air. Then his back hit the steep side of the stalagmite. He skidded down. At the bottom, he flipped himself over and lurched to his feet.

He heard Paula.

In spite of the bedlam from across the stream, he heard her.

Her quick, shaky gasps. Her sobs.

Nearby..

Moving.

He moved toward her, felt the soft mat of the sleeping bag under his feet and knew where he was.

Paula was off to his left.

Heading for the stream?

Is she *nuts*? Doesn't she know what's going on over there?

Just doesn't care. Just wants to get away from me.

Kyle hurried after her, feeling his way through the dark, guided by the sounds of her terror. He waved his arms in front of him. Tripped, stumbled, but stayed up. Heard Paula splashing in the water not far ahead of him.

He rushed down the embankment. Kicked a rock and yelped with pain and flew headlong through the darkness. He landed flat in the stream. The cold water exploded under him. Though his foot burned with pain, he scurried up and heard Paula gasping and whimpering nearby. He lunged toward the sounds, reaching out for her.

And caught a handful of fabric.

Her blouse?

It tugged at his arm. He lost his balance and fell forward, but kept his hold on the blouse, hoping to pull her down on top of him.

As he dropped, the weight of her pulling body went away. He hit the water. He pushed himself to his hands and knees. All he had was her empty blouse.

He got up and staggered after her.

Tossed the blouse away, dug a hand into the tight wet pocket of his jeans and brought out his knife.

Pried the blade open.

They'll blame it on the crazies.

Paula wasn't splashing anymore. From the sounds of her ragged breathing and sobs, Kyle realized she had reached the other side and was scurrying up the embankment.

Gotta nail her quick.

Before she gets to the railing.

Or we'll be running straight into *them*.

A part of Kyle's mind warned him to forget Paula.

Not worth it. Christ, no. Go back and hide before they get you!

But he wanted her. Wanted to tear her down and rip her and chew her tits and fuck her.

He scrambled up the slope.

Heard a soft ringing sound.

Paula was at the railing!

Moments later, Kyle's wavering left hand struck the railing. He grabbed the cold metal, ducked beneath it, and rushed on through the utter darkness.

If I nail her right now!

He grabbed a fistful of hair and jerked it. The body came against him. He drove his knife into her back, pulled it out, struck again.

And again.

She flinched and shuddered each time he rammed the knife into her back.

He felt hot blood pouring over his hand.

She slumped against him, twitching.

He found her throat and slashed it open.

271

19

Chris gently tucked the baby's face against the crook of her neck when they found the body.

Hank set the pickaxe aside. He wouldn't be needing it; someone had already knocked a hole through Ely's Wall.

He crouched over the body. It lay sprawled on its back off to the side of the opening, away from the strip of water that slid through the narrow gap below the remaining portion of the stone wall.

It was a man. His hair was neatly trimmed. He was clean-shaven. He wore nothing except pale blue boxer shorts and shoes. His gaping mouth was full to the lips with blood. His cheeks and chin and neck were painted with it. Hank pressed his hand to the man's neck. The blood felt tacky and the skin beneath it still retained some heat.

'He hasn't been dead very long,' Hank said. 'Probably less than an hour.'

'I know him,' Chris muttered.

'What?'

'I mean, I don't *know* him. I saw him this morning. He was waiting for Darcy's tour to start.'

'God almighty.' He looked up at Chris. Her face was

contorted, nose wrinkled, lips peeled back, eyebrows pinched together. Her eyes looked feverish, a little wild.

'What's . . .?' She shook her head.

'I don't know. Somebody killed this guy. If he was on the tour . . . and he's on this side of the wall . . .'

'Did they try to get out this way?' Chris asked.

'And maybe turned back when this one was killed. Or maybe he was alone,' Hank said.

'Who *killed* him?'

'The girl, maybe.'

'Or . . . or maybe there are others. Others like her.'

And if so, Hank thought, where are they?

Where's Paula? What if she was with this guy and . . . She's all right. God, please. She's all right.

He felt as if icy hands were squeezing his heart.

'We've gotta hurry,' he said.

Turning away from the body, Hank braced a hand on the sill of the wall and leaned through the hole. He held the lantern out in front of him.

He expected to find the narrow, shallow stream on the other side. Instead, there was a lake, its still surface for yards around him shiny in the lantern light.

He saw two bodies floating face-down, their heads and legs below the water.

One wore a white sweater (Paula had put on her white sweater, telling him that the guide book warned of the cavern's chilly temperature) and Hank felt a twist of panic before he realized the body wore some kind of black pants, not a kilt.

The other body was dressed in a plaid shirt and blue jeans.

Though the heads of both bodies were submerged, he could see their floating hair through the clear water.

274

Long hair. The hair didn't necessarily prove that these were women, but their hips seemed to flare out and their rumps looked female.

Women, all right.

But neither one was Paula.

And neither wore a guide's blue uniform.

'What do you see?' Chris asked.

'They're not our kids,' he said outright to save her even a moment of wondering. 'Two dead bodies. Female.'

'My God. You're sure . . .?'

'Darcy wore one of those uniforms like Lynn?'

'Yes.'

'That's what I figured. She's not one of them.' He saw a square-cornered, metal boat a short distance to the left. Bundles of clothing rested on seats. 'And there's an empty boat. There's a lake over here.' he added.

'The Lake of Charon,' Chris said.

'What's it doing here?'

'Ely's Wall dammed the stream. They take you over the lake on those boats.'

From his perch on the edge of the wall, Hank could see inside the boat. He didn't see any oars or motor.

How big is this lake?' he asked.

'I don't know, it's maybe fifty yards to the docks. It's not very deep, though. I think Darcy said four or five feet.'

That was about the depth he would've guessed from the look of the rocky bottom, but he knew that the clear water could distort his perspective and the lake might be considerably deeper than it appeared.

'I guess we take a dip,' he said.

He climbed through the hole, sat on the wall's edge

and lowered his legs into the lake. Holding the lantern high, he scooted forward and dropped. The water wrapped him to the chest. Its chill squeezed his breath out. 'Uhhh.'

'You all right?'

'Colder than a witch's . . . nose.'

Turning around, he saw Chris appear in the opening. 'Just a minute,' he said. He waded to the boat. Draped across a seat near the front were a plaid shirt and blue jeans similar to those worn by the dead woman. Propped against the seat was a four-foot length of board, the upper half of it burnt black. Another pair of pants rested on a seat near the middle. He saw a grey sweatshirt there. And a green sweater (not Paula's).

Hank set the lantern on one of its seats, then returned to the wall and reached up. Chris handed the baby to him. He held the small, squirming bundle against the side of his face.

Chris crawled onto the edge of the hole. As she positioned herself to jump, she stared past Hank – a look of revulsion on her face. Then she glanced down, and leaped. She entered the water with a small splash. Her eyes went wide and she gritted her teeth.

'Nippy, huh?'

'Gawd.' She waded to him, moving stiffly.

'You okay?'

She responded with a stiff nod.

'You want the baby or the lantern?'

'Baby,' she gasped.

Hank passed it to her. She nuzzled the infant against her cheek. It made quiet cooing sounds.

She stayed at Hank's side as he waded back to the boat.

'That piece of wood there,' he said. 'Looks like they used it for a torch. See the clothes? Must've been at least two men in the boat. And those women.'

'And Darcy,' Chris muttered. 'She would've been with them.'

'Maybe not.'

'She's the leader.'

'She might've stayed behind. But even if she was here . . . whoever belongs to the second set of clothes must've gotten away. Probably others did, too.' He lifted the lantern off its seat. 'The whole group might've been here.'

'It takes two boats to hold everyone.'

'Well, the other boat doesn't seem to be around. Maybe the rest of them got away in the second boat.'

'Maybe.' Chris sounded doubtful.

'Wonder where the oars are,' he said.

'Aren't any,' Chris told him. 'Spikes in the walls. When I was on the tour yesterday, Darcy stood up and . . . pulled the boat from spike to spike.'

'Weird.'

'It's how they do it.'

'Why don't you climb aboard, I'll push.'

'Don't you think . . .? Quicker if we walk.'

'Probably, but . . .'

'Let's hurry.'

'Yeah.'

They walked, staying close to the side of the boat so Chris wouldn't have to pass near the bodies. Hank would've liked to take a look at them and see how they were killed, but he refrained for Chris's sake. Besides, she was right. They had to hurry. Every second might count.

Someone, he was sure, had come through the hole in Ely's Wall and murdered at least three of those who had approached in the boat.

Someone, perhaps, who had lived in that strange nest with the girl he'd killed.

He thought about how she had attacked him for no reason. With a weapon of bone and razor blades.

He thought about her teeth, filed to points.

Some kind of savage.

What the hell was she doing there?

Did others live in that place?

Was one of them responsible for the hideous display of human remains they'd found along the banks of the stream?

How *many* are there?

Where are they now?

He heard only the sounds of his breathing, Chris's breathing, quiet gurgles and coos from the baby, the soft sloshing sounds of their own movement through the lake.

He wished he *did* hear others.

Savages coming toward them out of the darkness.

Let them attack.

At least I'd know they're here and not chasing down Paula somewhere.

'I'm scared, Hank.'

'Yeah, me too.' He put a hand on her back.

'What if Darcy and Paula . . .?'

'I'm sure they're all right.' Sure I am, he thought. He was only sure of his hope. He knew that hope wasn't enough. You hope for the best, you hope *against* the worst, but what he'd learned during two tours in Vietnam was that the worst could happen and often it pushed beyond the boundaries of what he had hoped against, pushed into the black territories of the unthinkable.

But hope was all he had, so he clung to it.

'Even if they were here,' he said, 'it doesn't mean . . . How many people were on the tour?'

'Thirty or forty, I guess.'

'That many couldn't have been . . . And we've only seen three bodies.'

'So far,' Chris said.

Seconds later, as if to shrink the hope, they found another body. Chris saw it first, gasped and flinched back.

This body didn't float. It hung spread-eagled in the lake a couple of feet below the surface. Like the two women, its long hair was spread out, drifting around its head like a strange seaweed.

'A man,' Hank said. Stepping in front of Chris, he reached down into the water and grabbed the man's hair. It felt thick and greasy. He lifted. As the head came up dripping, he turned the face toward him.

One glimpse, and Hank knew that this was not a man from the tour.

Bushy eyebrows. A heavy black beard. Skin so white it may never have been touched by sunlight. Pointed teeth.

When Hank was a boy, his father used to frighten him with tales of the Wild Man of Borneo. He'd loved the stories and begged for more, though sometimes the Wild Man stalked him through nightmares.

Staring at the face of this dead savage, Hank felt as if he'd slid back into his childhood.

Shivers crawled up his back.

'The Wild Man of Borneo,' he muttered. 'In the flesh.'

'It's one of them?' Chris asked in a small, high voice.

'Just like the girl.' He plunged the head down into the water and pushed. The body glided away, feet first. Hank rubbed his hand on the leg of his warm-up pants. When he finished, it still seemed coated with an oily film.

They started walking again.

He kept his hand underwater, kept rubbing it on his leg.

He wished he had a bar of soap.

Forget about it, he told himself. So the guy had dirty hair. Real big deal. You were up to your wrists in a dead girl's guts ten or fifteen minutes ago.

But this. Such a little thing.

Like finding a stranger's hair in your soup.

'I wonder how many others . . .' Chris said. She was looking around.

Won't even see the ones submerged like that guy, Hank thought. Not till we're right on top of them.

Those with enough water in their lungs would stay below the surface, he knew, until they started to decompose and the trapped gasses popped their bloated carcasses to the top.

'At least he was on the right side,' Hank said.

'They might be all around us,' she whispered.

'The more like him, the better.'

'It's . . . almost worse than the other place.'

Hank knew she meant the madman's gallery. She was right. There, you could see the things.

And there, it had never crossed Hank's mind that one of the corpses might be his own daughter.

She could be here.

No!

She's fine. Darcy's fine. Others had been killed, not our girls. The horror stops there. It has to.

Hank, like Chris, scanned the surface of the lake.

And then, near the far reach of the lantern's glow, he saw the dull gleam of a square-cornered boat. A few steps more, and a dock came into view.

Chris moaned.

She saw it, too – another body. This one lying flat on the floor of the dock.

Cold dread seized Hank.

They waded closer.

A woman's body. Naked. Torn up.

Faceless in the distance and dim light.

She seemed taller, thinner than Paula, but . . .

Clothing lay scattered beside her.

A white sweater and blouse and kilt? A blue uniform?

He just couldn't see!

Chris began to weep.

Hank lunged forward, leaning into the chest-high water, trying to run. The water pressed against him like hands holding him off. But he waded closer and closer, leaving Chris behind.

The clothing.

Those were blue slacks in a pile beside the body's hip. Not Paula's kilt. But pants like Darcy's.

Oh God, no!

'Chris, stay back!'

'What?'

He trudged past the bow of the boat, rammed the lantern down on the dock, and thrust himself out of the water. On hands and knees, he crawled to the side of the corpse. The flesh gaped with deep wounds as if chunks had been chewed out. The left arm had been torn from its socket and partly devoured.

The face was intact.

A face frozen in a rictus of horror.

A face that had never been beautiful – not like Chris, not like Chris's daughter *must* be.

And it was the face of a woman who must have been pushing forty.

Hank let out a long, trembling sigh.

He looked over his shoulder. Chris was yards away, a dim shape in the faint glow that reached her from the lantern.

Hank was pleased; she'd done as he asked and stayed put.

'It's all right,' he said.

It's all right? The woman's dead. They ate at her. And it's all right?

'Not one of our girls,' he explained.

Chris nodded and started forward. Not wanting her to see how the body had been ravaged, Hank slid the severed arm against its side. He covered the body from the waist down with the slacks, then spread the blouse over the torso. He didn't try to hide the face.

Crawling to the edge of the dock, he reached down. Chris handed the baby to him. From the slow sound of its breathing, he guessed it was asleep. He marvelled that the child could sleep through a situation like this.

Lucky kid, he thought. Doesn't have the foggiest idea what's going on.

Probably thinks Chris is its mother.

Chris boosted herself up and scrambled onto the dock. She looked at the corpse. She sniffed and wiped her eyes. 'Why did you cover her?'

'She's . . . partly eaten.'

'They *ate* her?'

'Must've worked on her for a while. And I think . . . too much was gone for one person to have done it. I'd guess there must've been a few of them.'

'Aw, Jesus.'

'In a way, it's looking better.'

'How can you *say* that? They . . .'

'That guy on the other side of the wall, he hadn't been dead very long. An hour at the most. Then, some kind of struggle took place here at the lake. That used up some time. Then, those bastards didn't go straight after the survivors. (If there were survivors, he thought.) They stuck around for a while and had themselves a meal. So they probably don't have much of a headstart on us.'

'You think we might have a chance of catching up with them?'

'We might,' he said, though that was almost too much to hope for.

He picked up the lantern. They got to their feet and started walking quickly up the dock.

'Another thing in our favour,' Hank said. 'They probably don't have any light, and we do. That means they won't be able to move as fast as . . .'

He went silent.

Out of the darkness ahead came faint, human voices shouting and screaming.

We're too late!

Darcy trotted through the black, one hand on Greg's bare shoulder, the other hand gliding along the metal bar of the railing.

The belt around her midriff was starting to slip. Before

they left the dock, Greg had wrapped her with the belt to secure her folded handkerchief against her wound. She had argued against taking the time necessary to apply the makeshift bandage, but he had insisted.

'If you lose so much blood you pass out on me,' he told her, 'it'll slow us down even more – I'd have to pick you up and carry you.'

'It's not bleeding that much.'

'We aren't going anywhere until you're patched up.'

'Okay,' she said.

And so, standing on the dock in the utter darkness, Darcy opened her windbreaker and took off her belt. She dug her sodden handkerchief out of the front pocket of her pants and gave it to Greg. She felt his fingers gently exploring her skin. Winced as he touched an edge of the wound.

'We've already lost so much time,' she whispered.

'A couple more minutes won't make that much difference.'

'Might make all the difference.'

'Face it, Darcy, we're not going to catch up with them.' He placed the handkerchief against her wound. 'Hold that.' She did. She gave the belt to him. 'They've got too much of a headstart,' he said. 'They'll reach the others before we're even halfway there. And when they realize how many they've got to contend with, they probably won't attack at all. They might just watch for a while, or they might turn back. And run into us.'

'We've gotta go after them.'

'I know.'

'So many are already dead.'

The belt encircled her body, just below her breasts. Greg touched her fingers. 'Got it,' he whispered. Then he tightened the belt. It closed around her like a tourniquet and she hissed at the pressure on her raw flesh. 'If it's too loose, it won't do any good.'

Darcy nodded and then realized how foolish it was to nod in such a darkness. 'It's okay.'

She felt for him and found his shoulders and pulled him against her. In an instant, his cold skin turned warm where it met her chest and breasts and belly. She felt the rise and fall of his chest, and beating of his heart.

Greg stroked her hair.

If we go, Darcy thought, *he* might be killed.

'If we can't overtake the savages,' she said as she held him, 'at least we might be able to call out and warn the others that they're coming. If we're even too late for that, we can join in the fight.'

'You've done enough fighting,' Greg told her.

'We might save lives. Even if we save just one . . .'

But what if it costs Greg his life?

Maybe we shouldn't go.

'Whatever we do,' Greg said, 'there's no point in staying here.' He eased away from her. For just a moment, his hands moved lightly over her breasts. Then they found the sides of her face. He drew her forward, kissed the side of her nose, then her mouth.

'Ready?' he asked.

'Yeah.'

Darcy heard a quiet snap. 'What was that?' she asked.

'Elastic. I took the bone out of my shorts.'

She laughed and couldn't believe she was laughing. 'You actually . . . had that thing in your *underwear*?'

'Right in there with the other bone.'

'Uh.'

'Let's move.'

Her laughter died.

Greg led the way, Darcy keeping a hand on his shoulder.

Somehow, they managed to walk the length of the dock without falling into the lake. When the concrete walkway was under their feet, he guided Darcy to the left until they reached the railing. With its metal bar to follow, Greg picked up speed.

'Faster,' Darcy said.

Soon, they were jogging through the total darkness.

The belt remained in place until she began breathing hard. Each time she exhaled, it slipped down a bit. Now, it hung around her waist and she felt warm trickles of blood sliding down her belly.

It won't kill me, she thought.

We must be at least halfway there.

Halfway.

'Greg?'

He stopped.

'Let's try yelling. We're close enough, they ought to be able to hear us if we yell out a warning.'

'You think so?'

'Sound carries a long way in here.'

'All right. But it'll give away our position. As soon as we do it, let's get off the walkway. Don't want those . . .'

'Yeeeeah!' The far-off cry of a woman.

Other voices too faint to distinguish.

Then, 'Let go of me! What do you want?'

A chill spread up Darcy's back.

'I didn't think they'd really do it,' Greg whispered.

Someone screamed.

20

The black air shook with shouts and screams.

Katie started to cry.

'What's happening?' Jean whispered in a frantic voice.

'An attack,' Wayne whispered. 'Some kind of . . . I don't know.'

He heard growls, gasps, thuds, even laughter. And the crying of his daughter.

The three of them had sat there and kept silent until a few moments ago, as if, like Wayne, Katie and Jean understood that the silence was their protection, a shelter that hid them from the invaders. Now, the girl's crying threatened to give them away.

'Katie,' he said. 'Don't. Shhhh. Please, honey.'

If they hear us, they'll get us!

Who? Who's *doing* this?

When it began (a minute ago? five minutes? seemed to be going on forever) he'd thought it was a joke – someone taking advantage of the darkness to throw a fright into a girlfriend or wife. Then someone cried out, 'Oh sweet Jesus, *he's dead*!' and Wayne knew it wasn't pretend. In seconds, he was engulfed by cries of alarm and pain.

It'll stop soon, he'd told himself.

It'll just fade out and end, like the Los Angeles earthquake when he was a grad student there back in 1972. When the earthquake hit, he'd known he was going to die, but he'd done nothing, just sat there on his bed, and it had gone away.

It'll be like that. If we just sit real still and don't make a sound, it'll stop and we'll be all right.

But it wasn't fading. It was swelling, growing, getting worse.

Wayne felt as if he'd been sucked into the plot of one of his own grim novels.

And thought, those are books. What *is* this shit!

She's got to stop crying!

Reaching into the dark, he touched Katie and she yelped. 'It's all right, honey,' he whispered. He stroked the side of her face, reached beyond her and felt Jean. The girl must be sitting on her mother's lap, just as she'd been before the fires in the elevators died. 'Don't worry. Nothing . . .'

'Don't let them kill us, Daddy.'

What can I do? he thought. I'm a goddamn writer. I'm no Chuck Norris.

A fucking wimp.

'Daddy.'

'Lie down and keep quiet and don't move,' he said. 'Both of you. Jean, get on top of her.'

Then he twisted himself around, turning straight into an explosion of blood that slapped his face and stung his eyes and filled his mouth.

Got the fat lady, he thought.

They're close. Fucking close. We're next!

The blood kept spraying his face. He crawled into it. His hands met the woman's thick calves. Her legs were still crossed, but jumping as if she'd been plugged into a socket. Wayne slapped a hand down on her dress. Found the handbag. Hissed and ducked aside as a thread of fire streaked down his ear and cheek. But kept the handbag and tore it open and dug inside and grabbed the matchbook.

With palsied fingers, he plucked out a match and struck it.

For an instant, there was a bloom of light.

He glimpsed the woman sitting in front of him, bouncing and twitching. Her eyes were rolled back. Her slashed throat spat blood. The blood doused the match but before the darkness dropped over his eyes, Wayne saw a crouched figure lurch past his side.

Toward Katie and Jean!

He bit down on the matchbook and sprang forward, slamming the fat woman onto her back. Her head thumped the rock floor. Kneeling on her soft, shuddering body, he found her shoulders, found her cable-knit shawl, tore it off.

'WAYNE!'

Katie screamed.

He scurried backward, balling up the shawl. Whirled around. Struck a match and saw in the shuddering glow of the flame his wife huddled on top of Katie (did as she was told, for once) and a man crouched over her back ready to slash with a straight razor.

A man – a teenager? – with a face as white as bread dough, wild, tangled black hair and a bushy beard. He wore a quilted pink bathrobe trimmed in lace, its front soaked with blood.

As the match flared, he squeezed his eyes shut and turned his head away.

He seemed stunned by the light.

Then his other hand flew up to cover his eyes and he started to slash down at Katie but the shawl in Wayne's hands was already a ball of fire. As the blade whipped down, Wayne dived at him and shoved the blazing garment into his face.

He shrieked. Wayne smashed him backwards, landed on top of him, rolled clear, thrust himself up to his hands and knees and jerked his head toward the light.

The attacker, beard and hair afire, squirmed on his back and kept screaming as he struggled with the flaming shawl. It seemed to be tangled in his arms. By the time he flung it aside, the sleeves of his robe were burning. He lurched to his feet. He twirled and flapped his arms, then lurched past Jean and started to run. He dashed past sprawled corpses, past bodies huddled in terror, past someone lying prone who darted out a hand and tripped him. He stumbled, fell, shoved himself up and staggered onward.

Maybe hoping to reach the stream, Wayne thought.

He was still running when Wayne crawled over to Jean and Katie. 'Are you okay?' he gasped.

'Yes,' Jean told him. 'Yes.'

'Did you get him, Daddy?'

'You betcha.'

As Kyle slashed her throat, blood gushed over his hand. He let go of her hair and stepped backwards away from her shuddering body. A moment later, her head struck the rock floor of the cavern.

He clamped the pocket knife between his teeth and moved forward. Her blood splashed his pants, his jutting penis. When he was beyond the spray, he turned toward the place where she must be lying, and knelt.

Scooted on his knees until they bumped against her. Reached down and touched her bare leg. Her shin. It was trembling.

Still alive. Fuck her fast while she's still alive and shaking.

Before they *show up.*

He crawled over her and got between her legs.

Behind him, the chaos went on. The mad sounds of struggle and slaughter.

Kyle's whole body quivered with terror and need.

The crazies were back there, doing their number, and no one knew he was here with Paula. He was invisible. He could do whatever he wanted with her. No one would ever know.

They'll blame it on the crazies.

He slid his hands up her shaking thighs, slipped them up beneath her damp skirt.

Skirt?

What's . . .?

Pulling his hands out from under it, Kyle reached higher and touched more wet fabric. A blouse? He squeezed the soft mounds of her breasts through the cloth. From the feel of them, she wasn't wearing a bra, but . . .

Where the hell did she get the clothes?

He'd stripped off her kilt and panties before she broke away from him. Her blouse had come off in his hand when he grabbed her crossing the stream.

Paula's naked.

This isn't Paula.

He remembered the pursuit through the darkness. He'd been right behind her. She was just out of reach

291

when he got past the railing, and he'd stuck out his arm and clutched her hair . . . *someone's* hair.

Nailed the wrong person.

I'll never get her now, he thought. And then he thought, who cares?

He tore open the blouse and filled his hands with the big, warm breasts. Then, he shoved the skirt up her legs and felt for her panties. She wore none.

Great.

Who is *she?*

Who cares.

Kyle folded the knife and slid it into his pocket. Bending down, he rubbed his face on her breasts. He kneaded one of her breasts and took the other into his mouth and sucked it in deep.

There was a high shriek. But not from the woman. From somewhere behind him.

Big deal.

Another tourist bites the dust.

He bit this one, and felt blood swell into his mouth.

The shriek got louder.

Then there was light.

Orange, fluttering light.

Kyle thrust himself up, suddenly alarmed, and was about to look over his shoulder when someone with a burning head and flaming robe tumbled to the cave floor beside him.

No more than a yard away.

He felt the heat of the flames.

He thought, *Christ, now everyone can see me!*

The crazies can see me!

He started to get up.

And saw the face of the woman he had killed.

The face was shiny red.

But he knew that face, though he hadn't seen it in years.

His mind tilted.

Whimpering, he climbed off the body of his mother and ran for the darkness.

Calvin, standing on the debris inside an elevator car, watched the man in flames run through the group and fall just this side of the railing. A kid next to the burning body climbed off someone and ran away.

Other matches suddenly flared as folks from the tour followed the first guy's example. In the glow of the matches, Calvin saw people pull off sweaters and shirts. They started the garments on fire. In seconds, the area in front of the elevator was ashimmer with light.

Plenty of folks were down – some playing possum, he suspected, some killed.

If we'd stayed put, Calvin thought, we'd be in the thick of it. Maybe toes up, our own selves, by now.

But when Calvin had realized it was trouble and not just foolishness, he'd hussled Mavis through the dark and got her into the elevator. There, they were safe on three sides. Blocking the entrance, he'd whipped his cane from side to side until the fires started and he saw that nobody was coming at him.

He made out four trouble spots.

A gal that was bare-ass naked and didn't appear to have a weapon was being tackled by one of their people while the pregnant lady squealed like she was dog-bit.

A gal decked out like the queen of the ball in a satin gown was bent spraddle-legged over the fat man, skewering him in the guts with something that looked like a bone while he bellowed and bucked. Calvin no sooner glimpsed her than the two gay fellows hit her and took her down.

Takes care of her.

Over to the right, half a dozen folks were tumbling around, wrestling each other and yelling. They were starting to break it up, though. Calvin guessed that the light let them see they were only fighting others from the tour.

Just a few yards to his left, Calvin saw his old friend Slick in trouble. The kid was riding the back of some bearded yahoo in drag who had his knees on Slick and planned to ream the son of a whore with a good-sized pair of scissors. It was just the kid hanging onto the fellow's wrist that kept him from polishing Slick off.

Calvin leaped out of the elevator, hobbled over to them, and swung his stick.

The brass horse's head bashed through the yahoo's teeth.

He flopped backwards onto the kid.

Using his cane like a golf club, Calvin teed off on the fellow's nuts.

The kid got clear, snatched up the scissors, and rammed them into the joker's chest.

Calvin stepped back and looked around.

He didn't see any more trouble spots.

The bunch that had been fighting each other had calmed down.

The gay fellows were on their feet and taking turns kicking the gal that wore the fancy gown.

The bare-ass gal was on her knees, talking and nodding to the guy who'd tackled her. He was taking off his shirt for her.

Peculiar, Calvin thought. She one of ours?

He took another look around. Sure enough, the attack was over.

Now, folks were keening over their dead, tending to the wounded.

Calvin limped back to the elevator. He stepped through the debris and wrapped his arms around Mavis. She hugged him hard.

'Next time you want to see a cave, May,' he whispered, 'get yourself a picture book.'

Darcy heard quick footfalls and gasping, sobbing sounds – someone running toward them through the darkness. Greg halted in front of her. She tightened her grip on his shoulder.

They stood motionless and silent.

The sounds came closer, closer.

Someone from my group? she wondered. Or one of them?

Almost on us!

Greg made a sudden twisting move – swinging the bone weapon? It whooshed. His shoulder jerked at the same moment Darcy heard a soft thump. A grunt.

She couldn't see a thing, but from the sounds Darcy guessed that the bone had struck the person – not his head but maybe his arm. He was staggering off to the side, falling, hitting the concrete walkway.

Greg lunged in that direction, and she lost his shoulder.

'No! Please!' A frantic voice. Familiar.

'Greg, wait. I think it's Kyle.'

'Kyle?' Greg asked.

Darcy bumped into Greg's back and put her arms

around him. She rested her open hands on his belly. She felt him breathing hard. In spite of the chilly air, his skin was moist with sweat.

'Darcy?' the boy gasped.

'Yeah.'

'Alive. You're alive.'

'Are you all right?' she asked.

'It's . . . murder. Murder.' He sobbed. 'They're all being murdered. I got away and ran for it.'

'Did I hurt you?' Greg asked.

'Just . . . I guess I'm okay.'

'We're going on ahead,' Darcy told him. 'You can come with us or stay here.'

'No!'

'I'm sure you're safe here,' Greg said.

'Don't go! They'll kill you.'

'There're only three or four of them,' Darcy said.

Greg added, 'Maybe even fewer, by now. I can't imagine our people aren't fighting back.'

'But they're . . . they're crazies. They're insane. They're killing everyone!'

'Just calm down, Kyle. Greg, let's get going.'

'Wait! No! I'll come with you! Don't leave me here!'

'Can you get up?' Greg asked.

'Yeah. Yeah.'

Darcy heard moans and shuffling sounds as Kyle struggled to rise. She stroked Greg's belly. He wasn't breathing so heavily now. It felt good, holding onto him, and she didn't want to let go.

'Where are you . . .?' Kyle asked.

'Here,' Greg said. 'You're right in . . .'

'This you?'

'Yeah.'

MY HAND!

Darcy blasted her breath out.

Her arm jumped away from Greg's belly, trying to get her hand safe, wanting to free it from the sudden molten pain but the pain stayed.

She whirled around, doubled over with agony, went to clutch her wound and her left hand knocked against something protruding from the back of her right. Scalded by a fresh raw surge of pain, she flicked her hand. Whatever it was flew out and clattered onto the walkway.

Dropping to her knees, she thought, *A knife! He stabbed me. Tried to stab Greg but my hand . . .*

She heard sounds of a struggle.

Greg'll take care of him.

Stabbed me! Kyle . . . tried to kill Greg!

She rocked back and forth, pressing her pierced hand to her thigh, feeling the blood soak through her pants.

The fighting went on. She heard blows being struck, grunts and gasps.

Her arm shook, vibrating the hand against her leg. The pain seemed to fade a little, but she couldn't stop the shaking of her arm. She held the hand with her left, and that seemed to help. The pain faded to a dull throb, a throb that was only slightly worse now than her hurt from the pointed bone.

That's two from the bone, she thought. The one below her ribs, the other on her left thigh.

The leg wound's nothing, she thought.

But Christ, Christ, I'm being ruined piece by piece.

She *buzzed* with pain.

And began to weep.

Kill him, Greg, she thought. Kill the bastard!

Vaguely, she realized she no longer heard the sounds of their fighting. Just someone panting for air.

'Greg?' she asked. She sobbed. 'Greg, you get him?'

The breathing sounds came closer.

Something brushed across the top of her head, then patted it. A hand. She started to reach up for it with her good hand. A blow crashed her forehead.

Darcy's back slammed the walkway. Her head hit the concrete.

A weight dropped onto her hips.

She lay there, stunned, dimly aware that hands were moving over her, unzipping her windbreaker, opening it, touching her breasts, squeezing them, pinching her nipples but not so much that it hurt through the vagueness.

Not Greg. Greg wouldn't.

Kyle.

He must've hurt Greg.

The thought that Greg may have been injured blew through the fog in her head, cleared it a little.

She tried to move, but couldn't.

Gotta . . . pull myself together.

She felt wetness on her right breast. Kyle's mouth. Pulling, sucking.

She heard his moans.

His mouth pulled at her other breast.

The fuck, she thought. *It's what he's always wanted.*

His mouth went away.

His hands smeared the saliva on her breasts, then slid down her body and she jerked rigid when he touched the wound.

'What's this?' he whispered.

He dug a finger in and Darcy squealed and he laughed.

Shuddering, she felt him tug the belt wrapped loosely around her middle. Then he let go of it. He opened the button of her pants. Slid the zipper down. Started to tug.

The fog was gone. The bright bolt of pain when he'd stuck his finger into her wound had blasted away the last of it. Her head was clear.

She wondered where the knife was.

Had to be out of reach. It had fallen beside her, and then she'd been knocked backward. Had to be way down by her feet.

Kyle's weight wasn't on her.

She felt her pants jerk out from under her rump, felt the cold concrete.

Kyle pulled off one of her shoes, then the other.

With her left hand, she unbuckled the belt.

Her feet were lifted. The cuffs slid over them. The pants slid down her legs.

The belt was out from under her.

Kyle forced her legs apart.

She felt his trembling hands glide up her thighs, hissed at the pressure against the torn skin down there. He didn't dig into that wound – more interested in what was higher up.

He rubbed Darcy through her panties.

Then his fingers hooked the thin elastic band and she sat up, reaching for him with her gashed and burning right hand. He yelped when it touched him. Flinched rigid.

Her hand was on his shoulder.

'Kyle,' she said. Her voice came out as thin and frail as a tattered rag. 'Don't. Don't.'

'You're mine,' he said. 'All mine.' He made a strange

laugh. 'They'll think the crazies . . .'

'You're . . . not one of them. You're just . . . a kid. You don't want to . . .'

One of his hands went away from her panties and found her breast in the darkness.

'Leave me . . . alone.'

It rubbed. It squeezed.

Darcy punched out.

With her left fist.

With the belt buckle clutched tightly, frame down against palm, the metal prong jutting out between her middle finger and ring finger.

Punched through the darkness at the place where his neck should be.

Felt her fist pound against him.

He squealed.

Somewhere behind Darcy, a baby began to cry.

Hank heard a sharp, high squeal. The baby in Chris's arms, apparently frightened by the harsh sound, started wailing.

'Wait here,' he whispered.

Started to run.

Chris didn't wait, she ran at his side.

He dashed around a bend in the walkway.

The glow of his lantern lit a woman with wild blond hair straddling a teenaged boy. She wore a blue nylon jacket. Panties.

The kid had short black hair, no beard.

One of us.

And the gal was killing him. She had him by the ears, was lifting his head up and crashing it down against the

300

concrete. Again and again. His head made soggy thuds each time it hit.

Too late, he thought. Kid's a goner.

As Hank ran, he dipped to the side and let go of the lantern. Its metal base skidded, but the lantern stayed upright.

He sprinted toward the woman.

She kept bashing the poor kid's head down.

Hank saw another body – a big guy sprawled motionless on the concrete beyond the two.

Naked except for jockey shorts.

One of the guys from the boat?

She got him, too?

Had help from the others, probably.

The big guy moved, raised a knee.

Least he's not dead.

The woman turned her head. She looked at Hank through tangles of damp hair. She let go of the boy's ears and twisted around to face him.

Quick kick to the chin.

Her jacket hung open. He saw her breasts, her flat belly.

This one's not pregnant.

Blood all over her belly, a nasty wound just below her ribs. Blood spilling from her right hand. A gash on her thigh.

Took a licking, this one. Took a licking and kept on ticking.

He saw confusion in the blue eyes peering at him through the tangled hair.

Great eyes.

Familiar eyes.

But eyes of a savage, a cannibal.
For the kid.
He shot his foot at the point of her chin.
'NO!' Chris yelled.

21

'I thought she was one of them,' Hank muttered.

Chris held her daughter tightly, and couldn't stop crying.

'Mom,' Darcy said, 'you're hurting me.'

She was crying, too. So was the baby Chris had handed to Hank after he'd come so close to killing Darcy. That kick . . . it would've broken her neck.

If Chris hadn't yelled.

If Hank hadn't been so quick, so good, that he was able to turn even in the middle of that deadly kick and blast his foot through the air beside Darcy's ear.

'Mom.'

'I'm sorry.' She let go of Darcy.

Darcy turned around and went right into the arms of a big man who wore nothing but his underwear. He stroked her hair, her back.

'What'd he do to you?' Darcy asked the man who held her.

'Don't know. My head hit something. Thought I had him, and then . . . Are you okay?'

'That's a good one,' she said, and sobbed.

'You saved my life,' he told her.

'Guess so. My hand'll never be the same.'

'I love you, Darcy.'

Who is this guy? Chris wondered.

Hank patted her shoulder. She turned to him, and he gave the baby to her.

'Paula,' he said.

That was all he had to say, and Chris's gladness and relief shrivelled.

Darcy turned away from the other man. 'Paula?' she asked.

'My kid,' Hank said.

Darcy's mouth twisted, but no words came out.

'What?'

'She was . . . they were together,' Darcy said, and nodded toward the body of the teenaged boy.

'Is that Kyle Mordock?' Hank asked.

She nodded again.

Chris saw pain come to Hank's eyes.

He picked up the lantern and started to run.

Chris rushed after him. We're leaving them in the dark, she thought. She had the backpack loaded with flashlights, but the baby was in her arms. She couldn't leave the pack for them. But she heard them following.

Please let Paula be all right, Chris thought as she ran. *Darcy's okay, thank God, hurt but okay and it wouldn't be fair if Hank lost Paula.*

From the darkness ahead came sounds of wailing.

It's bad up there, she thought.

But Hank is so good. He'll nail anyone in our way. He'll get us to Paula.

Please God, let Paula be alive.

Hank's a good man. He's killed, but he had to. He doesn't deserve to lose her.

She quickened her pace. The infant in her arms, no

longer crying, tugged at Chris's ear.

She caught up to Hank.

Side by side, with Darcy and Greg not far behind, they raced through the cavern. Ahead was blinding tragedy or joy for Hank. No matter which, Chris would be with him.

Either way, she told herself, we'll be together.

That should count.

The anguished cries grew louder, but Chris realized that no screams, no shouts of alarm came from the darkness beyond the glow of Hank's lantern.

Was it over? Had the beasts from the bad end of the cave been beaten, killed? Or had they only retreated? Were they coming this way?

Dashing around a bend, she saw light ahead. The shimmering light of half a dozen small fires. She saw people standing near the fires, adding shirts and sweaters to the flames. Others milled about as if lost. Some huddled together in small groups. More than a few were sprawled on the ground. Of those who were down, some lay abandoned. Others were being tended to by people crouched beside them. Still others were being held, wept over, mourned.

Faces jerked toward the brilliant glare of Hank's lantern. Chris heard startled gasps, quick shrieks, shouts of warning. Hank came to a sudden halt. She stopped beside him and took hold of his arm.

'PAULA!' he yelled.

Silence fell over the group.

A few men began to approach, slowly, hunched over as if ready to do battle.

'PAULA?' he called again.

And a small, wary voice answered, 'Dad?'

From behind a shirtless man standing with a woman near the far end of the chamber stepped a girl. A girl with thick long hair that glowed auburn in the firelight. A girl in a plaid shirt that was much too large for her, its cuffs flopping below her hands as she walked, its tails draping her bare thighs.

'Dad!' Her voice boomed out, now glad and eager, and suddenly she was running, dodging the survivors in her way, and Hank was passing the lantern to Darcy and rushing forward to meet her.

Hank stopped. His daughter didn't. She slammed into him. Chris heard the soft impact, and tears blurred her vision as she saw Hank spin, crushing the girl against him.

Darcy refused an ambulance. She stood in the wet debris at the top of the elevator shaft, a blanket clutched around her body, and watched the cable roll off the squeaking reel of the winch. It should almost be to the bottom by now. But it moved with terrible slowness.

She had intended to be last out. It was only right, since she was the leader. First to be hoisted from the cave were the injured. Then the others, one at a time, had strapped themselves into the harness and been raised to the surface until only Darcy and Greg remained below. The Coleman lantern had run out of fuel. They stood together, only the beams of their flashlights warding off the darkness.

Greg had insisted that she go before him.

Just as well. Duty or not, she hadn't liked the idea of being alone down there with only a flashlight. Alone except for the corpses.

A voice rose faintly from depths of the shaft. 'Got it.'

'He's got it,' repeated the fireman kneeling at the other side of the opening.

Darcy heard the winch clank, reversing.

The cable began moving upwards slowly.

She imagined Greg, snug in the harness, starting to rise. Stepping closer to the edge, she peered down into the shaft. The faint light of dusk faded a few yards below the rim, and she saw no more than the cable creeping upwards.

'*Yeeyahhh! NO! God!*'

Darcy's breath slammed out.

The cable jerked, quivered, swayed.

'GREG!' she yelled. Flinging her blanket off, she leaped. She caught the rising cable, clenched it between her legs, started to slide down. The cable felt like fire against her stabbed hand, her torn thigh.

Snapping 'Shit!' the fireman grabbed her. He tore her from the cable, swung her clear of the shaft and wrestled her backwards as she struggled to free herself. 'Calm down,' he grunted. 'Christ, you nuts?'

'Greg!'

Twisting free of the man, she scurried over charred rubble to the edge before he caught her around the thighs, hugged her rump to his chest, stopped her.

She waited, gasping, staring down the hole.

Out of the darkness below came Greg, his head down, his body hunched over in the harness.

Darcy heard him moan.

He rose out of the shaft, naked except for his underwear, groaning and clutching his right calf. Blood was spilling from beneath his hands.

The fireman released Darcy. She lurched up, grabbed Greg and pulled him away from the mouth of the shaft.

As she clung to him, others freed him from the harness. She held him while he was carried to the grass and put down.

Paramedics pried his hands away from his blood-slick leg. Darcy glimpsed a torn patch of skin hanging off the back of his calf.

His small toe was gone.

'Aw geez,' Darcy murmured. 'What . . . ?'

He shook his head. His face was pale, sweaty, twisted with pain. 'Bit me. Came outa . . .'

'They were *dead*,' Darcy blurted.

'Others. Two of 'em. Maybe three. Not the dead ones. Others. Don't know where they came from.'

'They'll be taken care of,' said someone behind Darcy. Looking over her shoulder, she saw a big lawman crouching, staring down at Greg. He met her eyes, then rose to his full height and turned away. 'Clement! Groves! Baker! Standish! Get the pumpguns, we're going in the hole. Move it! We got some mopping up to do!'

Darcy leaned over Greg. With her uninjured hand, she stroked the cool slickness of his forehead. 'You're going to be all right,' she whispered.

'You, too.' He tried to smile. His chin trembled.

'I'm gonna be fine,' Darcy said.

'Me, too.'

She eased down, feeling the mild evening breeze on her bare legs, feeling it seep through her thin panties, knowing she was being watched by firemen and paramedics, by survivors and spectators and even her mother . . .

. . . but not by Kyle . . .

She didn't care what they saw.

On her knees, she sank down over Greg. She felt his breath on her lips. 'You're mine, now,' she whispered.

'I'm missing a goddamn toe.'

'It was my favourite, too.'

'You love me anyway?'

'You bet,' she said, and covered his mouth with her lips.

RICHARD
LAYMON
DARK MOUNTAIN

'BEWARE ON YOUR JOURNEY,
TREAD SOFTLY WITH CARE.
BEWARE OF THE HAG
IN HER DARK MOUNTAIN LAIR...'

Two families join forces for a camping holiday high in the
California mountains. It's meant to be fun – a break from city life, a
healthy interlude in the hills amid the wonders of Nature. If only
they hadn't pitched camp at Mesquite Lake, home to two of the
wilderness's most terrifying inhabitants – an aged hag whose
loyalty to the Evil One gives her gruesome powers, and her son, a
depraved half-beast whose unnatural lusts even she cannot
control...

'No one writes like Laymon and you're going to have a good time
with anything he writes' Dean Koontz

'A brilliant writer' *Sunday Express*

'Readers turn the pages so fast they leave burn marks on the paper'
Horrorstruck

A selection of bestsellers from Headline

THE HOUSE ON NAZARETH HILL	Ramsey Campbell	£5.99 ☐
THE KING'S DEMON	Louise Cooper	£5.99 ☐
HAWK MOON	Ed Gorman	£5.99 ☐
LORD OF THE VAMPIRES	Jeanne Kalogridis	£5.99 ☐
BITE	Richard Laymon	£5.99 ☐
THE STORE	Bentley Little	£5.99 ☐
TIDES	Melanie Tem	£5.99 ☐
REIGNING CATS AND DOGS	Tanith Lee	£5.99 ☐
ARASH-FELLOREN	Roger Taylor	£5.99 ☐

All Headline books are available at your local bookshop or newsagent, or can be ordered direct from the publisher. Just tick the titles you want and fill in the form below. Prices and availability subject to change without notice.

Headline Book Publishing, Cash Sales Department, Bookpoint, 39 Milton Park, Abingdon, OXON, OX14 4TD, UK. If you have a credit card you may order by telephone – 01235 400400.

Please enclose a cheque or postal order made payable to Bookpoint Ltd to the value of the cover price and allow the following for postage and packing:

UK & BFPO: £1.00 for the first book, 50p for the second book and 30p for each additional book ordered up to a maximum charge of £3.00.
OVERSEAS & EIRE: £2.00 for the first book, £1.00 for the second book and 50p for each additional book.

Name ....

Address ....

....

....

If you would prefer to pay by credit card, please complete:
Please debit my Visa/Access/Diner's Card/American Express (delete as applicable) card no:

Signature .... Expiry Date..............